Saudi Match Point

Saudi Match Point

Paul Ulrich

BLACKSMITH BOOKS

SAUDI MATCH POINT
© 2007 Paul C. Ulrich
ISBN 9789628673254
Published by Blacksmith Books
5th Floor, 24 Hollywood Road, Central, Hong Kong
www.blacksmithbooks.com

Typeset in Adobe Garamond by Alan Sargent

Printed and bound in Hong Kong by Epoch Printing
First printing April 2007

Registered with the U.S. Copyright Office, Registration Number TXU 1-200-014. All rights reserved. No part of this book may be reproduced in any form or by any electronic means, including information storage and retrieval systems, without permission in writing from the publisher, except by a reviewer who may quote brief passages in a review. The right of Paul C. Ulrich to be identified as the Author of the Work has been asserted as have his moral rights with respect to the Work. This is a work of fiction. Names, characters, places, and incidents are either the products of the author's imagination or are used fictitiously. Any resemblance to actual events or locales or persons, living or dead, is entirely coincidental.

DRAMATIS PERSONAE

Nicholas (Nick) Hansen **	Protagonist, a consular officer
Susan Butts-Bradley	Nick's boss in the U.S. consulate of Dhahran
Herman Gewalt *	U.S. ambassador to Saudi Arabia
Martha Fischbein	Personal secretary to Ambassador Gewalt
Errol Hart	Deceased former consular official
Hajar bint Saleh al-Qaatil **	Protagonist, daughter of radical sheikh
Tariq bin Saleh al-Qaatil *	Half brother of Hajar, low-level al-Qaeda operative
John Kaddish *	Telecom contractor, friend of Nick
Ma Ling *	Chinese liaison from China Oil to Saudi Oil
Fatima bint Sami al-Sayyid *	Friend of Hajar, love interest of Nick
Ahmad and Faisal bin Sami al-Sayyid	Brothers of Fatima, one in Saudi, one in the U.S.
Sami al-Sayyid	Senior government official, father of Fatima
Rasheed	al-Qaeda handler of Tariq
Izzat	Hajar's employer in a clothing store
Huang Lei	Driver of Ma Ling
Jia Guomin	Chinese ambassador to Saudi Arabia
Yang Pangzi	Chairman of China Oil
Stewart Morrison	State department official in Washington, D.C.
Layla	Mother of Hajar, 2nd wife of the sheikh
Aisha, Munira	Half-sisters of Hajar
Suheir (Um Tariq)	Stepmother of Hajar, 1st wife of the sheikh
Sheikh Saleh al-Qaatil	Radical cleric and father of Hajar
Muamar	Blind cleric and intended husband for Hajar

** Main characters: the two plot lines follow each of their lives over several months
* Supporting characters

Saudi Arabia and the Arabian Gulf

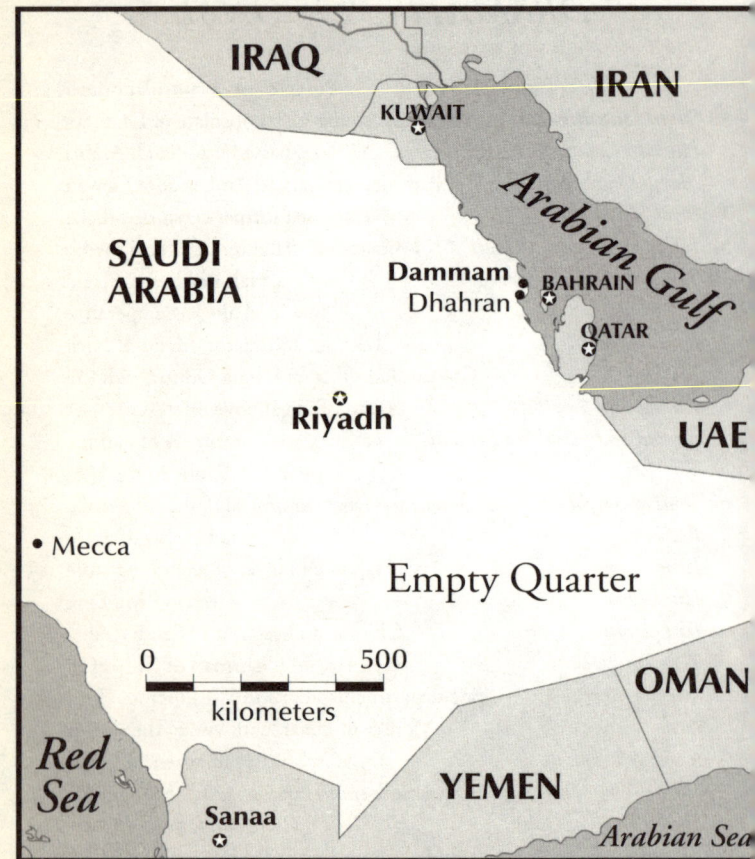

Dammam, Dhahran and Khobar

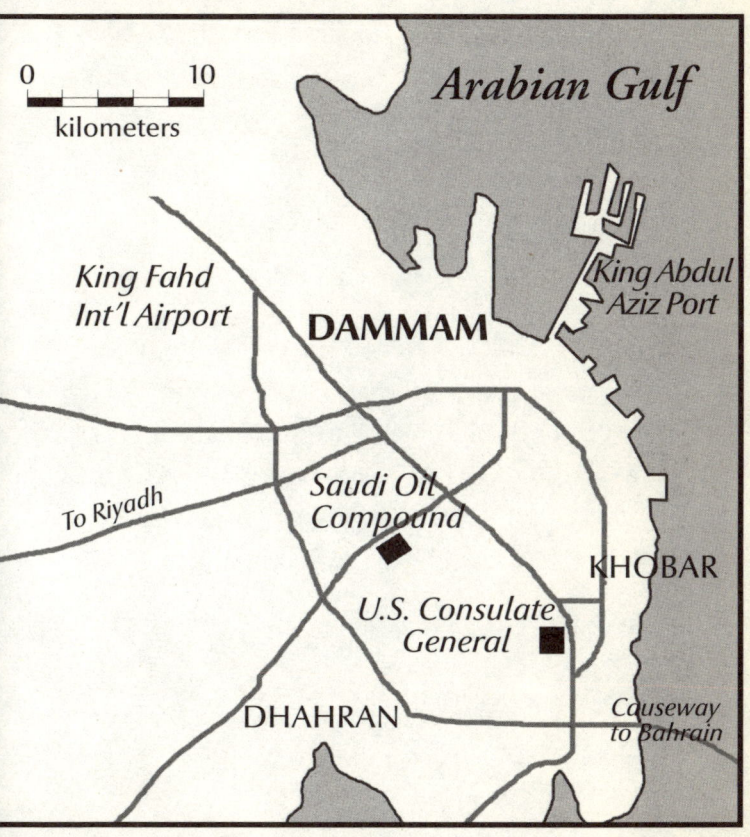

Prologue

CHRIST! WAS SOMEONE FOLLOWING him? Errol Hart's trembling hand adjusted the rearview mirror. He peered as long as he dared into the reflected scene unfolding behind his speeding vehicle. His own car was kicking up plumes of desert sand and stone, but weren't those flashes some kind of signal from the distance? He couldn't swivel his neck to look directly, but back on the horizon, what seemed like separate funnels of smoke or sand were rising into the desolate sky. Were they getting closer?

Hart was driving directly into the glare of the morning sun. Maybe those glints of light were the sun reflecting off car chrome. He wasn't about to slow down to find out. Hart's temples were starting to throb, and his mouth was parched. To steady his nerves and calm the morning shakes, he reached for a small bottle of Johnnie Walker balanced precariously in a bouncing, plastic car holster. He twisted off the cap with a free hand and gulped a mouthful. Diplomatic immunity had its privileges, he thought, and smiled at the recollection of all the smuggled alcohol he had brought in. Just for personal use, of course.

Did anyone see him last night, staking out the camp perimeter? But that was impossible. He'd taken all the proper evasive procedures. Was his cover blown? He glanced at his cell phone, but couldn't risk a call. They'd pinpoint his location. By the time anyone responded to a coded message for help, he might be dead, or hidden away in some prison. Diplomatic immunity didn't mean much if they caught him with evidence of spying.

As the alcohol took effect, Hart remembered that uppity bitch at the club a few nights before, implying he had a drinking problem. Hah! If she knew the stress he was under, she'd have one too. Just a few more months and he'd be ready for retirement. Hart still marveled at the thought. As soon as he reached the tender age of thirty-five, the CIA would put him out to pasture, or at least take him from the field and assign a cushy desk job in Langley. Time to settle down. Maybe he'd laugh about all this someday.

The plumes rising behind him like pillars in the desert were getting larger. They were gaining on him. If they were in cars, he might have a chance to outrun them. But only low-flying helicopters could be kicking up that much dust. He didn't have much time. In his white SUV he was easy prey from the sky. Better to ditch it, he thought. Head for the rough cover and go on foot. He'd be harder to spot, easier to hide. Hart was confident that, drunk or sober, he could outrun any of their foot soldiers. Time and again, he'd out-hustled guys ten years younger, over any distance. Better not take any water. He wouldn't go far and could circle back to the car after they passed by. Still driving, Hart slipped the two small bottles of Johnnie Walker into his pockets, just in case. Best not to leave any incriminating evidence, and the weight wouldn't slow him down—not like carrying a jug of water. Besides it was still relatively cool out. The killing heat of the desert summer was a long way off.

Hart skidded the SUV to a stop in the hard sand behind an outcropping of rock and climbed out. Shit! Was that gunfire? Or thunderclaps? But there were no clouds overhead. He didn't think anyone would be in this godforsaken place, but maybe there were people camped out. Could there be an oasis among the low-lying shrubs that he would be running into? It wouldn't be the first time he had needlessly ducked for cover after mistaking a Bedouin shooting celebration for something more sinister.

Regardless of the threat, Hart's desert-colored fatigues would be perfect camouflage in the brush. He knew how to cover his tracks and throw a search party off his trail.

The pillars of sand on the horizon were now a solid wall rising up into the pale sky. Jesus! Did they have the camp's entire fleet of helicopters after him? He paused to listen for the familiar whir of chopper blades, but heard only a distant roar, gathering in intensity. Was it just the wind, blowing hard from the north? He slammed the car door and set off at a sprint for the cover of rocks and desert shrubs. His pulse beat in his ears, and the wind howled. Grains of sand like tiny pinpricks hit the back of his exposed neck, his hands, and his wrists as he pumped his arms hard. Hart needed to get as far from the car as possible before they arrived. The noise was louder now. He glanced quickly up and back, seeing nothing but a rapidly darkening sky. They must be almost overhead. Had he been running for five minutes? That meant well over half a mile. He scrambled for the nearest bush, cutting his hands and khaki clothes on its sharp thorns, as he crouched down beneath it. The whirl of wind and sand was deafening now, the sky almost completely black.

Errol Hart had been in tight spots before and was not a religious man. Nevertheless, he began to pray.

Chapter 1

"Nicholas Hansen is not the right guy for this assignment," said the disembodied head that belonged to Stewart Morrison. His unseen hands, out of the camera's view, shuffled through pages of a dossier.

The U.S. ambassador to Saudi Arabia, Herman Gewalt, looked at Morrison's image on the screen of the ambassador's office wall in Riyadh, the Saudi capital. "No, but he's all we've got."

"We still haven't identified a suitable replacement for Errol Hart. Damn shame to add yet another anonymous star on the CIA's wall of fallen agents." Morrison coughed and cleared his throat. "Have you gotten anything conclusive from the investigation?"

The ambassador was annoyed. This deputy assistant secretary of state not only lacked the customary deference, but also had the temerity to question him. He played along. "No, we haven't. However, the circumstances seem suspicious . . . unless Hart just snapped. To leave a vehicle in the middle of the desert and wander miles on foot before succumbing—"

"Any signs of a struggle?" Morrison asked. "Any fingerprints in the car, or tracks next to it?"

Ambassador Gewalt shook his head, his patient veneer beginning to fray. "Look, you'll need to speak to others for the details. This is what I've heard—that there were no clues to go on. The sandstorm lasted nearly a week. It covered any footprints, or any possible perpetrator's trail, and prevented our satellites from spotting the body once we realized he had disappeared. Our team said the storm could also have interfered with the vehicle's GPS and disrupted cell phone signals, but they doubted that any telecom coverage extended that far."

Morrison's mouth moved; the words followed seconds behind.

Gewalt continued, speaking over them. "Everything went against Hart's training, but then again, I never could read the guy. That's what made him an effective covert agent. However, this new fellow, Nick Hansen—he's only been with State for a year, in country for maybe half that, and is barely out of college."

Gewalt looked down at a copy of the same dossier that Morrison held. "Well, okay, he had two years working as a China analyst at a California think tank. Still, I'm told he's like an open book: you can practically see the thoughts on his face as he forms them."

"Miss Fischbein, is the ambassador in?"

The long, gnarled fingers of Martha Fischbein paused over the keyboard, like a hovering predator waiting for the right moment to pounce. She stared at Nick Hansen, who came armed with pen, paper, and carrying case. Her eyes moved back to the computer screen, then again at the intruder. "And good afternoon to you, too. Do you have an appointment? There's nothing listed."

"Last night I got a message from Susan Butts-Bradley. She said I was to meet her in the ambassador's office, along with a Mr. More Something from the Near East Bureau."

"Susan is inside, but I don't see anyone else's name on the roster."

"The meeting's via video link, due to start at four-thir. . . ."

"Nick!" boomed the ambassador's voice as if shot from a battleship's turrets. "Come in, won't you! We're about to start."

The object of the previous day's critique opened the heavy wooden door, already ajar, and took a tentative step around it. A tuft of disheveled blond hair atop a pleasant, but nervous face appeared to the room's occupants. The rest of his lanky body entered the room while a trailing arm carefully closed the door. Seeing the broad chest of the ambassador, Nick squared his own shoulders and waited. He glanced quickly at Susan seated on a divan, at Morrison's head, adorned with square spectacles, on the wall screen, and back to the ambassador who was ruffling his crew cut with one hand from behind the desk and motioning with the other for Nick to take a seat.

"Stewart Morrison, this is Nicholas Hansen, who works for Susan, our acting chief of political affairs in Dhahran. Ambassador Gewalt frowned. "Nick, no need for any scribbling today. Everything is off the record."

Nick apologized and slid the black notebook and pen back into the satchel.

From the projection, the first noise emerged, again slightly out of sync with the jerky movements of the image: "Hi, Nick, great to meet you [inaudible]. I've read some of your cables, and [blank] that kind of perceptive political analysis we could use back here, too."

Having never before received any returned comments or questions on his reports, Nick was surprised that anyone had actually read them. "Thank you, sir. I —"

"In fact, the ambassador thinks you could help us with a new policy that we're testing in the region . . ."

Nick waited quietly this time, without trying to interject.

"... and I'm inclined to agree."

Gewalt turned to him. "Nick, I'm sure you've been wondering why State sent a China specialist to Saudi Arabia."

"I just figured it was the luck of the draw, sir. I—"

"The low man on the pole gets the hardest posting: Afghanistan, Iraq, Papua New Guinea ... you name it. If there's a simmering war on, pervasive threats from terrorists, or little of redeeming value, that job goes to the guy without dependents, especially if he's new."

Morrison piped in: "But in your case, it turns out there may be some rhyme or reason here, after all." Nick swiveled his lean frame again to face the screen. "We need to understand why we're losing so many big contracts to the Chinese in Saudi Arabia: not just in telecoms, but in oil, too."

"Nick, how's your Chinese?" the ambassador asked.

"Better than my Arabic, sir, but that's not saying much."

"Don't be modest." A deep female voice rose from the sofa. Susan Butts-Bradley was finally weighing in. Until then she had sat silently as if, in the presence of her superiors, she was trying not to dominate the discussion as she would have with just Nick alone. "You majored in that at Berkeley, didn't you?"

"Stanford, actually."

"Whatever. It doesn't have to be great. Just so long as you know the culture and have some rationale for going to events sponsored by the Chinese embassy."

Morrison added, "We're particularly keen to know how deeply involved the Chinese are on the ground: numbers of their personnel and staffing locations—that sort of thing. We'd like you to focus on the oil sector, which means getting to know Saudi Oil, the only game in town."

The ambassador said, "Work your Chinese contacts in Riyadh, then concentrate on the Eastern Province around Dhahran where the oil comes from. Since your consular duties should have you moving back and forth between visa services here and American citizens' services on the coast, this shouldn't disrupt the usual routine.

"You'll share your findings, which we'll need in a month's time, only with the three of us." Ambassador Gewalt looked across the calendar on his desk. "That will be due ... what ... April 15th." His face twisted into a pained smile. "I hope that deadline won't be so taxing on you as it is for me." The former bond trader, fundraiser for presidents, and now public servant scanned his audience for a reaction, but found none.

"In terms of the write-up, an earlier report by the embassy on the implications of an opening in the Saudi telecom market could serve as a useful guide, but you'll need to delve more deeply for this one—by talking to people rather than merely rehashing previous findings." Gewalt paused. "I take it that economics is not your strong suit, but you look like a quick learner."

Nick reddened beneath his freckles. The air-conditioned room felt warm, and a trickle of sweat rolled down his back. He wondered whether Susan had spoken ill of him or claimed as her own an economic study she had praised when he turned it in to her.

The U.S. embassy's visa section had not yet opened. Already waiting patiently were a crowd of forty or fifty applicants, mainly men in white robes and checkered head covers, and a few women, shrouded in shapeless, black, floor-length robes, headscarves, and veils. Even after four months in country, the sight of these black forms, entirely hidden, still unsettled Nick. He walked quickly past, through a door, and into an office nearby.

Soon after, a tall, young woman, with no veil but clad in the customary black silk, entered the waiting hall. Her gown was tighter than most and clung to the outlines of a slim frame. Within the relative freedom of the U.S. compound, she had let her headscarf slide from atop unmanageable ringlets of dark hair. Her bright eyes surveyed the room, as she held the arm of a companion, a youngish man of similar height, slightly stooped, narrow-shouldered, and sallow in complexion. He wore thick glasses, dark slacks, a white shirt, and thin black tie. The two found adjacent seats at the back and waited. The man read from a thick textbook filled with formulas and fragments of software code; the woman listened to music from a small, white device on her lap. With her hand still resting on his forearm, she offered to share one of the two tiny earphones. He declined. Then, too loudly, she said in Arabic, "I'm sorry to drag you all the way here, from your work, but Father thought—"

"Don't mention it. Whether I work in Riyadh or Dhahran, by day in an office or at home at night makes no difference. That's why I prefer technical to managerial jobs, despite what he says."

They continued to wait.

"Fa-ti-ma bint Sa-mi al-Sa-id." A woman's voice from behind the glass enclosure at the front of the room sounded over the intercom, with each syllable of the name drawn out in an American's southern drawl. The man gently tapped the woman's knee and slowly detached his gaze from the end of a page. Louder and with impatience, the call came again: "Fatima bint Sami!"

Fatima had pulled out her earphones and hurried to the front of the room. A buzzer opened a heavy, metal door to let her through, while her companion followed close on her heels and waved the passports to the marine sentry behind the glass.

Nick stood outside the doorway of a small, windowless office nearby and came forward, hand outstretched. Fatima pressed his palm with hers, smiled, and said, "That's the first handshake I've had in a while." Her voice rose and fell in a soft cadence.

Nick returned the smile, smitten. Fatima accepted his gaze directly, almost boldly, without the shy, often downturned, eyes he had heard that local women use when addressing a man. He laughed, and said, "Sorry. I forgot I'm not supposed to do that in Saudi Arabia, or so they tell me. I could burn in hell for touching a woman unrelated to me."

The man behind her said, "Don't worry, and there's no need to apologize. We don't believe that nonsense."

"I'm sorry. You must be the esteemed husband...."

When Fatima and the man giggled, Nick noted the resemblance in their smiles.

"No, just the little 'big brother.' Ahmad bin Sami al-Sayyid."

"Well please come in, Mr. and Miss al-Sayyid." Another *faux pas,* Nick thought. Which name is it that one uses to address Saudis upon first meeting? He always forgot.

"Please, just call me Fatima or 'Fat' for short." Fatima winked. "And you, Brother? Dr. Ahmad?"

Nick noted that they both spoke American English flawlessly, with only a trace of an accent in the rhythm of their words. He carried a third chair into the office and apologized for the mess and cramped quarters. Two stacks of papers and files weighed down both sides of a simple desk. The cream colored walls were bare.

"Is that doctor of medicine, or. . . ." Nick looked at the binding of the book in Ahmad's hand: *Enterprise Resource Planning*.

"Computer science. It's my sister who's in health care."

Now safely behind his desk, Nick opened a folder with Fatima's name on it and leafed through the contents in search of any red flags a predecessor might have highlighted. "As you might guess, I'm new here and still learning the basics. We're understaffed now and, unfortunately, with many Americans trying to return home, foreign visas are not currently a top priority. You may've heard we had to evacuate non-essential personnel." And with his voice falling to almost a mumble, "Although why they consider me essential, I've no idea. At any rate, I'm just a cog and not a well oiled one at that." *I'm sounding like an idiot and rambling. Steady . . . she's unattainable, anyway.*

Fatima and Ahmad exchanged puzzled glances, as Nick found his footing and got back on track. "Beginning with the World Trade Center bombing, and now with the escalating attacks on foreigners in this country, we've adopted new procedures that require not only in-person interviews here, but also clearance by our Department of Homeland Security for your in-country host sponsor. Not the institution, but the person or persons who vouch for you."

"Yes, Mr. Hansen, I think I understand the new procedures. When Ahmad went to study at MIT and later, when I enrolled in Johns Hopkins' nursing school, a travel agent had taken care of all the visa requirements with the U.S. embassy. That, of course, has all changed.

"You know I started my first classes just days before 9-11. I was so upset, I almost came back soon after, but my brother Faisal urged me to stay."

"Faisal. Yes, I see he's your local sponsor in Baltimore. But you left last spring after finishing your junior year. Tell me, why *did* you come back to this country?"

"I knew it might be difficult to return to Baltimore once I had left the U.S., but I had to be in Saudi Arabia. My dear mother was dying of stomach cancer, and I wanted to care for her at home to make her final months as bearable as possible. Afterward, I thought I should stay to be with my father and brother. With Mother gone, they no longer had a woman at home to look after them."

"And now you're working as an intern at Saudi Oil's clinic in Dhahran?"

"That's right. Ahmad works for Saudi Oil, too. He's with the information technology group. In fact, my father—who's with Telecom Saudia here in Riyadh—also has ties to Saudi Oil. They're naming him to the board of directors."

"Of course. Sami al-Sayyid, the deputy minister or permanent secretary. I didn't make the connection. There was quite a stir among the fundamentalists when the news came out. If I'm not mistaken, your family are Shi'ites."

Fatima sighed. "Yes, you're right, although we cannot worship openly. The Wahhabis—you know, the militant Sunnis—consider us infidels, no better than non-Muslims.

If it hadn't been for Ahmad and my father, I would've been unable to find work outside the home—being young and female, and a Shi'ite, as well."

"Your father must be an impressive man to have risen so far against such prejudice."

"We think so. I hope you can meet him. He knows the U.S. well and, like us, admires your country."

With that cue, Nick remembered the purpose of the interview and went through the series of mandated questions while jotting down Fatima's responses. As she and her brother rose to leave, he urged them to be patient. He would do what he could to expedite the renewal of the visa in time for her re-enrollment in the fall term.

"I'm sorry, once again, to have you both come all this way. Our consulate in Dhahran deals only with American affairs."

Despite the many other interviews he had to conduct that day, Nick didn't want to see them leave. Fatima rose, inclined her head in parting, and reached for her brother's arm. "I hope we'll see you there, Mr. Hansen. Perhaps in a social setting."

Chapter 2

From the air, Riyadh's slum of Suweidi looked no different from the rest of the city: it had the same grid of streets, boxy white and tan buildings, tile-roofed residences surrounded by high walls, and the occasional tree barely distinguishing one block from the next. Up close, the visitor saw migrant men, dressed in the garb of other Middle-Eastern countries, of North Africa, the Indian subcontinent, or Southeast Asia. Perhaps more males in Saudi dress were apparent than elsewhere— some running small roadside shops, a few toiling with deliveries of goods, but most lounging together at tea houses or cafes, unemployed, smoking from water pipes, drinking sugary tea, and conspiring to get a better life. Occasionally, a lone man accompanied a shrouded black figure on an errand. Presumably, these were Saudi women because most slum dwellers could not afford the immigrant servants, drivers, and maids that did the work for the more affluent Saudis living in the rest of the city. Even if a Filipino or Indonesian girl hid beneath the shroud, one would not know unless she spoke. Only a foolhardy woman would dare walk uncovered and risk the wrath of the *mutawwas,* the bearded and ill-mannered religious police who patrolled the streets in search of moral laxity. "Cover yourself, woman!" they would scream while beating the offender with a stick. If accompanied by a regular policeman, as was often the case, they would haul the criminal off to prison.

Westerners, and particularly Americans, did not venture into this part of this city. Nevertheless, the most visible signs of their fast-food culture had long ago spread even here, and as in other parts of the country, served as an obnoxious reminder to locals of their dependence on foreigners.

The state also feared the religious zealots, and this neighborhood was their stronghold, these were their people. On Friday sermons, the local clerics railed against all manner of evil—from the West and from the ruling royal family itself, which was desperately trying to appease two masters in conflict: foreign governments, the buyers of its oil, and conservative mullahs, from whom the ailing king and his extended family of several thousand princes claimed their precarious legitimacy. At the urging of the U.S., these members of the ruling elite made token reforms, pursued homegrown al-Qaeda terrorists, or muzzled particularly obnoxious preachers who were inciting still further violence. To many, the efforts seemed perfunctory, perhaps even staged. Not free to voice concerns in public, wary foreigners made their views known in private and left. An exodus of Western specialists, some of whom had lived in the country for decades, had begun.

One cleric of Suweidi who exulted in these departures was Sheikh Saleh al-Qaatil. A large, heavyset man in his early fifties, Sheikh Saleh wore his thick head of hair dyed jet black atop a leathery face frozen in a near-permanent scowl. Perhaps the mask-like features marked the onset of Parkinson's disease; more likely, as his hands shook only when he became agitated, the rigidity reflected a man set firmly in his views. The product of a "weekend marriage" in Cairo, where a Saudi visitor married and divorced his mother in the space of a weekend, Sheikh Saleh came on the hajj to Arabia as a young man and never returned, but instead renounced all things from his home country except the accent, which he couldn't shake.

Now at home, lord of a cramped four-room apartment divided between two wives and their five children, he was speaking to his only son in the one room, the largest, that served as the men's quarters. "Tariq, what did you think of my sermon today?"

"Your finest and most inspiring. Afterwards, the worshippers continued to murmur angrily, and some that I know vowed they would take action. I'll do what I can to help them."

"Good. Just don't tell me what plans you have. Those same two men who came last week again warned me to stop." The sheikh paused, thinking. "But I won't, even if it means going to al-Hair prison. If they *do* take me, it'll be hard for you. The brethren may provide the family with some financial support, but not so much as my usual wages."

Although the women in the household busied themselves with chores in the adjacent rooms, they strained to hear through the thin walls.

Sheikh Saleh continued, his voice rising, "It's high time we marry off your half-sister. At twenty, she's becoming an old maid like Aisha. I've put up with Hajar's pleas long enough. An unmarried woman is useless to a family—consuming food, taking up space, requiring constant vigilance."

His words carried into the neighboring rooms; in one, Aisha fumbled with the piecework knitting that brought some income to supplement the sheikh's salary; in the other, Hajar sat frozen beside her mother.

Tariq asked, "Who do you intend for Hajar? With her beauty, she could fetch a handsome dowry."

"I've already spoken with Sheikh Muamar. He's willing to take her."

Next door, Hajar clapped her hands over her mouth to stifle a scream. She collapsed into her mother's lap.

"But Father, isn't he the blind cleric who taught her Islamic studies at school? The one she was rude to and made fun of?"

"Don't 'But Father' me! I've already decided. Muamar wants a younger wife and has the connections we need for our cause. His other two are too old to bear sons, and he'll pay what I require." He gestured toward the door. "You can go now."

With eyes downcast, Tariq mumbled goodbye and, careful not to show disrespect, backed away as he groped behind for the doorknob to leave his father's presence. As soon as he had safely closed the door, Tariq swiveled on his heel, looked to his right, and glared at the mother and daughter staring at the floor. A young girl, oblivious to the previous conversation, tugged at her older sister's dress. Tariq fixed his gaze on Hajar, was about to speak, but thought better of it and strode out the room on his way to the street. Tariq's stride had a jerky motion, almost a limp. One leg was too short.

"Oh, Mama!" whispered Hajar, her eyes moist with tears. "What will I do?"

"Hush," said Layla, the cleric's second wife, while Suheir, the more senior spouse reclined on a couch in an adjacent room, looked at them through the open doorway, and smirked. Suheir's eyes had followed her son's profile, as if to ask whether she might accompany him outdoors. But she had not dared to speak, and so would be stuck inside like the others.

"It's for the best, my child. You should leave this household. I don't like the way your half-brother looks at you. His harsh words might turn worse."

"He's already struck me for being 'provocative' around him."

Alarmed, Layla knit her brows. "If only we had a maid with whom he could relieve his frustration, or the dowry money so Tariq could marry someone.

"Here you've nowhere to hide, although, thank God, I'm always nearby."

"But, Mama, Sheikh Muamar is so old and ugly! Fatima and I used to laugh at him and mimic his pompous words." Hajar's hands covered her face, now wet with tears.

"Don't mention her name here. You should know by now how your father hates that family."

Hajar thought of her former best friend Fatima whose visits stopped when she was twelve. Sheikh Saleh's direct questions to Fatima about whether her menses had started embarrassed them both. Why must he be so quick to insist that children veil? Father's learning that Fatima was a Shi'ite ended any further contact.

"Could you please speak with him? I'm happy to marry, but someone closer to my age."

"I'm afraid I've little say in the matter." Layla glanced across the passage at her rival for the Sheikh's attentions. "He's always favored Suheir. She at least gave him a son. With my childbearing days long past, what's the use? I just hope he doesn't insist on marrying off your sister, as well."

"But she's only eight!"

"He thinks we need the money, or will sometime soon. But if he won't let any of us leave the apartment to work, even if there were work to be found . . . and Tariq won't, or can't, get a job."

"Is Aisha so undesirable? At thirty-three, I suppose she's no longer of any interest."

"Only a poor man might make an offer." Hajar's mother lowered her voice still further. "Your father shouldn't have rejected that marriage proposal so long ago. To refuse merely because someone came from the wrong tribe. Word of that kind of attitude taints a woman and scares others away."

Layla looked again across the adjoining room and sighed as she contemplated Hajar's half-sister. "Such difficulties . . . and your Munira's medicine costs so much."

Temporarily forgetting her own troubles, Hajar said, "Mother, I read that blood disease can come from intermarriage. Since Suheir is Father's first cousin, could that be the reason?"

"Don't be silly. It's God's will. Or else someone cast the evil eye on the baby. Speaking too carelessly will do that."

They both fell silent to the sound of a clock ticking, punctuated by female laughter from the other room and by a roar from Sheikh Saleh to keep quiet as he composed his thoughts for the next week's tirade in the mosque.

Hajar rose wearily and shuffled to the side of the women's sitting room that doubled as a bedchamber. She lay down on the mattress that she shared with her younger sister. Soon tiring of staring at the ceiling, she reached above her head and pulled out from behind the base of a simple bureau a crumpled paperback missing its original racy cover and with dog-eared, yellowed pages. She opened it near the middle, idly fingered the pages and looked at the lines, but nothing sank in even when she mouthed the words slowly. It was a Harlequin romance novel smuggled into the country years ago, and in English. "Oh, what's the use now...." Her thoughts turned to the heroine who still awaited her rescue.

The front door opened and her brother came back. He snatched the paperback. "What's this?"

"Just a book," she said to the hem of his *thobe,* the loose white tunic dangling above two sandaled feet.

"What kind of book?"

"English. If I'm ever to work, it may be useful to continue my studies." She rolled over, facing away from him.

"You can forget about that." And he dropped the book in the garbage pail. "Don't let me catch you reading this filth. Father has the Koran, the Hadiths, and the Suras in his study. Those are all you need."

In a small act of defiance, Hajar got up, walked to the alcove by the apartment's entrance, and picked up from the middle of the pile an old copy of *al-Arabiya,* the newspaper her father or brother bought each morning. She usually took little notice of it, as the fare was either bland—reporting on some prince's presiding over a ceremony—or shrill, in its critique of Western and Zionist conspiracies that even she could see were exaggerated. Rarely was there a story Hajar could relate to her reality. As she feigned exaggerated interest, to annoy Tariq, she glimpsed a headline buried near the back: DEPUTY HEAD OF TELECOM SAUDIA TO JOIN BOARD OF SAUDI OIL. The article mentioned Sami al-Sayyid and quoted him as looking forward to spending more time at the family home in the Eastern Province. Wasn't that Fatima's father? Have they moved from Riyadh?

Hajar realized she had lost touch not only with this friend, but with virtually all those whom she had played with as a schoolgirl. Now dependent on an indifferent father and hostile half-brother to take her out of the home, she lived as a virtual prisoner, shut in from the world outside. Marriage might be a welcome escape, if only not to Muamar, whose ridiculous, almost loathsome, image made her shudder.

Chapter 3

JOHN KADDISH BREEZED into Dhahran main camp, the Saudi Oil compound, and the manicured grounds of its clubhouse complex as if he owned the place. Although not a member, he was a regular visitor, invited by this or that employee or spouse to liven up a party or act as partner, sporting or otherwise. Sometimes he came uninvited, and the Saudi guards ushered him in, assuming—rightly, in most cases—that whoever was around would welcome his visit. Not infrequently, he also came to work, under contracting assignments to integrate computer and telephone systems, and that probably smoothed his entrance, at least through the outer perimeter into the closely guarded walls of Saudi Oil's dominion—a small town in itself within Dhahran, part of the sprawling oil capital and tri-city metropolitan area extending to Khobar and the port of Dammam on the Arabian Gulf.

As usual, the guard waved in "Sheikh John," the honorific added in deference to Kaddish's facility—albeit imperfect—with spoken Arabic and his all-around bonhomie. In return for impromptu Arabic lessons, John taught them the peculiar pronunciation of the New Zealand dialect. Lately, Kaddish looked the part of a sheikh, sporting the traditional *ghutra* head gear and *thobe* of the Saudi man—"for 'safety's sake' when I'm driving in these Allah-forsaken lands. Can't be too careful. These days, driving in the desert to check an oil-flow meter that has stopped sending remote signals back to station is no longer child's play, believe you me." Other times, he would appear with a white skullcap and Indian dress to blend in with the workers milling about the coastal towns. He would explain to whoever was within earshot, "Last thing I want, mate, is to have al-Qaeda targeting *me*. Criminy, Kiwis are everybody's pals. We didn't support the assault on Iraq. Had only sixty engineers there, tops."

In his more reflective poses and Western garb, old film buffs would swear he had the appearance, air, and manner of a young Clark Gable in *Gone With the Wind:* thin mustache; dark, wavy hair; strong, handsome jaw with a dimple that collected a permanent five-o'clock shadow.

Today, the late Wednesday sun was inching closer to the horizon, signaling the start of the Islamic weekend. In the outer Saudi Oil lot, Kaddish parked his four-wheel-drive SUV, which doubled as a traveling office, filled with gear. As he climbed out of the vehicle, his trim figure, like the car, glowed white, capturing the fading bursts of the spring twilight. Kaddish stood against the lengthening shadows in tennis whites—long slacks, sneakers, and shortsleeves—a modern-day Bill Tilden sprung to life, and loped casually, racquet in hand, across to the snack bar outside the courts. "John! Over here!" called out the waving arms of two smiling women—one blonde, the other a redhead, both tanned. "Sit with us before your game." Kaddish trotted over.

"Here's our John," whispered one to the other.

"Just for a minute, ladies. I believe I'm late."

"What's the rush, *mon chéri?*" said the redhead, a French Canadian, as she rested her hand on Kaddish's muscular shoulder, giving it a squeeze and a purr of pleasure,

"Mmm, the Adonis returns." Likewise, the blonde caressed his knee in a one-two barrage of *verboten* physical displays that caused him to swivel his neck to either side and assess the reaction of any Saudis that might be nearby. None were. Kaddish laughed and in a mock plea, cried, "Help, male harassment! Female madness!" The women smiled, and one said, "We're just glad to see you."

"The pleasure is all mine."

The bleached blonde, an American, said, "Where have you been hiding yourself, Johnny? It's so *boring* now with the kids away at school and the hubbies on a business trip to Houston. There's nothing to do. Can you think of anything, Marie?"

Marie made a long face and shook her head.

"There's shopping," John said, "so long as you keep your lovely profiles low." Or, he thought, going back Stateside where you belong.

"That reminds me. We were at the mall in Khobar, visiting our Saudi—our Magic Kingdom's—version of a favorite shop back home. You probably have them in New Zealand: Victoria's Secret."

John nodded.

"Anyway, they're so uptight here, but wouldn't you know it, the store's shop windows display mannequins wearing nothing but risqué teddies, bras, and lace panties for all to see."

Marie chimed in. "And the shop attendants were all men!"

"That doesn't bother us—in fact, it's a bit of a turn-on—but it was hilarious to watch the local women, all in black and tightly covered up, coming in and acting like teenagers at home buying condoms in the drugstore. As fast as possible, not saying a word, in and out, if you know what I mean. Under the veils, I bet they were beet red."

To peek at his watch, John stretched his arms with hands clasped in front, but the women noticed the purpose of the gesture. They got to the point. "So, John," said Marie. "Stacey and I are having a get-together tomorrow night: Movie, dinner. All on the compound, of course. Would you like to come?"

Before he could answer, Nick tentatively approached and cleared his throat. John looked up and motioned him over before jumping up and wrapping his arm around Nick's shoulder, "My tennis pal, Nick. Ladies, if you'll excuse us. I seem to be ten minutes late for our game."

Stacey persisted. "Or make it a fourth, Johnny. Bring your friend. Like a game of doubles. We used to have such good times with you and Errol."

"I'll call you," Kaddish called out over his shoulder as he hustled Nick off to the farthest court.

"What's up with that?" Nick asked once the two were out of earshot. "They look nice, a bit old perhaps."

"They're not your type, my friend." To drive home the hint, John tapped his ringless ring finger and made a wry expression as he looked at Nick, "Get my drift?"

"Still, I'm impressed. So far, the only ones to flirt with me in the Kingdom have been the old Bedouin market women that come in from the desert to sell their trinkets. They ooh and aah over my blond hair."

"That's right, mate. Once they're old and considered undesirable, they can do as they please here. And I'm talking about the market women, not our friends over there."

"I've heard that the Bedouins are aggressive, and these old, how shall I say—hags?—were, too. A vendor translated for me at the *suq* as the old women gathered around, shyly at first. Then they clamored for me to sit with them. One woman held my hand and offered a silver pendant and chain. Her fingers were chapped, stained with henna, and she dangled the necklace in front of me. Not for sale, but in exchange for letting her touch my hair. Can you imagine? The vendor said she believed the touch would bring them all good luck. The woman said, 'Pendant for your wife. No? Okay for your pretty girlfriend.' I didn't have the heart to say I had none, but told my interpreter to say there would be no charge for a fondle. They insisted, he told me, and would be insulted if I refused to take the offering. Now I carry it around in my wallet, waiting for someone to give it to."

"Sweet."

"So, I guess you're going to brush off that proposition back there."

"Yup. I'll make up something or else forget to call. Hmm, instead maybe you and I could take a trip up to Riyadh, go to 'chop chop' square, and watch an execution on Friday. Or better yet, if the vice patrols don't mind, we could invite the two gals, as they seem to be in the mood for something physical. Wouldn't that be fun? Drama in real life—the severing of heads, the chopping of hands. Not to be missed, I'm told. And not for the queasy. If we happen to stray into the area—that's by the main mosque, mind you—the crowds will be sure to push us up front for a ringside seat."

"Let's take a pass on that one. To think that it happens on their holy days, and by their places of worship. I wonder whether, after the Salem trials, the Puritans hung witches on Sundays in front of the church?"

Kaddish shrugged. "That's your history, mate. Not mine."

Chapter 4

NICK HANSEN AND SUSAN BUTTS-BRADLEY were driving the four hours from Dhahran to Riyadh to attend an official reception that evening in the capital. Susan had said they would get to see the countryside, that going by car was almost as fast as the plane door to door, and that they could discuss confidential matters, if necessary. The one drawback of going overland these days: driving was riskier than air travel.

Nick had hoped to get some reading done during the flight to prepare, but instead was chauffeuring Susan, who sat in the back of his tiny Toyota. She felt it only right to adhere to Saudi custom, if not law.

The motor-pool attendant had said the consulate was unexpectedly short of drivers and cars. Ordinarily they would have provided one for a division chief. Susan was put out, she told Nick, but consoled herself that it had been her idea, not his.

After an initial silence, Nick spoke more loudly than usual so that his voice would carry over the din from the highway traffic. "I'm sorry about the limited space back there, Susan. It must be worse than economy seating, but it's all I could afford to bring from the States. You can always fly back to Dhahran after your meetings." But he'd still have to drive the damn car.

Staring glumly at the passing monotony, Susan prattled on about work, her life, plans for the future: retire in a few years, raise kids, let the man of the house get a real job. Apparently she didn't remember she had covered much the same ground when she and her hen-pecked husband Bob, who worked as a glorified office boy at the consulate, had picked up Nick at the Dhahran International Airport when he first arrived. She had seemed anxious to win Nick over as an ally before any of the others at the consulate had a chance to indoctrinate him. Nick liked Bob, felt sorry for him, and wondered how he could stand a woman who refused to let any man she deemed inferior, including her spouse, get a word in edgewise. Must be the women's-lib credo that caused her to tag on the maiden "Butts" to a perfectly good surname. The English-speaking staff had nicknamed her "Susan butts in badly," which usually drew howls of laughter when someone whispered it for the first time to those familiar with her ways.

Nick hoped to salvage some use from his time alone with the boss. When she paused for breath, he asked, "Susan, what do you think we should try to get from this reception? What would be a job well done? I mean, in the past two weeks, I haven't been able to gather any firsthand, verifiable numbers for the Chinese workers in Saudi Oil's oil fields and facilities. I've got some overall figures—guesstimates by the CIA from last year—but nothing solid or current. I sense there has been a build-up of personnel in recent months that Washington will want to know about."

Taken aback by Nick's shifting gears from her personal concerns to the work at hand, Susan paused before replying. "The Minister of Petroleum and Saudi Oil Chairman is hosting the function, and from what I hear, he has invited a full Chinese delegation, so I expect the key players will all be there. I'll work one side of the room;

you work the other. Use standard protocol for diplomatic glad-handing. In other words, find out what a person does within the first minute of meeting, and if he—or in the rare case, she—doesn't sound interesting, be sure to move on to the next. If you see me chatting with someone for longer than five minutes, make an excuse to extract yourself from your conversation and join me. They probably didn't teach you at orientation in D.C. how to make an effortless exit from the small talk, but watch Gewalt do it for the first two or three times. He's a master."

Nick was impressed. "Thanks for that. I'll stick close to the ambassador after we arrive, but I don't want to seem like a poodle tagging after him."

"Why not? How else do you get ahead in this world?"

Nick and Susan arrived at the American embassy's guesthouse, changed into formal attire, and met the ambassador and other embassy staff before attending the reception. The group drove in armor-reinforced cars with an escorted motorcade to the ministry's offices and proceeded past security to the function rooms where a hundred or more invited guests had already gathered. For Nick's benefit, Susan recalled aloud, but without indignation, how she had once come to the ministry on her own, and the guards had insisted she enter by the back through the women's entrance. Needless to say, that entry was not nearly so grand as the main gate for men. Separate but unequal, thought Nick, remembering his high-school civics lessons. Nick also noted that Susan, as the only woman from the U.S. delegation, was playing it safe and wearing a headscarf and an *abaya* over her dress. For some shapes, he supposed, such a formless cloak was a blessing in disguise.

As this was an official function, not a private party, the Saudi version of cocktails consisted of sweet carbonated and juice drinks, *laban,* a milky concoction, and cardamom tea served in glasses in silver holsters. Waiters balancing trays of *hors d'oeuvres* wove in and among the knots of men in their traditional white *thobes,* black tuxedos, or dark suits. The contrasting black-and-white color scheme reminded Nick of Chinese Go, a game he someday wanted to learn. There were only a handful of women, all from foreign delegations, and all in black *abayas,* as if in mourning. Susan had chosen the right outfit. As the Saudi men in the room studiously ignored the female guests, the women tended to converse among themselves or with foreign colleagues.

Nick shadowed the ambassador, hoping he wouldn't notice, while Susan made a beeline toward the small gaggle of other females. Nick's initially positive impression of Susan's diplomatic savvy quickly faded. So much for her working the room.

One lady, a petite Asian balanced precariously on high heels, did seem to break through the ever-present, but unacknowledged, wall of segregation. She talked with a succession of Saudi officials, some of whom had approached her to say "hello." Her high-pitched laughter floated across the room, and she gestured with tiny hands or nodded emphatically as if her interlocutors were the most insightful persons present.

Hmm, the life of the party, if not exactly the belle of the ball. Nick kept her in the corner of his eye, as he stood politely a few steps away from the ambassador.

Gewalt beckoned with an expansive gesture. "Nicholas, come here for a minute, let me make a formal introduction." As Nick scuttled to his side, he said, "Your Excellency, allow me to present the newest member of our foreign-service team, Nicholas Hansen. Mr. Hansen, I believe, attended your *alma mater.*"

The Saudi Minister to OPEC and Saudi Oil Chairman, Mr. Abdul-Zayyat, shook Nick's hand. "And what did you study at Stanford, young man?"

"Chinese, your Excellency."

"You're in good company then." He pointed toward a cluster of East Asians. "You might want to keep an eye on those Chinese tonight to see why they're so successful. Perhaps you Americans, our old friends, can learn from the Chinese, our new ones." Nick was about to make a suitably decorous reply, when the minister, having scanned the rest of the room, said, "And you might start with that one in particular, a charming woman who seems to have captured the attentions of one of our rising stars." With that, he turned from Nick, clapped the ambassador on the shoulder, and walked away.

Left holding his drink, Nick watched the Asian woman chatting with a tall, trim, and impeccably dressed Arab in a tuxedo. His once black head of hair had turned almost completely silver, yet a thick mustache, goatee, and eyebrows retained their former color. As they both seemed at ease, Nick bucked himself with a gulp from his glass, forgetting there was no alcoholic boost in the beverage, and made his way slowly through the crowded room to the pair. He stood nearby and hoped one of them might notice, turn, or smile some form of invitation to join in. Neither did.

Nick overheard their conversation. "Saudis have to learn from you Chinese. We're moving backward, as your country makes its great leap forward. In the past twenty years, our per-capita GDP has shrunk by three fourths; yours has quadrupled.

"It's time for a closer arrangement. We've got the oil; you've got the skilled, cheap labor. Send more Chinese here to train our people."

"That shouldn't be a problem. Our government is encouraging technicians to work in places like Saudi Arabia." The woman leaned toward the man and asked a question that Nick couldn't hear.

"It's down to Huawei and possibly Lucent."

Nick recognized both firms. Despite a weak international brand name, China's leading vendor of telecom equipment was pricing its products so low that well-established U.S. companies like Lucent Technologies could no longer compete.

The woman looked pleased. "Someone from the embassy or I can accompany you to Hong Kong to meet with Huawei's senior management. Their headquarters is just across the border in Shenzhen."

"That will have to wait until the summer after the board meeting."

Nick was embarrassed to continue eavesdropping. "Hello, I'm Nicholas Hansen," but his soft voice did not carry well over the background din. Still no response. Oh, what the hell. *"Nin hao ma? Nin shi cong nali lai de?"* Ma Ling turned with a start, irritated, *"Shenme ne?"* Then, blinking at Nick, she laughed, "What? Oh, I thought it was one of my co-workers acting like an idiot and asking where I was from. I'm sorry. You speak Chinese very well."

"*Nali, nali?* Where is this good speaker?"

"Ah, and just right with the modest denials. You must have lived for many years in China, Mr. . . . ."

"Hansen, Nicholas Hansen from the American embassy." Nick addressed the older man. "Excuse me for being rude, but neither of you noticed when I tried out my English."

"That's quite all right." He held Nick's hand in the gentle way that Americans, accustomed to more vice-like grips, mistake for a lack of manly fortitude. "Let me leave you two young people together to reminisce about the Orient. Ma Ling, we can chat again at any time." With a bow, he left them.

"I didn't mean to drive him away."

"Don't worry. I know him quite well . . ." Ma Ling hastened to add, "in a business sense."

Nick studied her birdlike features, which had a trace of Western about them that he couldn't quite place. "He seemed genteel, almost courtly."

Nick's mind compiled a silent inventory: oval face, small, aquiline nose, hooded, almost hawk-like eyelids, small, graying teeth . . . probably the result of too much tetracycline, he thought, remembering others about that age, nearing forty, and showing vestiges of misguided health care from China's harder years.

"Dr. Sami? Yes, she—I mean, he—is a favorite among many. When I tire, my English is the first to fly from my head."

"So that's the Sami al-Sayyid I've heard so much about. Now I do regret his leaving."

"But you still have me to talk to." Her lips compressed to a pout. "It is strange to find a Chinese-speaking foreign devil in this land." Ma Ling laughed, overcome by her own wit. "Will you be long in Riyadh, Mr. Hansen?"

"Mainly I'm in Dhahran, but I've only been in country since the start of the year."

"So that is why I have not seen you before. I live in Dhahran, too, which means you and I will become good friends."

"Dhahran has no Chinese consulate that I know of. You must be with Saudi Oil."

"Good guess!" More twittering.

"Are there many Chinese at Saudi Oil?"

"That's a secret," she said with a frown that changed quickly to a mirthful smile. "You will have to torture it out of me." She jostled Nick's arm causing some of the fizzy drink he was holding to bubble over. "Sorry! Oh, I cannot be serious tonight. You are a serious man, Mr. Hansen. What do you do for fun?"

Nick thought, Fun? In Saudi Arabia? "Tennis."

"Great!" Ma Ling clapped her hands in delight. "I love tennis. Let's play together." Then, collecting her propriety, she said, "You must be very good. Do you have a partner?"

"Yes, but he's a bit of a hack."

"Just like me! But my girlfriend Fatima plays well, so let's make what you call a double date. I'm with you, she's with him. It's okay. At Saudi Oil, everything is easy."

"Fatima, you said? Is that a common name?"

"I would not know, Mr. Nick. She is the daughter of that gentleman you met."

After the formal speeches by the minister and ranking diplomats, as the reception was breaking up, Susan buttonholed Nick to compare notes. "Any progress?"

"Some. I had a friendly talk with Ma Ling. I believe you spoke with her, too." Nick had seen Susan's wide bulk towering over the petite woman for several minutes, engaged in what seemed a one-sided monologue, as Ma Ling smiled, nodded, and gradually backed away until a familiar face had come to her rescue.

"Was that her name? Ma? That's what I call my mother."

And I bet Mom is a pseudo-feminist like you.

"Ma Ling's surname translates as 'horse,' which is common among the Hui ethnic group. The Hui are Muslims and originally came to China a thousand years ago on horses from the Middle East. I suppose that's why they posted her here, under the assumption of some natural affinity."

"Hmmph. Horse. Hardly looks like one. Let me know what you dig up in Dhahran. The ambassador will want something fairly soon."

The next day, Susan went home from Riyadh by plane. Nick drove.

Chapter 5

SHEIKH SALEH'S PREMONITION came true, for he did not get a chance to deliver his next sermon. The same two men accosted him on his way to the Suweidi mosque, seized his notes for the week's harangue, and, after a quick glance through them, hustled the cleric into the back of a nearby van. Since Saleh usually preferred to walk alone to the mosque while composing his thoughts, Tariq had not accompanied him, but arrived early to perform the rituals of prayer at the back of the large carpeted room. He preferred the rear as it afforded the best vantage point from which to observe the listeners' reactions.

Today, however, Tariq felt an unusual disquiet start from the front of the chamber and ripple backward in a low rumble toward him. Instead of his father, a hastily installed cleric was about to give the morning's speech. As in previous weeks, murmurs erupted among the audience of disaffected men, but this time they muttered angrily at the replacement of their spiritual leader. Instead of fiery words, the soothing bromides of a government stooge were floating down from the pulpit. None recognized the new cleric, a wizened man who seemed to have been pulled into service after many years' retirement, and few sat through the entire delivery. Most looked around to assess others' reactions; some got up to leave.

Tariq sprang to his feet to see if his father was seated elsewhere on the mosque's carpet. Perhaps Saleh was introducing some older mentor to lend further credence to today's speech. But Father was nowhere to be seen, and the old man's weak voice made no mention of him. Before the cleric completed the first invocation, Tariq had lurched for the exit door. Once outside, he paced to and fro, unsure what to do. Several young men soon followed, and one placed his hand on Tariq's shoulder.

"Is your reverend father unwell?"

Tariq's voice shook. "No, Rasheed, I don't think so. But he spoke recently of threats. They must have taken him— to one of the prisons around Riyadh."

"We'll help you find him. Tell me what you need." Rasheed motioned to the others to stand apart as he and Tariq, with heads bent, walked slowly together across the tiled square surrounding the mosque.

"I'll have to do this alone, my friend. The authorities probably won't provide information to anyone except immediate family members."

"Then go now, Tariq, and let us arrange things here. We won't confront that old cleric in the holy place, but after he finishes, we'll ask him what he knows."

"Not much, by the look of him." With that, Tariq clasped Rasheed's hands and hobbled off in search of a cab.

In his agitation, Tariq had not thought through how hard it might be to locate Sheikh Saleh. He spent nearly an hour and cab fare he could ill afford to reach al-Hair prison, only to find the administrative office closed for the weekend. The young man cursed himself for not thinking that all would be shut on Friday. He did, at least, note the phone number for inquiries and resolved not to make the same mistake twice.

The placard on the shuttered office door outside the prison gates gave an appearance of efficiency and order that did not exist, or at least not for the common detainee. The Saudi government had never invested much in its prison system; with dwindling oil revenues and monies siphoned off to prestige projects or princely kickbacks, little was left for services that officials begrudged to those who ran afoul of the system.

The king maintained power through fear and stoked that fear with the uncertainty engendered from capricious rulings, double standards, or no standards at all. Rules and regulations were unwritten, or if codified, honored only in the breach. For the elite, the state turned a blind eye to even the more egregious crimes, but kept the laws in reserve to bludgeon those who fell from favor. Unlike the case precedents, statutes, and codes of the West, Shar'ia law was subject to endless interpretation, a shifting quicksand that could send a person to doom for looking the wrong way at another, a casual remark, or an ill-advised fashion statement. Not surprisingly, a similar murk clouded the administration of the penal system.

To Tariq's dismay, when the office reopened, it had no records of any arrest or detention of a Sheikh Saleh al-Qaatil. The officer responding to Tariq's telephoned request and then to a second visit was neither brutal nor callous; he even affected an air of concern and suggested other prison addresses to contact. No, there was no central database of records and even if there were, it would take weeks, if not months, for the entry of the appropriate file. As traditionalists, the al-Qaatils shunned all graven images as un-Islamic, so Tariq had no photos of his father to show and ask, "Have you seen this man?" A name and description, that was all.

Tariq cursed his ill luck to have only women in the family. Useless! They could not disperse throughout the city and help with the search nor, in fact, leave the house without him. Even if Tariq had the right phone numbers to give them, no prison official would take their phone calls, but would demand to speak with the man of the house, and there was only so much that he, the remaining man, could do at one time.

After days of fruitless effort, the resignation to fate that guided much of his actions had settled in. Tariq's mind circled back over the same thoughts, each an added burden to the weight already on his back. With no father, no income, no savings, and rent due at month's end, how were they to continue to live? Confined to the home, the women could earn but a pittance. He could sell off Hajar to Muamar but, under the circumstances, that was not right and not proper. As only the temporary head of the household, he was in no position to conclude the betrothal contract with Muamar. Perhaps it is for the best, he thought. Hajar will have a reprieve from marriage, at least until Father returns. Such an ill-advised union, even if profitable, could end in sorrow. She is not submissive, and would doubtless use some tricks to betray or shame the blind man. And such scandal would redound on them all.

"It's settled." Tariq gathered the two household's females into the apartment's largest room and made the announcement. The women, on edge from the week's uncertainty, eyed one another and waited for his explanation.

"Since Father is away for God knows how long, we have to divide his family. We can't afford to live here any longer." Each wife sat with her daughters, and expressions of relief flitted across the senior women's faces at the thought of no longer sharing the same roof.

Tariq went on, "I've spoken to Layla's brother, and he has agreed to take her and the child. The rest, including Hajar, will come with me to al-Khobar."

Hajar's elation at no mention of marriage to Muamar passed quickly to fear. She gripped her mother's hand. "But, Brother, I should stay with my family."

"What family? We are all your family, and you do as I tell you."

Suheir asked, "My son, do you have any news of your father?"

"Mother, I've heard he is in al-Hair, but they won't let me speak with him," Tariq said. "The brothers at the mosque have arranged an assignment for me in the East. They'll provide an apartment where we can live and money to cover some of the expenses. Soon they'll try to smuggle a message to Father in prison through their contacts and will let him know where we have gone.

"Until I have instructions from him about Muamar, I plan to keep an eye on Hajar. So for now, she comes with us—with you, me, Aisha, and Munira, whom she can help care for." Tariq looked at the wasted figure of his disabled sister, who sat mute in the corner, and added, "I don't know what we'll do about the medicine or the blood transfusions. God willing, there must be free clinics in Khobar. It's not just a fishing village any more."

Chapter 6

"WAIT A MOMENT, MUSTAPHA. Pull over." Nick instructed the driver to bring the consulate's vehicle next to a beat-up car with its hood propped open and a man in Indian dress bent over the engine, peering inside. Nick had noticed the same broken-down sedan on the roadside of Dhahran twenty minutes before while en route to the commissary.

"Can we give you a lift?" Nick called out.

A bedraggled man straightened himself and wiped the sweat from his face with a dirty sleeve. "Thank you, that is most kind, good sir, but I do not wish to leave my car. I think the battery has died."

"Hold on, we'll help you jump start it."

First, at Mustapha's suggestion, they tried the easy way, seating the man behind the wheel, shifting the car to neutral, and pushing. But the engine still failed to turn over and catch. They then opened the back of the consulate's vehicle to fish out some cables for a jump start. As Mustapha and the stranded driver began attaching them, with Nick looking on, a second SUV pulled up.

"Nick, what are you doing in this heat?" It was Ma Ling, unveiled, in the front passenger seat. "Get in. We'll give you a ride."

"I'm trying to help out this fellow. . . ."

"Your driver seems able to handle it. You haven't forgotten our game, have you?"

"No, Mustapha was going to drop me at the club. I suppose your taking me will save time and leave him with one less thing to worry about." Nick grabbed his bag, climbed into the back seat behind Ma Ling, and gave his driver some final instructions. "If the cables don't do the trick, please stop at the nearest service station and have them send a tow truck for this guy." Mustapha did not reply but cast a bemused look at Ma Ling and back at Nick.

As they pulled away, Nick asked, "Ma Ling, don't you think this might seem improper?"

Ma Ling turned with her elbow propped on the front seat. "Oh, you are an old ninny, Mr. Hansen. I always sit up front. We Chinese are egalitarians."

"Not just that. I mean, driving with an unrelated man. . . ."

"Who? You or Mr. Huang?" she said, looking at her driver who was decked out in a tan cap, matching gloves, and loose-fitting Mao-style jacket. "That is one of the local inconsistencies, isn't it? If the religious police found me alone with you—a non-related man— they could take me away to be whipped as a prostitute. But I'm not allowed to drive, so must have this unrelated man take me all over town.

"Of course, with Huang Lei, no one would dare insult me in such a fashion. Please introduce yourself. He'll be amazed to hear you speak Chinese."

Nick greeted the silent driver, whose broad bulk and close-cropped, gray hair reminded him of a calmer Ambassador Gewalt. Huang's face lit up in a big smile. He looked at Nick in the mirror and replied in a deep voice that Nick couldn't understand. Ma Ling translated. "His accent is very strong, so you won't catch much of what he says, but he follows you perfectly."

Nick said, "If it weren't for that driving outfit, I'd think he might be a bodyguard."

"And you'd be right! Oh, you are clever!" Ma Ling laughed. "I tell Huang the gloves are a bit much, but he is too vain about the scars on his hands."

"I'll have to be more careful around you."

"Before my husband left, he would often drive me when I needed to go out, but Huang has been a good companion since then."

"I didn't realize you were married...."

"Divorced and, fortunately, there are no children to fight over. We came out here three years ago as employees of China Oil and I became liaison to Saudi Oil, but there was little for my husband Ruan to do."

Nick tried to imagine what Ruan was like. He must have had his hands full with this one.

Ma Ling continued. "He is a Party member and did some work for the embassy in Riyadh, but I think resented my getting on better than he could. I guess my being Muslim and knowing Arabic helped. Or could it be my vivacious personality?" She turned around and winked at Nick.

"So you're not in the Party? Isn't that the way to get ahead?" Nick asked.

"Certainly, but to be in the Communist Party, you must be an atheist. That is incompatible with my religion. Even though I'm not devout, it wouldn't be right. But like the other Hui, I support my country and will fight for it." She clenched her tiny fists to make the point and shadow boxed with Huang's large shoulder.

"Did you know that one of the five stars on China's flag stands for us Hui?"

"But it's still one of the four smaller ones, right?"

"Yes, but unlike the other Chinese Muslims—the Uighurs—we do not harbor terrorists and we look Chinese, so the government trusts us."

Nick nodded. "I doubt I would ever see any Uighurs posted here. Your embassy would assume they would be scheming with al-Qaeda. The last thing you need is to turn Xinjiang into a Chinese Chechnya."

"Actually, I grew up in Xinjiang and have many friends who are Uighur. There are only a few bad pears—or what you call—'apples.'"

"So you must be a natural for this place. Oil fields and deserts are nothing new to you. Tell me, how does China view the U.S. in the Middle East?"

"The same way I view you—warily." Ma Ling laughed. Then turning serious again, she said, "Although we keep our heads down, we are a proud people. You know, the West humiliated us for centuries." She glanced at Huang. "But now, like a sleeping giant, we will one day stand up and challenge America."

Nick took this comment as an idle boast, borne of feelings of insecurity, and thought of his stay in Beijing in 1999 as an exchange student. Then the U.S. bombing of China's Belgrade embassy had led to government-organized street protests that subsequently fizzled. What if something similar happened now? Despite aggressive U.S. policies in recent years, neither side could afford to rattle its sabers any more.

The two fell silent as the car reached the Saudi Oil club. John, Fatima, and Ahmad were already suited up and waiting for them. Approaching from behind, Nick overheard Fatima chatting with John: "When I first told Ahmad I wanted to play tennis here, he said, 'Well, I don't know. What you and Faisal do in the U.S. is your business, but when Father is away, I am responsible. Let me consult the Koran to see what it says about games with sticks.'"

"I was joking!" Ahmad protested. Then turning and seeing Nick, followed by Ma Ling, Ahmad waved at Ma Ling and shook Nick's hand in both of his. "Mr. Nicholas. Good to see you again. I came with Fatima."

Nick grinned at them and said, "Yes, it's a good idea for Fatima to have a chaperone, particularly with John present."

Kaddish parried the barb. "Now, now, boy. Ahmad and I go way back at Saudi Oil—don't we, mate? We're both propeller heads—technical nerds, that is," he explained to Ma Ling's puzzled expression. "Although this is the first time he has introduced me to his sister, or even told me he had one."

"Well, John, your reputation preceded you." Ahmad laughed.

Fatima kept John on the defensive. "And I was safely hidden in the U.S. for much of that time."

Kaddish turned to Nick to deflect the ribbing. "And you are escorting. . . ?"

Nick introduced John to Ma Ling, who gave a mock curtsy to his exaggerated bow.

All five then walked to the courts, Ahmad climbed into the referee's chair and said, "Now someone tell me how to keep score."

John called across the net, "Nick, shall we go for the usual thirty-point spot per game?"

"Let's see how the rallies go."

In the milliseconds that enabled him to rate another player by the swing of the first stroke, Nick noticed that Fatima had the graceful motion of someone naturally gifted as a late learner or brought up from childhood with lessons. He suspected the former to be the case. Ma Ling, on the other hand, hacked at the ball as she had warned she would.

After some limbering up, Nick won the racquet toss for first serve. "Okay, we'll start each game with a love-thirty handicap." He consciously downgraded his serving speed to enable Fatima to return the shot.

Before Nick's serve to John in the backhand court, Ma Ling backpedaled from the net to the baseline. "Thanks for the vote of no confidence, Ma Ling. I've made some bad shots but never hit my partner in the back."

"Oh, I trust you, Nick. It's just that Mr. Kaddish shoots his balls like rockets."

"Don't worry. Only a few of them go in, so there's little chance of one heading straight into you up there."

Unlike John, Nick didn't go for winners. He preferred to keep the ball in play and would rather lose with both sides playing well than win if the other played badly. Nick made sure to congratulate opponents on their good shots. Not aggressive enough, his coach had said.

In the end, the ball boy got the best of the workout, chasing errant shots across the empty courts on either side. The only damage done to Ma Ling was self-inflicted: a volley deflected from her racquet's edge off the side of her head and miraculously landing back over the net, a feat that had the others laughing, her smarting, and Ahmad climbing down from his perch to help settle the point.

"Time for some drinks," John called out, and handed the ball boy a fistful of bills as a tip, equivalent to a day's wages for the youth. The boy beamed as John thanked him. "*Shukran jazeelan, ya walid.*"

They all went to the clubhouse patio and sat at a shaded table. Nick noticed Huang seated with his eyes closed, apparently asleep in the corner, and asked Ma Ling to invite him over.

"No, he's meditating. Besides he doesn't speak English so would not understand the conversation."

Ahmad ordered a round of *carcadays*—a purplish drink made from hibiscus. When the sweating glasses arrived, John, ever the showman, sipped first as if sampling a fine wine and said in an affected southern drawl, "Mmm, that packs a twang." He then promptly leaned next to Ahmad and ignored the others to talk about work. Glad to have the women alone, Nick thought of how to draw Fatima out. He asked how she and Ma Ling knew each other.

"We met at the Saudi Oil clinic. Ma Ling came in with a twisted ankle from. . . ."

"Sticking my high heel into the wrong place."

". . . and we talked. I think you had already met my father then, right?"

Ma Ling nodded and Fatima continued. "Mother had recently died, and Father wanted me to have the steadying influence of an older woman, so since that time, Ma Ling has become a regular at our home in Dhahran."

"And I was alone—Ruan had returned to China—so I enjoy the company."

Nick said, "It doesn't seem easy for women to fraternize—er, socialize—like—um, you know, to mix with friends, as it is for men." His cheeks colored as he tried to choose the appropriate words.

"Having lived in the U.S., I've become a bit of a feminist. I often ask Ma Ling about women in China," Fatima said. "It's not so easy there, either."

"Our society considers women inferior," Ma Ling said. "When I was young, some parents didn't even bother to name the baby girls and just referred to them as 'Number 2' or 'Number 3' depending on their order of birth."

Nick remembered his stay in Beijing and laughed. "One of my friends in China—an old chauvinist—still refers to his grown sisters like that."

Neither Ma Ling nor Fatima seemed to appreciate the humor.

Fatima sighed. "At least Chinese women are allowed to drive."

Ma Ling made a subtle dig at her Saudi friend. "Not everyone grew up in a wealthy family—or one that could afford a car." The three fell silent. As if to emphasize her point, Ma Ling looked around at the opulence of the Saudi Oil club before continuing. "Here, at least, the embassy brought hundreds of drivers for us." She gestured toward her slumbering Buddha. "Like the dependable Mr. Huang over there."

Fatima's voice rose, losing its musical lilt. "In Maryland, I don't have to ask Faisal to take me around. I drive myself to college every day, but in this country I have to have a driver. Saudi men say it's because they treat us like 'queens,' because we all deserve chauffeurs. That's absurd. What did the prophet ever say about automobiles? And what about women who have no money to hire a driver? Women in every other Muslim country can drive. Why not here?"

Ahmad and John had stopped talking and were listening. Never quiet for long, John butted into the conversation and assumed the role of raconteur. "Ah, driving in Muslim countries. That reminds me of my days traipsing about North Africa and Yemen. Part of my self-styled graduate education, you might say—a one-year, global tour. We Kiwis go for long vacations 'cause it's so damn far to get to everywhere else."

Ma Ling asked John why he had come to Saudi Arabia, but he didn't answer directly.

"I had to get out of New Zealand: the job was too boring. Pulling telephone cables through office buildings—that wasn't for me. I am, after all, just a self-taught computer hack—no genius programmer like my friend here." He patted Ahmad on the back. "So I went to see what the rest of the world might offer.

"Skipped Asia completely, which means I have no China war stories to tell. But I did get to Europe and at one point found myself on a steamer from Gibraltar to Morocco with a small-time thief and drug dealer. Managed to shake him and avoid having hashish planted in my knapsack." John patted his pockets as if to see whether he was still carrying any.

"Got waylaid by the usual carpet hucksters who don't take 'no' for an answer even though it's impossible to carry a six-by-nine-foot carpet in a forty-inch backpack. Apart from some *Arabian Nights* adventures with ladies along the way, I managed to stay out of trouble, avoided the prisons, and befriended some people who showed me the famous Arab hospitality."

Nick saw Fatima and John smiling at each other and wanted to take him down a peg. "So you repaid the hospitality by dallying with their daughters . . . or wives."

John ignored the comment.

"What about the driving?" Nick prodded. He cupped his hands behind his head.

"That was in Yemen, but let me get there first, mate.

"So I bummed around Morocco and did some odd jobs in Casablanca. It didn't look at all like the movie, believe me. Next stop was Algeria, soon after the killing had ended. That place had some horror stories—fundamentalists slaughtering people. You better hope it doesn't happen here one day."

Nick was tapping his feet, "Uh huh, uh huh. . . ." He knew his interruptions were childish and felt like a little kid clamoring for attention, jealous of another's charms.

"Okay. Let's fast forward to Yemen. Not the safest place a few years back, but I could speak a bit of Arabic and wanted to hike in the mountains. If you can handle a rifle on your back, you're okay—not that I carried one, though sometimes wished I had. Instead I slung a curved Yemeni dagger around my waist and drove from one hilly range to the next in their bus taxis—big, old, American station wagons belching exhaust and crammed with a dozen passengers who smelled like goats.

"On those long drives with your arms wedged to your side between two guys that look like they'd slit your throat on a dare, there's not much to do but talk. During one ride, the two on either side of me seemed to like my appearance. A little flattery is okay, but I didn't enjoy the way the conversation was heading, so I steered it to my favorite topic—women. That got them going. One had marriageable daughters and asked if I was Muslim. I hesitated, said I respected Islam, and might even consider converting if I hadn't been born a Christian. They got even more excited at that, and by the end of the trip had me witnessing three times that there was no God but

Allah, no prophet but Mohammed, and some other mumbo jumbo. To their minds, I had converted—a simple process, actually."

"You're a Muslim?" Fatima squealed. Her voice rose to a pitch beyond her normal range.

"Not exactly. I had my legs and arms crossed, and for good measure, a couple of fingers and toes. So I remained faithful to Lord Jesus." He winked.

Ahmad and Fatima frowned, and she said, "You lied then."

"Nick, explain to them what it means if you do this when you speak." He held up his crossed fingers.

Fatima said, "I know, but still it's not honest."

"I just wanted to keep these guys happy and off my back—literally. Besides, they were delighted to think they had a new convert. The two were all set to have me move into one of their homes—after some back and forth as to which house was better—and marry their daughters. If they had thought I was rich enough, they would have sold me four of the girls—that's the Muslim limit, isn't it?

"You're terrible," Fatima said, smiling.

John let the comment pass. "When we arrived at their squalid village, and I saw my fate dangling before me, I begged off. Said I had an urgent appointment in the next city, but would be sure to look them up when back in town."

"You, devil, Mr. Kaddish," said Ma Ling, whose grin belied her words.

"Yes," he winked back. "And remember that's spelled with a 'K,' not a 'C.'"

"Despite what you say, I think you may in fact be a Muslim—just not a practicing one," said Fatima. "With the right outfit, you'd look like Omar Sharif."

"No, no. I'm still a man of the cross. In fact, to prove it, I have a tattoo that says 'I love Jesus' on my lower cheek." He leaned forward and patted his butt. "If I ever do convert—and my grandparents would be rolling in their graves to hear me say that—they'd have to sand this off first."

"Can we see?" Fatima giggled.

"Fatima!" Ahmad was not amused and got up to pay the bill. "We'd better be going before such talk gets you in trouble."

John jumped to his feet and put his arm around Ahmad, "No harm intended, mate. Don't go away mad. Besides, I wanted to invite you and Nick to a Hash House Harrier run next weekend. Sorry, ladies, here in the Magic Kingdom, it's just for guys."

"A Hash what?" Ahmad furrowed his brow.

"It's a regular run in the countryside that expatriates do—mainly Brits and Americans with their invited guests. As a Kiwi, I'm an honorary Brit, and the Americans—the less cultured ones than Nick—don't hold their noses toward me as they do with the French. The run is easy going: some 'hares' or rabbits mark a trail a day in advance, and the rest—the harriers or 'dogs'—go barking mad chasing after it to see who can find the clue—the marker—to where the trail leads. We hold these runs as an excuse to go into the desert and drink some bootleg brew. Of course, you didn't hear that from me. Most of us camp overnight and then drive back the following morning after the smell of alcohol has gone from our breaths. Wouldn't want any *mutawwas* catching a scent of that. It's all great fun, really."

"Thanks for the invite, John. I'm game," Nick said. "But are these social outings for drinkers with a running problem, or vice versa?"

John paused to parse Nick's meaning. "Both. But you don't have to be in shape to participate."

"I'm afraid I'm even worse at drinking than at tennis," said Ahmad.

"No matter, mate. Come along for the desert air and a bit of exercise. We'll share my tent—it's big enough for three."

"Go on, Ahmad," Fatima said. "You can tell me all about it afterwards." And with that, the matter was settled.

Dusk had fallen, and the group broke up. John and Nick lingered in their seats as Huang took Ma Ling to her apartment. Ahmad and Fatima drove to their family house.

"Sorry to give you a hard time today, John."

"Oh, I was showing off. Need to be put in my place now and then."

Nick fingered his empty glass. "No, really. I guess I'm on edge. The initial thrill of my culture shock at being in Saudi Arabia—of things new and different—wore off months ago, and now the drab reality is sinking in."

"What you need, my friend, is a woman. Do you have any prospects?"

"No."

John looked east at the silhouetted horizon. "How about you and me taking some R&R in Bahrain sometime? Ma Ling seems to like you. Why not get to know her better?"

"What about Fatima?"

"Oh, I'd stay away from the Saudi women. Not worth the risk. You saw how even Ahmad reacted to a playful jest, and he's about as easy-going and Westernized as they come."

"She seems keen on you," Nick said.

"If this were another country, I might try to make something of it. But here? No. Ma Ling on the other hand. . . ."

"Forget Ma Ling. You already have your hands full with the expatriate contingent. If any tire of the Kaddish charms, pass one on to yours truly."

"Frankly, I'm not sure what they see in me. I've heard it's a man's hands that catch a woman's eye." John splayed his fingers and inspected his nails. "But in my case, it's probably another appendage that keeps her interested."

Ahmad opened the door to the palatial house that for months had seemed empty. Servants still guarded the gates, tended the cars, cooked the meals, and weeded the garden, but with his mother gone, it was no longer the same. Muslims are not supposed to mourn the dead who have passed to heaven, but that did not mean the al-Sayyids did not miss her. They no longer held dinner parties at home and rarely attended others. A large photo of an attractive, middle-aged woman was the only human image on display in the house. Tasteful, abstract art decorated the high walls, and wooden ceiling fans, augmented by air conditioning, kept the carpeted marble floors and contemporary furniture cool, but conveyed the atmosphere of a mausoleum, not a lived-in home. Sami al-Sayyid now spent most of his time in Riyadh while both brother and sister worked long hours at Saudi Oil, often eating out together and returning to the house late, only to sleep.

On this night, a light was on in Sami's study. Fatima peeked inside, gave a squeal of delight, and rushed in to hug her father. "Papa, you weren't supposed to get back until tomorrow!"

"My child, I missed you and your brother, so I came back early. What have you been up to?" he said, as he stroked her unruly hair.

Fatima told him of the mixed-doubles match and spoke glowingly of John: "He's charming and funny and very handsome."

A look of concern spread across Sami's face. "When in Arabia, you should act as a Saudi. I don't want you interacting with men, particularly foreign ones."

"Oh, Father. This is only on the Saudi Oil compound. It's like a little piece of America."

"I'm not sure the Americans are still our friends."

"John is not American," said Ahmad.

"That at least is in his favor. And what about the other one? Ma Ling, I know."

"A quiet American," said Fatima. "Sometimes he seems awkward, but he's nice enough."

Sami glanced at his son. "You never can tell with those quiet types."

Fatima examined her fingernails. "He's a junior diplomat with the embassy and helping me renew my student visa."

"I wouldn't expect much of them these days, so you may have to go to a different country's school to finish your degree. In the meantime, perhaps we should talk again about arranging a marriage. It worked out well for your mother and me."

An image flashed across Fatima's mind. She was plucking the strings of a wooden lute and singing softly a traditional Saudi song for her mother. The prematurely aged woman lay ill in bed in the room that the family now kept closed. She asked Fatima to stop for a moment to talk. With her daughter's help, the mother propped herself on the pillows. *Fatima, find a good man like your father—one who works hard and is kind. He doesn't need to be handsome or even a Saudi, but don't rush.* She took a sip of water, her voice hoarse, little more than a whisper. *We are proud of all our children, but you're special and dear to me above the rest.* As Fatima stroked back the sweaty hair from her mother's forehead, the woman's weak grasp on the daughter's arm faltered. *I have asked your father not to force your hand, so look after him and Ahmad when I'm gone.* Oh, Mama, don't talk like that. You're not leaving us. *When you go back, and I hope you will, take care of Faisal. None of you may want to stay here forever. . . .*

Sami persisted, startling Fatima from her reverie. "Why is your generation so against it? Two grown sons and a daughter, with none married. How do I explain *that* to my colleagues?"

"We're just choosy. Save this gloomy topic for another day, Papa. Tonight let's have fun. I'll play some music for you and Ahmad."

Chapter 7

"It will work out for the best. Trust in Allah," said Layla as Tariq pulled a sobbing Hajar from her mother's embrace. Rasheed was waiting outside at the curb in a pick-up truck partially loaded with suitcases he had roped down. Its motor was idling. One half of the truck's back was empty; a frayed blanket, folded double, covered the metal ridges of its flooring. Tariq patted the top of the head of his little half-sister, who had come outside to wave them off, and led his mother Suheir by the arm to the vehicle. She had trouble seeing through the heavy veil that blocked almost all light from view. He sat her on a puff cushion atop the blanket. After lifting his crippled sister Munira, Tariq let Aisha and Hajar climb in unassisted. The younger women used thinner veils, which still obscured their faces, but enabled them in the day's sunlight to make out more than just shadows. Their ankle-length *abayas* tangled with the ropes and rough corners of the truck's contents as the three crouched uncomfortably beside the older woman. With everything packed, Tariq slammed the back door shut, got into the front cab beside Rasheed, and they were off.

Before leaving Riyadh, Rasheed stopped at a local animal market to buy a baby goat, which he placed between him and Tariq in the front. The goat's legs were loosely bound to prevent it from scampering about the cabin. They would slaughter the animal that evening in celebration of Tariq's new life in al-Khobar.

Once on the highway, the rushing wind made speech all but impossible for the women in the open back of the truck. They clasped the folds of their flapping gowns, gripped a taut rope or metal siding, and thanked Allah that this big, wide road seemed to have no painful bumps along it. The special cargo made Rasheed drive with more caution than normal, and he stayed in the slow lane following pick-ups and small cars laden in similar fashion. Most of the traffic honked and whizzed by, jockeying for position, shifting lanes, or straddling two lanes at a time.

"We will initially employ you as a scout, Tariq," he said. "We'd like you to watch the foreign compounds around Dhahran, so once we arrive, you can use this vehicle to take you to and from al-Khobar."

"But I don't know how to drive."

"Never mind. Here I'll show you. It's easy." Rasheed's pudgy index finger tapped on each of the instruments in front of him, while he explained what they did. Tariq tried to make a mental inventory, but was sure he would forget.

"After we get to Khobar and drop off the stuff in the back, I'll take you into the desert and give you another lesson, with you behind the wheel.

"We can't pay you much at first, so you'll need to get work for your sisters. You said one can sew?" Tariq grunted yes. "When you're not watching the movements of the infidels, you might take some samples of her work to the local stores to see if they will buy it.

"The other one—the one that speaks English—might have a better chance of an income, at least until the marriage goes through. Khobar still has lots of foreigners who need services, and many of them only speak English.

Their wives shop in women-only malls that have recently begun hiring Saudi women as store clerks. You should take her there."

Tariq stopped stroking the head of the goat, crossed his arms, and scowled at the thought of letting Hajar out among such people.

Rasheed glanced at him. "I can't think of any other way." Tariq made no reply, and Rasheed looked into the rearview mirror to check that all the bundles were still in the back.

"You'll need to be especially vigilant. With so many foreign *kafirs,* the coastal areas are looser in their ways than the Saudi heartland. You'll be shocked by some things you see there, but don't worry: one day soon we'll push them all into the sea to sink into the slime they created."

After several hours on the road, they stopped for a brief break to let the women relieve themselves, and then continued on. The sun beat down mercilessly, and despite the cab's air conditioning, made the right side of Tariq's *thobe* uncomfortably hot. He was tempted to slide into the middle of the seat and shift places with the goat. That would show weakness, he thought, so he stayed put.

After a while, Tariq's jaw slackened, spittle dribbled out, and his head dropped down, bouncing up with a start before nodding slowly down again, a process repeated for much of the remaining ride. The goat bleated occasionally, but had stopped fidgeting.

Rasheed nudged Tariq. "We're almost there." Tariq looked up, to the right, and in the distance saw a plane lifting off, its tail fins sparkling in the glare. An oasis of buildings appeared beneath it.

Rasheed pointed. "That's Dhahran. Khobar is a few miles ahead." On the horizon in front were more buildings and beyond the deep blue of the Arabian Gulf stretching below the pale sky.

Hajar sensed that the air was heavier, more humid than at home. She smelled the salt of the sea, an unfamiliar scent for one who had never before left the central desert of Riyadh. The sweat that has been pouring from her body no longer evaporated so quickly, and her plain cotton dress under the *abaya* felt damp. "After you, Um Tariq," she said to Suheir, whom she respectfully referred to as the mother of the eldest—in this case, the only—son. All but Suheir's own offspring used this term with her and thereby honored the mother through association with the son she bore.

Hajar rubbed her sore legs in the few moments it took Tariq to help the older woman climb out. Hajar then clambered out ahead of her sisters, who appeared to be equally stiff. The apartment was on the first floor of a three-story tenement that extended from one end of the block to the other. The windows had blinds drawn and metal grates across them. Rasheed had already unlocked the front door, flipped on a light, and was back at the truck untying the luggage. "Go in," he said, motioning to the doorway and remained outside with Tariq to carry in the suitcases and the few bundles of items the women thought indispensable.

Simply furnished, dusty and covered with cobwebs from long disuse, the accommodations evidently pleased Suheir who clapped her hands to her face and exclaimed, on behalf of the others, their thanks to Rasheed. A windowless room, little bigger than a walk-in closet, would serve as Tariq's quarters; the women were to share the main space that combined with a tiny kitchen and eating area to form a self-contained studio.

After a quick survey of the lodging, Tariq said, "I'll be back tonight with some food. In the meantime, you can unpack and straighten up the place." He drove off with Rasheed.

The unpacking and cleaning largely fell to Hajar. Suheir plopped down on the sofa, removed her sandals, and propped her feet up while Aisha made some tea, and at her mother's bidding, kept her company after the water boiled.

"I worry about Tariq," Suheir said, blowing the liquid to cool it down. "How has he come into this wealth so suddenly?" No one ventured a reply, and hoped the question was merely rhetorical. As if to herself, Suheir mused, "Why is that Rasheed so helpful, and what will he have Tariq do here?" Aisha looked uncomfortable and was about to rise to help Hajar arrange the clothing in the only wardrobe available.

"Hajar, stop that," Suheir snapped. "Let Aisha do it. You help me with my feet." The stepdaughter dutifully knelt beside her and began kneading the middle-aged woman's feet.

"Be careful, girl! Gentler! Hasn't your mother taught you anything?" Hajar's head was bowed, and she did not look up. "That woman—I hope her brother has a firmer hand with her than your father did. The sheikh was always giving in to her pleas—not circumcising you and the little one, for instance. Being able to experience pleasure in the sex act makes women wanton. I can already see how you will turn out, you little hussy. You're already provoking my son, aren't you?"

Hajar dared not make a sound, but shook her head.

"If your mother hadn't fallen at your father's feet and pleaded, if he hadn't had a soft heart for her beauty, now long gone, he would have done the proper thing, as he did with my daughters, as my parents did with me. What matter, if the cutting and blood almost killed the crippled one? At least, she's assured of being virtuous.

"And that woman—" Suheir spit back into her cup. "—she could have aborted your sister once she knew it was a girl to have another try at a boy, but again she cried." Suheir mimicked Layla, "'Oh, please, please, my husband.' And again he relented. And now, look, she can have no more children, no possible sons, will never be known as an Um—she is in fact useless and lucky that your father didn't divorce her."

"Please stop attacking my mother, Um Tariq. I will miss her so," Hajar raised her face, lined with tears, and received a slap for the perceived impudence.

"Go finish unpacking. I've had enough of this."

With her cheek red and stinging, Hajar looked away and went to the other side of the room. No one said a word.

Later, when the sounds of Suheir's snoring assured the women she was deep into her nap, Aisha touched Hajar's hand and confided in her. "My sister, I really hope you have better luck than I've had. Try to find happiness as best you can."

Chapter 8

Ahmad pushed the spectacles back onto the bridge of his nose and settled into the comfort of the swiveling Aeron chair that made tolerable the late nights in front of the terminal screens. He was working from home to test the ERP systems that Saudi Oil was deploying at its five locations of Dhahran, Abqaiq, Ras Tanura, Udhailiyah, and Tanajib. Ahmad needed to ensure that the company's virtual private network linking the sites was impervious to external attack.

As one of the country's most skilled computer scientists and with his father's connections, Ahmad could have quickly risen to a senior management position after returning from M.I.T. However, he disliked what he perceived to be the main function of managers—telling others what to do—preferring instead the intellectual rigor of his discipline. Both the Saudi intelligence service and the National Security Agency of the U.S. had tried unsuccessfully to recruit him for operations in signal intelligence—the intercepting and decoding of electronic communications—a subject he had briefly dabbled in as an undergraduate.

With a keen and restless intellect, Ahmad quickly tired of a subject once he had mastered it. Fortunately, to his thinking, the fast pace of change in software and computer networking presented a challenge that forced him to read voraciously to keep up with advances in technology coming from the U.S.

The Internet served as Ahmad's online library, although for many Saudis much of it was off limits. The government tightly controlled the Internet by censoring access to sites deemed immoral or politically sensitive. For Ahmad, the blockages presented only a minor annoyance. To get unfiltered versions of the news, Ahmad simply routed around the censors and connected to host servers abroad. He also used the technique to simulate computer hacking attacks against Saudi Oil from outside Saudi Arabia.

Ahmad chose several overseas Internet service providers to test as sample sources of incoming malicious Web traffic. After finishing with one ISP in the U.K., he looked at another in the small neighboring island state of Bahrain. Before routing his own sample attack via the overseas servers, Ahmad checked how secure the ISPs themselves were from eavesdropping and scanned a sample of the e-mail that their facilities stored and forwarded. Choosing a random topic of interest, he typed in the phrase "al-Qaeda" to a computer script to see whether the ISP's security prevented a computerized search. The security failed, and his screen filled with hundreds of recent entries sorted by relevance and date. One item near the top of the list caught Ahmad's eye. The e-mail's subject line read "Al-Qaeda compromises Saudi security services," and the message appeared to have originated from the U.S. embassy in Riyadh with recipients in the U.S. embassy in Bahrain and an offshore facility of the U.S. Department of Defense.

Ahmad assumed someone was spoofing the addresses as a joke, using a simple technique to forge the sender's identity and dupe the unwitting recipients. Since Ahmad knew that foreign governments and the U.S., in particular, did not generally send their internal communiqués across the public Internet, such a hoax would fool only exceptionally gullible recipients. Yet, the body of the message was encrypted. Intrigued as to why any prankster would bother to encrypt such a ruse, Ahmad decided to decrypt the message. He quickly determined that the code relied on a technique known as "Pretty Good Privacy"—a freely available encryption algorithm, sometimes used commercially, but definitely not of the industrial strength required by government agencies.

Ahmad's desk at home had a bank of three workstations, on loan from Saudi Oil, so that he could harness, when needed, the combined computing power of their multiple processors. Here was such a case. Ahmad used a few of his own custom-designed programming algorithms to speed up the calculations. Even so, decrypting even simple messages took time, and it was late. He was ready for bed. Although Ahmad admitted he shouldn't waste his resources on this sidetrack, there were few puzzles he could resist. So he started the program script and resolved to check in the morning whether it had cracked the encryption. If not, that would be the end of it.

Fatima's knocking and voice woke him in the morning. "Ahmad, it's time to go, and you're not even up."

"Give me a minute," he called back. Rolling over, Ahmad reached for his glasses, and noticed that a blinking icon had replaced the cascading pipes of his computers' screensavers. He pulled on the clothes left strewn on his chair and looked closely at the blinking message: DECRYPTION COMPLETE. Munching on an impromptu breakfast of the previous night's uneaten snacks, he scanned over the e-mail of interest, now plain to see. It looked intriguing, so he printed out the page, crammed it into his briefcase, and rushed out the door to join his sister on the drive to work.

Before shutting down the terminals, Ahmad had also scrolled through the computer log: it had completed the work in only an hour. Had he used the more powerful computers at the office, it might have taken just a few minutes.

"Brother, what are you reading and re-reading so intently?"

Distracted, Ahmad looked up at the Filipino driver's shaded eyes in the mirror and then across at his sister.

"Nothing," he said and folded the sheet of paper to put in his pocket. On this morning's ride, he didn't feel like talking, but stared through the glass, past his own reflection, at the street gliding quietly by.

The e-mail's contents contained nothing extraordinary, but the more Ahmad thought about it, the odder the e-mail seemed. The message referred to the compromising of the Saudi government and its intelligence services by al-Qaeda sympathizers at the highest levels and speculated on crackdowns by government troops in the country's Eastern Province in the event of any more terrorist operations there. Due to the infiltration, it hinted that much of the current intelligence on Saudi intentions and motives was now coming from a well-placed mole in the Saudi government—a secret source recruited by the U.S. or a sympathetic ally. Given the nature of the information, the writer, who appeared to be in the embassy's political-affairs division, emphasized that, if leaked, this would be denied by Saudi intelligence in private and vehemently refuted by the Saudi government in public. The sender repeated instructions to the U.S. 5th Fleet in Bahrain to stand down and not assist in any crisis, such as a hostage taking, unless specifically requested to do so by the Saudi government.

Although Ahmad knew that some in the Western press had previously said the same about al-Qaeda sympathizers, hitherto the official U.S. government line had been that the Saudis were doing excellent work in the war on terror. Was the U.S. government telling its citizens and the world one thing yet secretly pursuing a different agenda? Who did it intend this weakly "classified" information for, and why was it so easily available? If Ahmad could decrypt it with his homebrew equipment, most intelligence services, including the Saudis, could do the same. Why was the writer speculating about a hostage taking? Ahmad's logical mind ticked through the possibilities. Thoughts of a possible disinformation campaign came up, but he dismissed them: he could see no reason for such an effort by the U.S. or others. The sender could also readily deny the message because few, if any, foreign agencies would want to admit to reading another's private traffic, if only so as not to provide information on their sources or methods. He also rejected the idea of informing Nicholas Hansen, whom he did not know so well. In the end, he filed away the disquieting item along with the other unpleasant aspects of recent life in his country.

"Nicholas! Please make yourself at home!" Ahmad said as he made an expansive gesture toward the large sitting room. As on many such weekends, only he, his sister, and a few servants shared the house. Their father was back in Riyadh. "Fatima and Ma Ling will keep you company while I gather my things upstairs."

"Thanks, Ahmad. John will come in a minute. He's clearing a space in the backseat of his car for you."

As Ahmad left, Nick heard Ma Ling speaking rapidly in Chinese on the phone. She appeared to take no notice of him and was scribbling notes on a pad. His eyes adjusted to the room's dim lighting, and he saw Fatima approaching to greet him. The room had a pleasing scent of smoky perfume. Fatima drew near, and he realized the fragrance came from her. "Wow, you look great!" Neither she nor Ma Ling was wearing an *abaya,* and both were elegantly dressed. Fatima stood tall in heels, wore a diaphanous wrap, and her neck and wrists were covered in gold and sparkling stones. "And you smell wonderful," he said.

"You're too kind, Nicholas. Since you boys won't let us join you on the desert run, we're going to a ladies-only party at the home of Ma Ling's friend. The hostess is a distant relative of the Saudi royal family: at such events, how one dresses takes on the manner of a competitive sport. Hence, the jewels." But it wasn't the jewelry that Nick's eyes were admiring.

"The musky scent—I can't quite place it. A French perfume?"

Fatima laughed. "It's frankincense, a homegrown Arab product from Oman. You put the crystals into a lit incense holder and then stand over the smoldering crystals while flapping the folds of your dress to let the smoke— how do you say—aerate the body. Here, I'll show you."

Fatima led Nick into the next room, and he was thrilled to be alone with her. On a low table in front of a couch stood a small, circular urn filled with what looked like yellow rock candy. They both sat. "It's no longer hot. You can take a closer look." Nick gingerly picked up the object to examine the fragrant contents. His fingers felt the warmth of the hardened clay.

"I've never seen one before."

"Then you must have this as my gift. When you return to the States, you can show your female friends how their sisters perfume themselves in Arabia."

Fatima would not accept Nick's refusals. When Nick glanced at the lute leaning on a chair in the corner, Fatima said, "I'd play it for you, but one of the strings needs replacing." As if an afterthought, she asked about the renewal of her visa.

"I recently forwarded the papers to Washington. Sorry for the delay, but I have a vested interest in keeping you here," Nick said.

Fatima's brow furrowed in a look of puzzlement. "What do you mean, 'keeping me here'?"

Nick stared at his feet, then turned shyly, and addressed the curve at the nape of her neck. "I've grown fond of you—more than fond. I really like you, Fatima, and would be sad to see you leave." He looked down again and did not see the expression of alarm that flashed across her face, but felt her quickly shift to the end of the couch before rising. Nick then stood and sheepishly faced her.

"If you *do* like me, shouldn't you do what is in my best interests?" Fatima asked. Nick was awkwardly holding the small urn as if to block the anticipated rejection.

"No such relationship is possible, Nicholas." Her mouth was smiling, but not her eyes. She seemed worried. "This is Saudi Arabia. I should not even be alone in this room with you." They heard the front entrance door close as John let himself in and called upstairs to Ahmad not to rush. "Any foreign suitor must be Muslim . . . like our Sheikh John, for instance." Nick did not reply to her attempt at levity. So John was a rival for her affections. "Besides, you have a most . . ." she searched for the word, ". . . *difficult* name for any Arab woman, or man."

Nick didn't find his name hard to pronounce. What did she mean?

Her voice dropped to a whisper. "It sounds too much like 'Nick, handsome.'" For the first time, Fatima seemed truly embarrassed in his presence.

"What?" he demanded.

"'Nick, handsome.'" Have any women in America said that to you?"

Nick was confused, and annoyance crept into his voice, particularly as Fatima struggled to keep from laughing. "Okay, I don't have movie-star good looks, but I'm not that ugly."

"Nicholas, that's not what I meant. You *are* handsome." Fatima began to blush. "But in colloquial Arabic, your nickname sounds exactly like the crudest possible expression for 'making love.'" By this time, she had stepped back into the living room. Nick followed, feeling like an ocean buoy buffeted by waves from all sides. Ma Ling was off the phone and watching them.

"John spent some time in Egypt and speaks a bit of Arabic. Maybe he can explain to you what I mean."

For once, John acted the part of the straight man.

"John, think of your repertoire of swear words in colloquial Arabic," said Fatima. "Tell Nicholas what 'Nick' means to an Arab, but don't say it out loud."

"What is this, charades?" It was John's turn to be puzzled. He repeated to himself. "Nick, nick, nick . . . Fuck! That's it. Fuck Hansen."

"John, I said whisper it!" Fatima hissed.

An awkward silence ensued, before Ma Ling burst out laughing.

"Oh Nick—Nicholas—your name won't keep *me* away from you," said Ma Ling.

John slapped Nick on the back. "Be careful how you introduce yourself, mate. Maybe you and I should swap names for a while."

Nick smiled, unsure whether to feel pleased or offended. "That explains some of the embarrassed looks I've gotten over the past few months. Why didn't anyone tell me before?"

Nick thought of his father. "Maybe I should call myself 'Duke' like my dad. His army pals in Vietnam started calling him that, and the name stuck."

John tried to cover for his previous slight. "It sounds like he must have earned the nickname, my friend. Before you leave this kingdom, we may be calling you 'Earl' or 'Prince,' or simply 'Sir Nicholas.'"

The sound of Ahmad's footsteps down the stairs marked an end to the conversation. He was carrying a small bag on his back and had an open cardboard box full of provisions in his arms. "Tea before we go?"

"No, thanks." said John. "If we linger too long, we'll miss the rendezvous point."

The back of John's SUV was cluttered with gear—laptop satchels, cables, a rolled-up tent, poles, plastic bottles of water, bags of clothing, thermoses, and a plastic icebox full of food preserved temporarily from the heat. There were even golf clubs and a 12-inch, circular patch of green AstroTurf on the backseat beside Ahmad, who silently marveled at the mess.

"You can toss that into the back," John said as Ahmad held the artificial grass in his lap. "That reminds me. You guys should join me in a round of golf. The Saudi Oil course doesn't look so inviting, but it's not bad."

"A golf course made entirely of sand—at least you won't lose the ball in any high grass," said Nick, who sat in the front passenger seat. He was an indifferent golfer, but keen for weekend diversions.

"There are a bunch of maps back there, Ahmad. They're mainly in Arabic, which I can't read, so you're the designated navigator." While not taking his eyes from the road, John handed back to Ahmad a folded printout of instructions for reaching the first Hash meeting point. Due to security concerns, the numbers of Hash participants were way down from previous years. John expected just twenty or thirty men to show up. To avoid attracting unwanted attention from the authorities, the runners carpooled, met at designated points on the outskirts of town, and drove off into the desert in clusters of at least two, but no more than four, vehicles at a time. The new two-car minimum began only recently to prevent a repeat of the mishap that claimed the life of Errol Hart, a popular and founding member of the runners' group, who foolishly—for reasons unknown—had driven into the desert alone and without informing others of his destination or route.

At the first sign of a shamal, a sandstorm from northerly winds, the drivers would regroup to decide whether to call off the outing. Where possible, they communicated via cell phones, and at least one car per group usually had a global positioning system to pinpoint locations. Because the local weather forecasters had trouble predicting the storms, the Harriers could not plan around them in advance.

Another change of late, prompted by the spate of kidnappings and assassinations, was the carrying of firearms. A small contingent of marines guarded the U.S. consulate, and at least one of them took part in the runs. Some others—foreign private contractors and a few Saudi Oil employees—had also received government permission to carry small arms for self-protection. Their work required them to travel into remote, potentially dangerous areas.

"Most of the runners are not fit," John said, addressing Ahmad. "So don't worry about keeping up."

In front, Nick sat silently chewing his fingernails. John glanced across at him. "You're in great shape, Nick. What are you nervous about?"

Nick tried to cover his thoughts, which focused on the day's earlier events, not on what was to come. "What me, worry?" he said.

When neither John nor Ahmad reacted to his allusion to *Mad* magazine, Nick tried a different, more scholarly, tack. "Nail biting does not necessarily express anxiety. The human nail contains keratin, the same ingredient found in the rhino's horn, a famous Asian aphrodisiac. I'm just trying to keep my supply up, as there are few rhinos in the desert."

"There are also few females, unless you're into camels and goats." They all laughed at John's retort.

When they reached the interim meeting point near the start of Route 10 heading southwest toward the town of Buqayq, John saw that some of the regulars had already arrived. One of them, a large unshaven Brit with a beer belly protruding beneath his T-shirt, noticed the occupants in

John's car. "I see you've brought some inductees," he called out in a loud voice and waved for John to come over to speak with him. In an undertone, once John had approached, he asked, "Is that fellow in the back a Saudi?" He already smelt of beer.

"Yeah, but he's cool."

"We don't want Saudis along. What if he rats on us?"

"Don't worry, buddy. I'm vouching for him. Besides, he's a Shi'ite, which is like being a Jew in Nazi Germany."

The heavyset man didn't seem happy with the explanation, but grunted as he moved off. "You're responsible for him."

After the drivers checked their bearings, the small clusters of vehicles continued, driving in intervals a few minutes apart, on Route 10 toward the town of al-Hofuf, before going off onto small roads, then tracks, and lastly into unmarked space to the southeast of the small Saudi Oil camp at Udhailiyah toward the Empty Quarter, the largest desert in the world.

John's group had started in the early afternoon from the al-Sayyids' home in Dhahran, but would not reach the destination until about four o'clock. The ninety-minute run would start at 5 p.m. when the desert sun had begun to sink toward the horizon and the sands gave up some of the heat collected during the hottest period of the day. Remaining behind in camp with the cars during the run would be two of the three "hares" who had prepared the trail hours before with markers of piled rocks, yellow ribbons tied to shrubs, and colored powder splashed onto rock outcroppings. The route started and ended at the camp. Their job complete, they finished setting up tents for the late arrivals, collected the drinks and food, prepared a cooking fire, and awaited the evening's rituals to welcome new members.

The tally of twenty-five all arrived safely and changed into short pants for running. No one had made the mistake of changing into such forbidden clothing until far from the city. At first, Nick thought he might try running barefoot, but thought better of it when he saw that the seemingly fine sand was full of stones. He wore running shoes like the rest and mentally divided those present into "lard butts" who would bring up the rear and the "hard asses" who would set the pace. He resolved to stay up front, particularly as one of the fatter ones wore a T-shirt in tatters that positively reeked. Most of the others were giving this guy a wide berth. Shouldn't someone tell him to change his shirt?

With the sounds of a whistle and bugle, they were off, scampering toward the first marker several hundred yards away. As Ahmad slipped off the front of the pack and joined the latter group, John downshifted his gait to stay with him. As further insurance that no one fell too far back and got lost, one of the original markers of the trail acted as the sweep and jogged behind the slowest.

The frontrunners, amid self-congratulatory fanfare, finished the trail in about an hour, followed by razzing and hoots for those who came in last, nearly thirty minutes later: Ahmad, the sweep, an obese driller from Texas, and John, who had not broken a sweat.

The Hash's four-member executive committee, which included John, called forward the inductees: Ahmad, Nick, and two others. A keg of bootleg beer on tap, brewed from a mix at home and foul tasting to connoisseurs, was propped up on a makeshift table, and the toasts began with the inductees drinking a plastic cup 'bottoms up' in turn to each of the other twenty participants. Nick spat out part of his first cupful: the obnoxious heavyset man who had objected to Ahmad's presence had apparently saved a dead desert fly and put it in the cup he poured Nick "for taste"—apparently to haze him, as if drinking oneself silly were not enough. The group sang some mindless ditties and bestowed or re-instated inane titles to members. Nick feigned good humor, but decided he would not be a frequent participant in the future. After the ninth or tenth cup, he lost count and by the end of the obligatory rounds, Nick felt his movements slow as his gaze lingered on individual faces longer than normal. He wondered if he was swaying as he walked, and he paid more attention to simple movements. Nick was drunk for the first time since arriving in Saudi Arabia. Meanwhile, Ahmad had had trouble with his first cupful of beer, looked concerned at the second, and ready to bolt at the third. John, seeing his discomfort, stepped forward early, declaring, "Pinch hitter. I'll drink for my friend here." Those watching shouted "Not fair! This is already your third initiation, and you hold your liquor too well." A grateful Ahmad stepped aside from the center of the group.

For his breach of protocol, and by coming in last, although tied with others, John received the Hash's smelly time-honored T-shirt, which he was to keep safe and wear at the next run unwashed. They did not insist, as had sometimes occurred, that he put it on immediately.

With the heavy drinking out of the way, the cookout began. Beef burgers and chicken fillets hit the grill, but no hot dogs: the government banned all pork products as severely as alcohol and it wasn't worth the trouble to try to smuggle any into the country. The men at this week's Hash ranged in age from the off-duty marine, barely twenty, to one fellow, who must have been well into his fifties. When drunk, Nick became sleepy and quieter than usual, but alcohol had the opposite effect on John; he was laughing and mingling amid the groups clustered around several cooking fires. Another boisterous boozer, talking loudly to Kaddish, wore a white T-shirt emblazoned with a large red maple leaf in front and, in big letters on the back, "Don't shoot. I'm Canadian."

"So Don Je-wan. . . ." The guy apparently couldn't make up his mind whether to call Kaddish John or Juan, didn't know how to pronounce the latter, and decided it didn't matter anyway since he was slurring his words. "Tell us about your latest exploitations . . . expoloits."

"I helped a friend install the country's first wireless local-access network."

"Not those kind of expoloits, *dummy*. With women—our scarcest commodity," he said, whirling both arms like a dizzy dervish, as if to say, look, there are none. "You and Errol—gosh—what a pair you were. Always in the clubs, with a different set of gorgettes lolling on your arms." He paused, recalling the better times. "I guess you miss the poor bastard."

John didn't reply, but looked into his cup.

"Aw, forget it." Yet, the Canadian wouldn't take his own advice and said, "But I don't for a minute believe that official bunk. Some buggers took the guy out. They didn't videotape the killin', and didn't lop off his head, but somebody had him offed."

"You spinning conspiracy theories again, mate?" John said.

The drunk spat onto a hot stone next to the fire's embers and watched the spit slowly sizzle. "Pshaw, this country—this part of the world—is one goddamn conspiracy. If Errol's American president, what's his name, had the cunning of Bismarck, he would hold another conference like that one in 1880-whenever that carved up Africa. This time they could divide the Middle East—you know the parts with oil—and give them back to the great powers. Leave the deserts for the locals and their animals."

"Would Canada be at the table?"

"Why not? Any civilized country could get its take. Even New Zealand, I suppose."

"Let me chew on that for a while," John said and rejoined the saner conversation of Ahmad and Nick, seated in the sand nearby. He twirled an index finger by his temple, "See what the solitude of the desert can do to a man."

Nick, struggling to stay awake, felt the effects of the beer and a full stomach. "John, you've never told me why you have stayed so long in Saudi. Five years already? Now that it's so dangerous, don't you want to leave—wouldn't it be easier?" He settled back to hear John spin another yarn.

"My friend, where would I go? This is about all I know. I don't have the skills like this guy . . ." He put his hand on Ahmad's knee, ". . . or the organizational structure like you have that could ship me off tomorrow to another country. I'm on my own, living by my wits. I could go to another Arab-speaking country since I know the language, but those wouldn't be much safer."

"Why not back home? I hear New Zealand is beautiful."

"If you're a tourist, sure, but unless you raise sheep like my Poppy, there's a limit to how much forest and greenery you can stand. On the south island there, we don't have many people. Even in the bigger places like Christchurch, they're really just small towns, not cities. If you're trying to sell your services, the place is not close enough to the international markets."

Ahmad contributed his two cents' worth. "John, if you are ever ready to settle down and raise a family, go back. We'll set up some business together, with me here and you there, collaborating over the Internet."

"To address your first point, when it comes to choosing a Mrs. Kad-DISH . . ." He stressed the latter syllable, ". . . if there is to be one, I'm still reading the menu. As for your second suggestion, I'll keep that in mind. Since the tech bubble burst, I haven't thought seriously about my earlier schemes for an online business and world domination."

As night fell, the talk around the campfires died down. With little else to do, and only a few kerosene lamps, candles, and flashlights giving off light, those still watching the smoldering coals drifted off to their respective tents to sleep. Apart from occasional stray scorpions, there were no other threats from wildlife to concern the sleepers. They would awake at dawn, make a quick breakfast, break camp, and then drive along the sunken path of a nearby *wadi*, a dry riverbed, to one of the few oases in the area. Nick had seen photos of the aqua waters in the oasis and was looking forward to a swim, if only to clean off the sweat and dust that had collected on his skin and caked his hair.

The following day Nick flew to Riyadh to brief Ambassador Gewalt on what he had learned about deployments of Chinese staff at Saudi Oil's facilities. He took the earliest flight from Dhahran to have time for some visa interviews at the embassy in the morning before meeting with Gewalt in the late afternoon. The consulate in Dhahran kept a list of staff members' birthdays, and Nick had noticed that Martha Fischbein's was coming up the following week. Thinking he might soften up the ambassador's surly secretary, he brought the spinster a box of chocolates. The gift didn't melt her heart, but she smiled and thanked him for the thought.

Nick was nervous about the meeting. He hadn't been able to nail down hard numbers and had only secondhand estimates. He was on time, but the ambassador had not yet returned from an appointment at the foreign ministry. Martha waved Nick in and had him take a seat in the same plush office as a month before. Nick had already rehearsed how he would put the best possible spin on his providing only a meager amount of intelligence, supplemented by suppositions and estimates. While waiting, he had time to study Gewalt's office, first from his seat and then after twenty minutes of nail biting, from walking along the walls to look at the book titles, mementos, and photos hanging nearby. Nick knew the ambassador wasn't a reader, so was glad to see he didn't have books on his shelves merely to impress visitors. The few in his office were ones he probably reached for on occasion to better understand Saudi Arabia or the Middle East. Unlike many of the staff, Gewalt actually kept a photo of his wife on the desk. Nick had met her once before she returned to the U.S. He wondered whether the ambassador was lonely without her. Also on the desk were equally large pictures of what looked like the ambassador's sons, apparently with their wives, and even bigger snapshots of the faces of four small kids, who had to be the grandchildren. On the opposite wall were three photos of Gewalt in casual settings: with the U.S. president, with the U.N. secretary general, and with a third individual, presumably prominent, but whom Nick did not recognize.

The room was light and airy, thanks to a large window overlooking the compound's grounds. Next to the window hung a picture of a catamaran moored in front of a clapboard beach house and a red-brick mansion behind, with the inscription *I'd rather be sailing* underneath. Was this his home on Long Island? If Nick sat in the ambassador's chair, he'd be tempted to stare at the photo all day long, but didn't dare try out the seat. He moved closer to the image, examining its details, when behind him, abruptly came the ambassador's voice. "She's a beauty, isn't she? Fast as the devil."

At the first sound, Nick jumped, confused and wondering how long Gewalt had been watching him. Martha must have left early for the day. "Sir, I . . . it was just that . . . is this your home?"

"Yes, but I was referring to the boat."

Nick saw that his boss Susan was not with the ambassador. She had said she would come to Riyadh, but in fact, he hadn't seen her all day, and Gewalt made no mention of her nor did he turn on the video screen that they had used before to connect with Morrison. Gewalt looked tired, dark and puffy under the eyes. Or was this supremely self-confident man worried and losing sleep? Nick noticed ridges on his brow where none had showed before.

"It'll be just you and me today. Tell me what you've found out, and I'll decide whether and when to bring the others back into this."

The two sat, and Nick pulled out a small notebook to make sure he got the numbers and location names right.

The ambassador had not wanted anything sent to him in writing. Already he was frowning.

"Sir, my sources tell me that the Chinese have increased their presence at all five Saudi Oil camps in the Eastern Province, but particularly at the smallest, most remote location of Udhailiyah. The current estimates are as many as 200 Chinese personnel at Udhailiyah and several dozen, perhaps as many as fifty, at each of the other sites. The build up seems to have occurred uniformly, beginning six to nine months ago, when at most only a handful of Chinese were working at each location."

"Who were the sources?" —the question Nick knew was coming. His breathing now shallow, Nick spoke quickly to defuse the ambassador's first reaction to what Nick construed as a failure.

"I didn't actually get inside information from the Chinese themselves." He hastened to add, "But I have befriended a key contact, China Oil's liaison to Saudi Oil, Ms. Ma Ling. She wouldn't answer my question. I tried to be casual about it and didn't want to push. It might have made her suspicious. The relationship seemed important to cultivate, and I've met with her several times in Dhahran where she's based." He scanned the ambassador's face to see his response. The ambassador rubbed his nose but said nothing.

Nick went on. "Most of the information comes from a friend, Mr. John Kaddish. He installs communication systems for Saudi Oil so is often visiting all five sites. He said he had noticed a lot more Chinese at Saudi Oil, particularly in Udhailiyah recently. The numbers I gave you were his estimates."

Nick waited for a response. In the ensuing silence, the heartbeat echoing in Nick's ears raced past the much slower tick—tick—tick of the clock on the office wall.

Apparently deep in thought, Gewalt finally spoke. "That confirms our satellite images of increased activity at Udhailiyah. However, we needed some on-the-ground confirmation: with the protective covering that most of the oil workers wear out there, we couldn't identify from the photos any particular ethnicity, let alone nationality. He's sure they're Chinese?"

Nick nodded. "He seemed to think so."

"I assume you didn't tell this Kaddish why you wanted the numbers."

"No, sir. I just asked if he knew, and he didn't probe for why. Truthfully, sir, I myself don't know—"

Gewalt cut him off. "All the same, we'll run a check on him.

"You've done well not to push the Chinese woman, but be careful about fraternizing out there. The old-timers in the service may have told you of the State Department's former policy against that—particularly for those stationed in communist countries during the Cold War. China is now ..." He searched for the term, "... a strategic competitor, so we don't enforce the non-fraternization rules so strictly. Nevertheless, the Saudis do it for us—at least so far as men and women are concerned. If handled improperly, such a relationship can prove fatal, literally."

"I have no romantic involvement, nor prospects for any." An image of Fatima at home flashed by.

The ambassador smiled and seemed to relax. He leaned back and was no longer studying Nick closely. After a pause, he unlocked a drawer of his desk, reached for a folder, and sat down on the divan next to Nick. "Son, you've done well. In fact—and I hope you don't mind—I had a supplemental security check done so that we can bump up your clearances."

He pulled out a pair of eyeglasses from his pocket and read aloud. "Father, Daniel 'Duke' Hansen, realtor in Atherton, California. Served as a lieutenant in Vietnam for two tours. Originally assigned to the central highlands pacification program under John Paul Vann. Stayed on as a civilian with USAID and was one of the last to leave in '75. Your mother, Thong Hansen, a Vietnamese, older sister Tranh." He glanced up. "You don't look part Vietnamese. Explain that one, please."

"She was—is—my stepmother. Duke Hansen—my dad—is actually my uncle. They adopted me as a young child when his younger brother, my real father, and my natural mother died in a car crash. Somehow I survived it, but have no recollection.

"Dad met and married my stepmother, who already was a widow and had an infant girl when they met in Saigon. Her husband, whom my dad had known, had died in the fighting. It's all rather confusing."

The ambassador seemed to agree.

"My father, Duke, never talks about Vietnam, particularly after he and Thong divorced when I was ten. I stayed with him, and my older sister went with her."

"Yes, I see that one, Tranh, was a concern in your first clearance and again this time. She's in and out of psychiatric wards and a drug user."

"We're not close and I haven't seen her or my stepmother for years."

"And your father...."

"Dad got me into Stanford on a tennis scholarship but wasn't happy about the Asian studies."

Gewalt leafed through several pages of the file. "Seems he was even less enthusiastic about your joining the department. His comments about that to the FBI almost kept you from getting in."

That was news to Nick, but it didn't surprise him. "He came home disillusioned by Vietnam. In fact, he hasn't been outside the U.S. since then and was always saying we should avoid 'foreign entanglements.'"

"Well, now you're in the thick of it. As you know, I haven't yet given you the whole story. This was a test: Morrison and I didn't want anything inadvertently to slip out in the course of your investigation. Not even Susan or anyone else in this embassy knows the rationale, but they will in due course.

"Listen, I'm going to be in Khobar for a working vacation the first weekend in May. Usually, I'd go in the other direction—to our consulate in Jeddah to do some fishing in the Red Sea, but there are things to take care of in Dhahran. I've got a boat at the Half Moon Bay Club outside Khobar on the Gulf, so we'll go for a little sailing and have another talk then." The ambassador walked him to the door.

Nick had long since forgotten his relief at not having failed this assignment and felt flattered by the ambassador's personal attention. Maybe he wasn't doing so badly after all.

Chapter 9

Rasheed and several cohorts set up shop in a run-down part of Khobar not far from the tenement building where Rasheed had installed Tariq and his family. Ostensibly, the men ran a small kiosk selling mainly newspapers. They manned the stand in shifts, almost around the clock, with one person, and sometimes several, loitering there at night long after the other shops on the street had closed.

The day that Tariq arrived, they all went to a local restaurant, slaughtered the baby goat, and had it cooked on a bed of rice. The following morning, Rasheed took Tariq in the pickup to a secluded spot in the desert north of the city. The sand off the highway was firm and flat, so they drove on it perpendicular to the path of the road for several minutes until they were out of sight and earshot from any passing vehicles.

Rasheed stopped the vehicle and reviewed his previous lesson on the functions of the various dashboard instruments. He also gave Tariq a five-minute sketch of the rules of the road. "You probably know these already," he said, "but just don't attract attention to yourself while driving. The last thing we want is for a policeman to pull you over for a traffic violation." The pickup truck had an automatic transmission, so Tariq didn't have to contend with the complexities of shifting gears.

They switched seats. "Make sure you can see directly behind you through these three mirrors. If it's getting dark, turn on the lights, like so; if someone cuts you off, use this to honk—no, better not: don't call attention to yourself; if this gauge drops to here, it's time to buy gas.

"Now start the engine. Remove your right foot from the brake and slowly push the gas pedal. Don't do anything with the left foot. Just keep it there. That's right. Go faster. Slow. Stop. Turn to the right. Okay, that's it. You've graduated."

"What about parking in a busy street?"

"I'll show you how to do that later. Turn off the engine." Rasheed reached under the driver's seat and pulled out a long plastic case. The two stepped out of the car. Inside the case was a semi-automatic submachine gun. Tariq's eyes widened as a moment of fear gripped him. Had he done something to offend Rasheed?

"It's loaded, so watch me first. Very important: this is the safety latch. Never, never undo this until you have to fire the gun at someone. Hopefully, you won't. Now, you see that tree?" Rasheed stood with legs apart, gun braced at his hip, and fired several rounds. The gun cracked with each burst, tearing pieces of bark and wood from the trunk, but no echoes returned.

"Now you try. Be careful. There's a backward kick you won't expect if you've never fired one. Go ahead, take it."

Tariq gingerly cradled the weapon, initially surprised at its weight. He mimicked Rasheed's stance, and pointed at the same tree.

"Okay, fire."

Tariq's shots went higher as the bullets forced the gun muzzle up, but a few hit the top of the tree trunk and tore at the lower branches.

"You're all set. We have a commando in the making." Tariq carefully replaced the safety latch, and with both hands, gave the gun back to Rasheed. He wondered what they were planning, but knew not to ask. Rasheed would tell him only what he needed to know, when the time was right.

After the Hash outing, Ahmad had invited John and Nick to a social event—a prince's party at the palatial estate belonging to one of the king's many grandsons, whose father was governor of the Eastern Province. Ordinarily, Ahmad would not have attended. He disliked these functions and found them decadent, but certain invitations one could not refuse. This one came from a director at Saudi Oil for whom he worked. Ahmad asked if he could bring along a few friends. Yes, of course. Ahmad knew that John had been to several such events and was not thrilled with them either, but they both thought it might be a good introduction for Nick—an eye-opener into a part of Saudi life one heard about, yet seldom saw.

Nick was grateful for the invitation. His social life seemed to be picking up, and he wondered how he could top this. What could he offer to the guys in return, where he played host? He asked what to wear. Casual. Should he bring anything? He usually brought wine, but that was out. "This is not a Tupperware party," said Ahmad. "No need to bake a bundt cake." The three met on Thursday evening to go together, but drove in separate cars so that each could leave when he liked. "There will be plenty of parking," Ahmad said. "The home is on the outskirts of town, so we'll have the entire desert as our lot."

The palace was enormous. One could see its outline illuminated by night-lights from miles away. Up close, whimsical turrets, spires, and what looked like the minaret of a mosque competed for the highest point of the building. A huge structure, reminding Nick of the Berlin Wall, surrounded the grounds. They had parked their three-car convoy outside, and Nick asked about the wall as they approached the ten-foot-high cement barrier topped by another two feet of barbed wire. Ahmad explained. "For those not admitted into your property, such walls convey your status. The lesser ones put shards of glass on top to keep out intruders, those higher in the pecking order cover it with electric wire, and once you've reached the pinnacle, you station armed guards like those." He pointed to the sentry boxes placed at strategic intervals around the enclosure.

"As for me," John said, "I'd prefer to have nothing worth stealing."

"Tonight we are privileged." Ahmad smiled. "Ordinarily, common folk like us share in the royals' wealth only by viewing their magnificent palaces from afar. Now we can see one up close, from the inside."

Ahmad spoke to the guard at the main entrance, who let them in past the wide gateway through which drove a non-stop procession of cars moving in both directions. Once inside, Nick surveyed the grounds. He imagined the prince paid a hefty water bill to keep the grass, trees, and gardens lush in the middle of the desert. Sounds of American rock music came from one side of the building, and Nick felt the earth vibrate to the pulse of the bass.

"Let's go in this way," Ahmad yelled over the din. "It'll be quieter. You might actually be able to hear what someone is saying."

It was after ten o'clock and the foyer, like the parking area outside the estate, was crowded. John pushed inside, creating a gap for the other two to follow. Chandeliers and marble columns gave off an air of opulence. Nick's hand rested briefly on one column, which was not cool to the touch. Maybe it's fake, he thought.

An open bar with several male attendants occupied one end of the room. Behind them in a glass cabinet was a rack of bottles labeled with the familiar Western brands of alcohol. The barmen served a crowd of Saudi men gathered around.

"They can bring in what they like," Ahmad explained. "Customs agents do not dare search the luggage of the royal family." Then he added, "Selling smuggled liquor to others in the country can supplement their allowances, which have remained fixed at $30,000 per month per person. And that includes each child in the family."

"Hard times," John said.

"The bigger the family, the larger the allowance. So they have incentives to procreate," Ahmad added.

"Do the royals still make their fortunes from kickbacks?" Nick asked.

John nodded. "Yes, but the senior members of the family sometimes crack down if an upstart gets too greedy and asks for more."

Focusing again on the party, Nick noted that, while most were in casual Western or Saudi dress, he saw no other obvious Westerners. Was that why men turned to look at him? He felt uncomfortable and made for the bar. Before reaching it, John grabbed his elbow and whispered in his ear, "Just ask for seltzer water or a soft drink. Don't give them an excuse to hold something against you."

Plush, but gaudy couches and chairs lined the walls, while open passageways and closed doors led to other chambers. Neither John nor Ahmad had yet met anyone whom either recognized, so the three initially sat together amid a leopard-skin ensemble of furnishings and nursed their drinks. Nick watched filing past a stream of men and some whose smooth faces suggested they were adolescents. Part of the crowd was pushing through one particular passageway, while a few came out again with plates of food. Despite the many lit cigarettes and a few cigars, the air was not noxious. Wisps of smoke rose to the ceiling where well-placed vents sucked it out. "Hungry?" Ahmad asked. They were and soon got up to follow the procession. A smell of stewing lamb wafted through the entrance. As if at a cafeteria, attendants in cooks' outfits were ladling out chunks of thick stew along with fragrant, saffron-colored rice and an assortment of side dishes.

Most men were eating with their hands in the traditional fashion and sat on cushions or directly on colorful carpets spread about the large room. John pointed to some knives and spoons if he needed them. Nick shook his head. "Remember, just use your right hand," John said. "In this part of the world, they consider the left hand unclean, and for some, you can take that literally." Nick didn't probe for an explanation, but sometimes forgot about that rule when drinking. He thought it inconvenient to hold a drink in the right and then try to shake another's hand. Always put it down first before mingling had been John's advice.

By this time, Ahmad had seen some acquaintances and nodded at a few, but made no introductions. After eating, they were about to go back to the main room when an older man came up and greeted him in the elaborate manner of Arabs, repeating the lengthy formula of well wishes, culminating in an embrace. He looked John and

Nick over and, while still addressing Ahmad, switched to English so that the others could share in his wit. "I see you've brought two dates." Then in an undertone, he said to Ahmad, "Would you like to share one?" Ahmad laughed it off, but looked embarrassed. The man ignored his discomfort, and said, referring to Nick, "The boy with the girlish face looks exotic."

Ahmad made an excuse to move them away. The other two, who had overheard the exchange, made forced smiles, and quickly followed him. John said to both, "Remember that story about the tattoo? Part of it was true. I've got a set of temporary ones in my back pocket that you can affix to your butts. Once in place, the image acts like garlic to a vampire in case you find yourself in a pickle."

Behind a door, Nick heard the sound of female voices, of men and women talking together and laughing. Ahmad said, "I had warned you guys about this place and the potential for decadence. Once at such a party, I even saw—what you call—transvestites."

"You mean men in *abayas?*" John joked.

Ahmad ignored the sarcasm. "The government normally punishes such behavior by imprisonment, lashings, or worse, but in the privacy of royal households, anything goes."

A smell of burning leaves, reminiscent of high school, reached Nick's nose.

"Hashish." Ahmad confirmed his guess. "We should not stay long."

A short young man in a Saudi *thobe* but no headdress stepped out of the side room. He appeared drunk. Even Nick could see that his hair was dyed black—not to cover gray, but to obscure the light reddish brown that was his natural color, visible along his thin beard, temples, and in a one-inch strip along the part of his hair. "Excuse me, this is our host," Ahmad said and introduced Nick and John. The Saudi prince spoke unaccented American English. He thanked them for coming and hoped they were having a good time.

Afterward, Nick asked Ahmad about him and his fair coloring. "Some of the princes are like that. This one may have had a foreign concubine as his mother. He lowered his voice and moved closer. "He is about thirty, so was born in the early 1970s at a time of new-found riches when our oil prices skyrocketed. I have heard that is when some princes began bringing in Western sex slaves—beautiful young women, some from Scandinavia, to sire their children." He looked at Nick. "Fair skin is highly prized in Saudi."

Nick thought of the lecher's uncouth remarks, of the smooth faces from earlier, and wondered if he should grow a mustache to blend in and appear older. He had never succeeded in growing a beard, so doubted it would be worth the effort. Would just look unkempt, he thought. Next he'd be thinking of dying his hair, too, or wearing disguises.

"How did the foreign women agree to come?" Nick asked.

"I expect they lured some with false promises; others they may have kidnapped. You don't hear much about it, just rumors."

John and Ahmad agreed it was time to go, but Nick wanted to stay a bit longer to look around some more.

"We'll wait here for you, so don't stray too far. Wouldn't want you to end up in someone's harem," John said.

Nick nodded and walked off. Curiosity got the better of him. After affecting an air of nonchalance, he made sure no one was watching and peeked in through the door from which earlier he had heard men and women laughing. The room was dark. Something glowed with an orange incandescence in the middle and he could make out the shapely forms of women, reclining with men in various stages of undress. Nick thought he heard European accents as one of the women spoke incoherently in English. Was she drugged? The last thing he wanted was to make a scene. Quickly closing the door, as if having opened it by mistake, he took several rapid steps from the room and once safely away, moved more slowly to discover what other passageways might contain.

Behind a second door was a large study, its shelves lined with books. Off to the side, four or five were playing cards, possibly poker, with piles of chips beside them. At a gilded table in the middle sat two older men smoking from pipes and playing chess. Several onlookers surrounded them, but took no notice of Nick apart from an initial glance. He approached, pretended to be interested in their strategies, and saw that instead of a queen, there was a piece beside the king that one of the watchers, speaking in English for Nick's benefit, called the "vizier." That figures, thought Nick. They wouldn't want to have a woman in a position of power and mobility, even in a board game.

He moved on, and looked into several empty rooms before tiring of playing the spy. Deciding it was somehow demeaning, he returned to Ahmad and John. The three left.

Chapter 10

TARIQ DROVE HAJAR to the new women-only mall in downtown al-Khobar. Located in the al-Halal, a newly built four-story building, the mall occupied the third floor, with the space above it containing leased private offices and the two stories below devoted to a supermarket and men's stores. The structure rested on top of a three-level underground parking garage.

Hajar sat in the open back of the pickup truck while the seat in the cabin next to Tariq was empty. Rasheed had insisted that Tariq keep the machine gun. Put it in a safe place, he had said. Tariq had none, so he kept the weapon in its case, as before, under the driver's seat. The gun felt like a heavy weight dragging on the wheels as the truck moved slowly along the city streets. Tariq was a tentative driver, made all the more cautious by the contraband weapon. He had turned the air conditioning to high, but sweat was trickling down the side of his face as he inched into the morning traffic. Cars slammed on the brakes, honked at him, then zoomed past with drivers or passengers staring through their windows to get a look at this bumpkin. One rolled down the glass pane and yelled to go back to the desert. Another cursed angrily. Tariq's first day driving was not going well.

Rasheed had pointed out the mall the day before when he had taken Tariq home and reminded him of the route before leaving the vehicle with Tariq and walking to his shop. He had also left a street map on the cab seat, but

Tariq had no spatial sense, was not good at reading anything other than well-reviewed verses of the Koran, and was now trying hard to avoid an accident. He could not risk glancing at the map, even at stoplights. The thought of opening the car window and asking a fellow driver or pedestrian for directions was not an option. He would find this place and not stoop to begging for help.

Tariq spent over an hour to locate the mall. During the next few days, he would reduce that time by half. A competent driver taking the most direct route and avoiding traffic could make the trip in ten or fifteen minutes. At the mall's pay-parking garage, Tariq faced another dilemma. He had been to one or two such places before but always as a passenger and had never paid attention to the process of getting the garage gate to lift open. Tariq angrily watched the barrier and wondered why it would not lift to let him pass. He thought of stepping outside to force it up himself. A patient driver behind him got out of his car, quietly walked up to the ticket machine behind Tariq's truck door, and pulled the stub. Like magic, the gate lifted. Tariq had not noticed the man's actions and felt he himself must have willed it open. He was about to drive through when the fellow tapped the window, got a surly Tariq to roll it down, and explained, "Hold onto this until you leave. Then exit through there and put in the bills or coins to match the fare shown on the machine. It will make you change." Tariq nodded acknowledgement and crept forward, the car surging and stopping as his heavy foot rode the gas pedal. He prowled through the lot until he found two empty adjacent spaces on the lowest level. He had lacked the confidence to park properly in a single one.

In the back, Hajar was oblivious to Tariq's turmoil. She was excited to be out of the apartment. Even the circling about the city center was thrilling as she watched the urban sights that men took for granted, but that she rarely experienced for herself. And she was going to be getting a job! She could hardly believe her good fortune. Only the occasional thought of Suheir, and less frequently, of the blind sheikh Muamar, dampened her good spirits during the ride. She bubbled over with enthusiasm, but adopted a brief dour expression once Tariq had parked and shuffled around the truck to let her out. Even through the veil, she felt he would sense her delight, if left unchecked. Such a mood would surely anger him, perhaps even make him change his mind and take her home.

Tariq explained again what she was to do. "Go to each shop in turn, ask for the manager, and see if they will hire you." He would wait for her at the entrance to the supermarket on the ground floor. If she took any longer than an hour, he would send a *mutawwa* accompanied by a policemen to get her, and that would mean trouble. Hajar nodded she understood.

Two elevators, separated by a staircase, went from the garage landings to the floors above. Signs showed that one elevator was for women—it went only to the third floor; the other was for men and went to all the rest. After standing apart from her brother, Hajar's good spirits re-emerged. She felt like bounding up the staircase beside the elevator rather than wait for the lift, but Tariq was still there watching her and waiting for his ride. Once inside, with the door closed, her thoughts turned to fantasies. She went over the plot of the romance novel that Tariq had dismissed as trash. He had even allowed her to bring the book from Riyadh: "It's English and will help me with my work." Maybe she, too, would find her knight. He would ride in from the desert on a white stallion and whisk her away. The elevator doors opened, and to her amazement, the women there were not only unveiled, some had even shed their *abayas*. Hajar was giddy.

Several shops surrounded the lift. She went to the clothing store immediately opposite. She was attracted by the shop's large size and bright, open spaces filled with racks of colored blouses and dresses from Europe. Hajar approached the cashier's counter. The short, squat woman behind the register and the customer she had just served looked at Hajar oddly. Two others with nametags giggled as they clipped skirts to hangars.

"Can I help you, madam?" the cashier asked.

"I'd like to speak with the manager, please."

"I'm the manager. Is something wrong? What do you need?"

"I'd like to work here."

The woman's manner changed from solicitous to gruff as she realized she had a young supplicant before her. "Come with me then."

Hajar followed her to a back office. "Sit down and remove your veil. Our staff do not hide their faces from customers."

Hajar did as told, and the woman sucked in her breath as she saw Hajar's features. Hajar's cheeks were flushed and eyes still sparkling with the happy thoughts of moments ago.

"Are you married or engaged?"

Hajar wasn't sure how to answer the last part. She said, "No." The manager seemed to mull something over and then said, "We do have a position, but you would start as a trainee. Do you have your father's permission?"

"My half-brother is responsible for me now."

The manager took two papers from a folder, rose, and handed them to Hajar. "Have him fill these both out or make a copy and return them to me. When can you start?"

"You will take me? Oh, madam, I. . . ." Hajar embraced the woman. She was too happy to speak.

"My word, you are enthusiastic. That's good. I will see you tomorrow then at 9 a.m."

She walked Hajar to the store entrance as the younger woman felt as if she were floating alongside, wanting to skip and twirl through the aisle and dance about the wide spaces of the mall.

As Hajar was about to leave, the manager said, "One last thing. Don't you want to know what you will earn?"

"Whatever you can afford will be marvelous." Hajar waved goodbye and raced down the stairs to tell her brother the good news.

The manager smiled, and the two store girls burst out laughing.

The next morning, Hajar wore a simple dress, the best of the three that she had, and appeared for work with her papers completed in the large script of the semiliterate. Tariq had labored over the page, cursing the government bureaucracy and Hajar for being a nuisance. She had offered to help with everything except the signature, but he shooed her away. His first question when she had told him of the job was, "So how much will you make each week?" When she didn't know, he had almost struck her in exasperation, then restrained himself and told her to ask for an advance on her first two weeks' wages.

"We don't do that, Hajar," said the manager. "But if you need something to tide you over, I will give you the equivalent of a day's pay at the end of today." The amount worked out to minimum wage.

"Thank you, madam."

"You may call me Izzat."

Izzat, who was also a part owner, had only recently opened the store, having run a similar business in Dammam. She rarely left the shop for more than a brief break: government regulations required her to employ the services of a male agent for any transactions with other businesses that could not occur by phone.

This was her first time to hire women as help, something she had long wanted to do. As the third hire, Hajar showed more promise than the other girls, whom the manager bemoaned as flighty, with empty heads. They were the twin daughters of a friend. She wanted someone to handle the register at the front of the shop and greet potential customers walking past. Neither girl, however, spoke more than a few words of English, so Izzat had to handle the questions of the few foreign women who stopped by. Moreover, both of the girls were hopeless at the register, making the same repeated mistakes as cashiers while Izzat looked on and tried to point out their errors. In exasperation, partly at herself for such a mistake in hiring, Izzat had secretly nicknamed the two "Dumb" and "Dumber." Perhaps Hajar could do better. This new one also had a pretty face and open, curious manner that might welcome in ladies. Her English could use improvement, but would pass for now.

During the first few days, Izzat trained Hajar in the basics of the store—unpacking, sorting, and hanging clothes, picking up after customers who had to size up items without trying them on, and making sure that nothing walked out of the store unpaid for. The last of the tasks was particularly delicate. Izzat did not want to insult her customers by asking that they leave any bags at the front with her, nor did she have the time to watch the parcels *and* run the register.

The Saudi authorities punished theft severely although first-time offenders usually received a stern warning rather than physical harm. Nevertheless, in the event of shoplifting, and only when the girls had clearly seen it with their own eyes, they were to signal Izzat, who would approach the offender and politely say she might be eligible for special discounts, which Izzat as manager could offer. Izzat would never prosecute nor even inform the police, but would ask to speak privately with the woman and look into her bag. Only if resisted, would she take the last resort of calling over one of the *mutawwas* who patrolled the floor, tapping their sticks as they paced the mall.

By week's end, Izzat thought Hajar ready for the big test, the cash register. She didn't do badly and learned quickly from her mistakes, rarely repeating the same one twice. Soon she was handling it on her own, with Izzat taking over only to start the day and in closing to count the cash and collect the credit card receipts. Hajar quickly sensed that the twins resented her. They took their breaks apart from Hajar, and when she was near, they wondered aloud to each other why she always wore the same dress. After Izzat overheard a snide comment, she upbraided them that poverty was no crime. The next day, the girls brought in a small vial of cheap perfume and, wrinkling their noses, quietly presented it to Hajar when the boss was away. "Here. It will help you with your job."

Hajar said nothing. She stopped talking to the girls unless absolutely necessary. When they realized they might have overplayed their hand, the girls changed tactics and adopted a good cop-bad cop routine: one remained aloof, the other tried to make peace and draw Hajar out, if only, as Hajar knew, to collect information they might use against her. About home life, she was consistently vague and mentioned not a word about Muamar.

"For one so pretty, aren't you old not to be engaged? There isn't something wrong with you, I hope," said the twin, feigning solicitude for Hajar's future marital well-being. "Perhaps our mother can help introduce you to the right man." Hajar pretended to be unconcerned and made an unconvincing attempt to laugh it off. When she saw the dart hit home, the twin began to play on Hajar's insecurity with expert precision, raising the subject of men and marriage at nearly every opportunity.

One day the girl said, "Did you know that young men—many handsome ones, too—gather outside the front entrance to this building, hoping to contact female employees as they leave work on Wednesday nights? The thought of the long weekends alone must drive them wild with illicit passions."

"But it is forbidden to speak to a woman who is not a relative."

"Don't be silly. They aren't so stupid as that. Those with cars will put a big sign in their side window and drive slowly past."

"Sign? What sign?"

"Oh, Hajar," the girl groaned, as if explaining to a child. "A sign pretending to sell the car, with the man's phone number posted in LARGE digits. Other men, without cars—you know, the poorer ones—linger at a suitable distance, write their name and phone number onto pieces of paper that they crumple into little balls to toss in the direction of a passing girl, whose ankle may have caught their fancy."

"Some girls show their ankles?"

"Don't be a prude. Haven't you seen the jewelry women wear down there? Sure, the *abaya* covers them, but if you turn your leg just right. . . ." The twin looked down at Hajar's bare ankles and plain shoes.

"If the girl likes the look of the suitor, she will call him. It's a kind of dating service for the repressed. This way you won't end up marrying your ugly first cousin just because his father is the only one *your* father knows and trusts."

"So parents don't object?"

"It depends. Many would, but the more liberal see it as something to try so long as they manage the process. They would dread a daughter's not telling them, chatting by phone in secret, and, God forbid, arranging a secret tryst. Not that it doesn't happen," she said with a grin, while looking at Hajar closely.

Hajar took the bait. "My brother always picks me up in the parking lot in front of the women's elevator, so I have never seen this phenomenon."

"Come with me tomorrow when we finish work. I'll walk you out the women's exit and then back around into the parking lot. It will be our little parade."

The next day the sisters arrived early.

"What are you two giggling about?" Izzat asked shortly after when she arrived to let them in.

"Nothing," they said in unison, but the whole day they were even more careless in their work than usual. Hajar had also not forgotten the appointment and noticed that even the aloof twin was smiling at her today.

Like many shops in Riyadh, the mall opened from 9 a.m. to 1 p.m., largely shut down for a four-hour siesta during the heat of the day, and reopened from 5 p.m. to 9 p.m. with mandated 20- to 30-minute closures during prayer times. The hypnotic voices of muezzins from the nearby mosques and an internal speaker system announced the prayers. Those with rides went home during the lunch break; the ones less fortunate like Hajar had to hang around. A driver usually collected the twins to take them home at midday for lunch and a nap. They never invited Hajar over or even offered a ride to her home. Izzat often stayed behind to work the books.

Hajar could have taken the bus, but it was an infrequent and bad connection with a lengthy walk from her apartment building. Moreover, Tariq did not want her riding public transportation even though buses had separate entrances and seating arrangements for females. He also begrudged her the fare and promptly collected her entire paycheck every two weeks, only agreeing to dole out a small allowance for "emergencies."

When Hajar hinted it might be nice if Tariq would occasionally pick her up at midday, he said, "What? Have I become your servant?" To his credit, at least, he faithfully dropped her off in the morning and collected her at night. Lately, as his assignments for Rasheed took more time, he began letting her take the bus in the morning, but insisted on always getting Hajar at night. On such occasions, when he did not personally drop her off, he would borrow a phone to call the shop and make sure she was there. At first, Izzat thought he was merely a concerned brother. Eventually, the calls became an annoyance as she realized he was mainly trying to exert his control over the girl.

The commutes and staggered hours, largely on her feet, made for an exhausting day. To make the break pass more quickly, Izzat loaned Hajar some of her old books in English. Like many malls, there were few chairs, and girls in similar circumstances often occupied them. Sometimes after closing up for midday, Izzat would return to find Hajar slumped on the floor, asleep and beside her a book, open to the same page as the day before. Izzat would take pity on the girl and invite her over for lunch and a rest. However, Hajar felt uncomfortable accepting the offer more than a few times, and even asking for a ride would be imposing on the older woman's kindness as Izzat lived in the better part of town, in the opposite direction from Hajar.

"If you won't come home with me, please remember to eat something. You're losing weight from too little food. Here, it is on me." Izzat handed Hajar some coins. "Now go to the market downstairs and buy something."

At the end of the workday, the gregarious twin known as "Dumber" came up to Hajar and said in a soft voice that Izzat would not hear, "Are you ready? It will just be you and me on the promenade; Mother has already chosen a man for my sister."

After descending to the first floor, the girl grabbed Hajar by the hand as if they were good friends, and the two stepped out through the sliding doors into the sultry evening air. The twin had made a point of going promptly at 9 p.m. so that they would be among the first of the stream of girls to leave the women's exit at the back of the mall. Being near the front of the procession might get more attention from the onlookers, as there was only so much that the flash of an ankle or the wearing of a tightly bound *abaya* would do.

"What about the *mutawwas?*" Hajar asked.

"Don't worry. I can spot those long-bearded goat herders from a mile away."

They made a pass slowly along the walkway, and Hajar was curious to see, through the thin screen of her veil, that indeed there were lots of men waiting and watching, both on foot and in slowly passing cars. Hajar thought one of those standing looked like her half-brother. His pose, one shoulder off-kilter, was the same, but he remained motionless, so she did not see the distinctive gait. She wondered whether Tariq might be among those lonely hearts. Her father and his mother had never seemed active in finding a match for him. Was the dowry the only issue, or could some girl's father have refused him for his disability, however slight it might be?

Hajar didn't find any signs in car windows and doubted she would remember a number posted there even if she had done so, but toward the end of their walk, a crumpled ball of paper bounced to her feet.

"You've got one," the twin hissed. "Let me handle it for you." She looked around and then kicked the paper to the side out of view as if it were so much trash. Then pausing behind Hajar, she bent over, pretending to tie an undone lace on her shoe and scooped the paper into the fold of the *abaya's* sleeve. The girl continued her amble, but Hajar, at her side, said that Tariq would be upset if she were late, so they both hastened to the parking lot through a side entrance. By this time, the twin had unrolled the paper and confirmed that it contained a man's name and number.

"I didn't see who threw it. Did you?" Hajar said under her breath.

"No, but never mind. It's worth an anonymous call to get things rolling. From the handwriting, the man appears courageous and smart."

Hajar doubted that she had any training in graphology. "You take it. I don't have a phone."

The twin seemed put out at this, but didn't argue. She shrugged, saying "Suit yourself," and walked off to her driver's car. Her sister sat inside waiting for the news.

Within a few weeks, Izzat no longer considered Hajar a trainee. By the end of her first month, she was quietly paying her more than either of the twins. She didn't formally promote her to avoid creating further friction, but explained to Hajar's grateful surprise upon examining her third paycheck that she was receiving pay commensurate with her duties. Izzat noticed that Hajar had a knack for drawing in more traffic to the shop. Her bright smile and her carefully rehearsed English phrase of "Won't you please come in to see our new fashions?" attracted an ever-growing stream of Western women, who in the past had tended to favor the larger stores at the other end of the mall. Business was brisk, and Izzat talked of bringing on another girl, specifically to run the register and thereby free Hajar to work full time as a greeter.

One morning a woman stepped from the elevator opposite the store's entrance. The lady was unveiled and had already removed her *abaya*. She was wearing a nurse's uniform with white shoes. Her hair was pulled back into a tight bow, but Hajar thought she recognized the ringlets of hair that had been the envy of her schoolmates. As the woman turned to walk down the mall, presumably to a pharmacy in its center, Hajar called out, "Fatima?"

Fatima paused, looked around to see where the voice came from, and catching sight of Hajar, yelped "Hajar! My dear!" The two embraced. The normally stoic Fatima wiped a tear from her eye and offered a perfumed handkerchief to Hajar, whose cheeks were also wet.

"I thought I would never see you again. My, you've grown! Such a full and beautiful woman. What happened to that mischievous little girl always getting into trouble?" Fatima surveyed her long-lost friend.

Hajar was just as impressed. "And you, my sister, so tall and graceful. You must have many suitors asking for your hand."

The two soon talked as if only a few days, not eight years, had passed. They reminisced.

"You were my best friend—the only Sunni girl at the Riyadh school who would play with a Shi'ite," said Fatima. "Now look at us. We are both working and still unmarried—can you believe our good fortune?"

Hajar smiled, but a touch of sadness around her eyes belied her vigorous nodding. She had refrained from any comments about Muamar even when Fatima had joked about the pranks they had played on the blind buffoon.

"What is it, child? Is anything the matter?"

"No, nothing at all."

"You must come for a visit." A brief cloud of concern passed across Fatima's face after she made the invitation. She then asked about Hajar's mother Layla and half-sisters Aisha and Munira but avoided mention of the men in Hajar's household.

"They are as well as can be expected, I think. Actually, I haven't spoken with my mother for many weeks. You see...." and she explained what had happened. She also mentioned Munira's worsening illness, and Fatima offered to get her the best treatment in Dhahran.

Hajar doubted Tariq would let her visit Fatima's house or accept her coming to see them. Fatima nodded, remembering how he and her brother Faisal, who were classmates, frequently got into taunting matches and then fistfights with each other.

"For starters, at least we can talk by phone. We shall work something out, even if it means sneaking off during lunchtime. When shall I contact you, Hajar? What is your number? If Tariq answers, I'll pretend to be your colleague."

"We don't have a phone at home. You could call me here at work."

Fatima seemed dissatisfied with this solution. "Here, take mine. I don't need it. She reached into her purse, handed Hajar a cell phone, and on a scrap of paper, wrote and underlined her name, noting down both her home and work numbers. On a separate piece, she did the same with Hajar's name written above the number of the cell phone, as if underlining that the phone now belonged to her.

Hajar protested. As she became insistent that it was impossible to take such a phone, even as a loan, the instrument began to vibrate in her hand. Startled, she gave it back, "You see, someone is already trying to call you."

Fatima glanced at the tiny screen. "It is just my brother Ahmad. He is the only one who calls this number, and I am with him much of the day. So what need have I for this? He just wants me to hurry up so he can drive us to work."

Hajar meekly accepted this explanation. After Fatima briefly explained the basics of operating the phone, the two parted, promising to get together as soon as possible.

The twins had been watching this exchange. Later, the one came up, made a hand gesture as if on a phone, and said, "Now you have your dating tool!"

"I hadn't thought of it like that."

"But you must. I still have that man's phone number. Haven't worked up the nerve to call. Why don't you take it?

"No, you keep it."

"Perhaps you're right. Better to get a good look at them first. Wouldn't want a smelly south Asian masquerading as an Arab stud. Egyptian or Syrian would be best. I hear they treat their women better than the Saudis do. Maybe even a Westerner. Now that would be exotic!"

Hajar shrugged and walked away. She realized she had forgotten to return Fatima's handkerchief. With a piece of string she carefully wrapped the phone in the perfumed silk and tied a bow around it before returning it to her purse. She also slipped in the note of paper with her name and the cell phone number as a reminder. Hajar hoped Tariq wouldn't nose about her pocketbook, for he would surely confiscate the phone if he found it. The handkerchief would provide some camouflage from his prying eyes.

Chapter 11

NICK KNEW IT WOULD BE A HOT DAY, so he lathered the sunscreen onto his face, neck, and hands. Just in case, he put some on his forearms as well. Looking like a D.C. bureaucrat in short sleeves and tie, he picked out a light-colored sports coat to wear with even lighter pants.

On this Thursday morning in early May, the roads between Dhahran and al-Khobar were empty. Nick parked his car at the Half Moon Bay Club just before 7:30 a.m., saw what appeared to be an embassy car next to several others, and went to the club's front door, which was still locked. The ambassador's secretary had left him a message the day before to meet Gewalt at the club but hadn't specified the topic and type of meeting. Nick assumed they would speak over breakfast or on Gewalt's boat. Guessing it might be the latter venue, he had put on his docksider shoes.

No one came to the door after Nick knocked, and he saw no movement inside when he pressed his face, eyes shielded, against the dark glass. Must be out back, he thought, and hustled around the lot to the marina with his coat draped over an arm.

"Over here, Nick!" The ambassador, in polo shirt and chinos, was undoing some ropes from the rigging. "Do you know how to sail?"

"The basics, sir. I've skippered a sunfish," Nick called back, referring to the tiniest of sailboats, not a thirty-foot yacht like the one he was boarding. He made his way to the dock.

The ambassador shouted through the wind, "Well, I won't let you scupper this one." He grinned, pleased at his own wit. "So long as 'tack,' 'jibe,' and 'watch your head' mean anything to you, you'll be fine."

Walking along the dock's wooden slats, Nick was checking his balance as the slender quay rocked from the morning surf. Was a windstorm brewing? He looked up and saw the telltales on the rigging already horizontal. There must be whitecaps on the waves by now. The ropes snaking up the masts of the boats were already snapping and the clamps clanging in an urgent beat. Nick hadn't eaten, but the pit of his stomach felt heavy as he recalled earlier scares on rough waters.

Two gulls were squawking overhead and took temporary refuge on Gewalt's boat before lifting off again. "Welcome to the *Holey Moley,*" Gewalt said, extending Nick a hand to pull him onto the deck.

When Nick smiled at that, Gewalt added, "It's a silly name that I haven't bothered to change after buying her from a previous owner."

Nick began loosening his collar, already damp, and thought about pulling off his necktie. The ambassador preempted him. "Put your coat and tie into the cabin to keep them dry and help me with these." Gewalt pointed to some tangled rope that looked like gray seaweed on the deck of the boat.

Nick wasn't good with knots, other than a half hitch, so he separated and pulled taut the individual rope ends and let Gewalt's expert hands tie them down.

By this time, a club employee had jogged across the sloping lawn from the clubhouse and was helping them cast off. The man tossed the mooring rope onto the deck, gave the boat's stern a push, and watched them drift away.

Gewalt lowered the engine into the water. "We'll motor out into the open and then unfurl the sail. Won't need the jib today. With this wind, we can get by as a catboat rather than a sloop." He then waved at two men on a motor launch halfway down the dock. Nick hadn't paid attention to them, but saw they were a marine from the consulate and a bulky American bodyguard who shadowed the ambassador wherever he went in Saudi Arabia. "They'll keep a discreet distance. I told them I'd have you on board to fend off any pirates."

As soon as they were past the first buoy, Gewalt said, "Take the wheel. You're going to be steering while I man the sail. Head for that marker over there."

However, Gewalt did not untie and hoist the mainsail. Instead, he climbed down in the cabin, emerged a few minutes later, and turned off the boat's engine.

"Have you got a feel for how she moves? Good. We'll let her drift for a while. I'd like you to go inside with me for a few minutes."

Nick looked around to see if there were any other boats or objects they might crash into.

"Don't worry. The tides won't carry us far from this position, and nothing will come close. My boys over there will see to that." He gestured toward the launch about fifty meters off to their starboard side. Nick wondered what measures they would take. A warning by megaphone? But did the bodyguard know the Arabic for that? A pistol shot across an offender's bow? What if the approach were intentional rather than accidental? Two men did not amount to much against a determined sea assault. The unsettled waters were stoking Nick's paranoia.

He bumped his head, forgetting to duck into the low cabin, and saw that Gewalt had laid out two maps on the long wooden table inside. Paperweights held the map corners in place, but the rocking and pitching of the boat had one of the weights about to slide off. Nick rested his hand on it, as much to steady himself as to keep the metal object from falling. He realized he should have eaten something that morning and felt queasy. Although not prone to seasickness, he looked through the port windows for a stationary object to fix his eyes on.

"We won't stay down here long. I just wanted to show you the maps without the wind flapping them all over the place." The two maps conveyed nothing unusual: one was of the entire world, one of the Arabian Peninsula and the Middle East. Was a geography lesson really necessary?

Gewalt's index finger tapped on the Arabian Gulf. "What does this look like to you?"

"The Gulf, sir."

"Yes, obviously. But what about the shape of it?"

Nick was stumped. He felt as if in a bad dream, attending an exam he hadn't prepared for.

"A stomach. The shape is like a stomach, for here along its lining ..." Gewalt's finger traced the Gulf's outline, "... is where 60 percent of the world's oil comes from. That oil feeds the economies, including ours, that would wither and die without it."

Nick didn't like the metaphor and felt sicker than ever.

"That lining is also home to sizeable Shi'ite populations—in Iran, southern Iraq, Kuwait, and here along Saudi's Eastern Province. The Shi'ites live on the land supplying the oil, but apart from Iran, the Sunnis—their enemies—rule the governments that control the oil wealth. Makes for a volatile situation, wouldn't you say?"

Nick thought of Fatima, but forgot to agree. If he could only just hold that thought. . . .

"Now pay attention. Here, here, here, here, and here are strategic choke points in the movement of the food—the oil—to the bodies that need it." Gewalt tapped the Saudi port of Dammam, the Straits of Hormuz, the Suez Canal, the Malacca Straits, and the Panama Canal.

He pulled out a black marker from his pocket and drew five circles next to each location. "Who do you think has recently installed a major commercial presence at each of these points?"

"Us?"

"No, the Chinese."

Nick was failing the catechism.

"Hudson Woosung, a major port developer and shipping conglomerate, now has port operations at all five locations." Nick was familiar with the Hong Kong company, controlled by Asia's richest tycoon, who had close ties to the Beijing government. "We have no direct evidence that Hudson has allowed PLA soldiers into these places, but it's not inconceivable. Several years ago we heard about thousands of PLA troops working in the Sudan to guard an oil pipeline that the Chinese were developing with the Sudanese government. According to other intelligence services with whom we cooperate, the soldiers were disguised as pipeline workers."

"Don't we do the same, sir? Protect our strategic investments?" Nick referred to the U.S. troops in Iraq and American bases elsewhere in the Middle East.

"You're right. There's nothing sinister *per se*. It's just the extent and rapid expansion of a Chinese presence that concerns us. For years they stayed out of the Middle East, but now they're crawling all over the place. The Russians' decision a few years ago to build their major pipeline to serve multiple Asian markets rather than China alone acted as a catalyst. That move seemed to have driven the Chinese into further entrenching their position in this region. Beijing has been searching for, and winning, oil contracts around the Gulf to fuel their economy's insatiable appetite. They've surpassed Japan in the magnitude of oil imports and are closing in on us."

"But, sir, haven't the Chinese promoted a policy of focusing on economic growth rather than projecting military power abroad?"

"Nick, nowadays you cannot distinguish economic from military power. The Chinese may not be engaged in combat themselves, but they're supplying surrogates, including states known to have supported terrorists. For instance, in the Middle East, China has contracted many of these oil deals or won drilling concessions by selling weapons." Gewalt glanced at him. "Let's go back upstairs and eat a bite. You're looking pale. We can talk more once you have something in your stomach."

On deck, the ambassador handed Nick a half-full box of donuts and poured some coffee from a flask. "I've already eaten. This will give you back your sea legs until we return to shore. I won't keep you out here long."

Gewalt pulled the halyard to unfurl the sail while Nick held the wheel and a half-full paper cup with one hand and ate a donut with the other. Soon the sail was out, and the boat surged forward as if kicked. "We'll let her run for a while," said Gewalt. "I suppose we might have put up a spinnaker, but then those boys in the launch couldn't have kept up."

Nick wolfed down two of the three donuts and set the box aside. He was concentrating on holding the boat steady to its course. With the wind behind them, he knew enough that he had better not get sloppy. Otherwise, the sail's boom might come about too quickly. He preferred to tack into the wind, a direction that held fewer surprises.

Gewalt leaned back to watch the sail. "It's time for me to spin the rest of the yarn, son. Now that you have the bigger geopolitical picture, we'll work through some of the details here in Saudi Arabia."

He paused to check that Nick was ready. "I'm currently taking part in an exercise—a war game, really—conducted at regular intervals by the Defense Department and increasingly involving State, as well. These days, to add to the realism of the gaming scenarios and to propound differing perspectives, they want to involve input from officers in the field. But this game is important. The president likes to review the results of our scenarios so that he knows what potential options he has available.

"In this year's exercise, China's role in the Middle East figures heavily, and so I'm bringing you in to tap your expertise on a country I know little about. I want you to make a well-informed and rigorous analysis in a draft cable that you and I will write next week. You are to write the political section as it pertains to China, and I will do the economic and financial scenarios.

"To make the best possible analysis, you need all available information. I have few hard facts to impart. Therefore, what I will tell you from now on is either hypothesis or conjecture, but all highly classified. You are not to mention to others any of what I say or even the fact that we had this conversation. Do you understand?"

Nick didn't, but nodded anyway.

"Here's a bit more background that figures into the scenarios. Earlier this year, the newly elected Iraqi government hinted, not too subtly, that they would like all U.S. troops, apart from a small contingent of advisors, to leave the country within 12 months. We have been drawing down our force levels there, but they want the reductions sharply accelerated.

"With Congressional talk of our re-instituting the peacetime draft, and the president's acquiescence, U.S. armed forces will have more men and women to work with. We need to train and keep those new soldiers sharp, which means stationing them near the field of action. The expected future battlefields are no longer in Germany, but in Asia and most likely out here. Some troops can go to South Korea, but many more should come to the Middle East. The question is where to put them. Only so many can fit into Qatar or Bahrain, or float around on battleships and carriers that patrol the waters in the region.

"Got it?"

Again Nick nodded, but wished he could have taken notes.

"Nick, did you know Errol Hart, from the Political Section in Riyadh?"

"I met him once, sir, but he died shortly after I arrived in country."

"Tragic, losing such a fine man. We ruled the death an accident, but what no one else knows—or should have known—including the *chargé*, was that Hart was working under official cover as an agent for the CIA. His handler in Washington and I do not believe Errol's death was simply an accident. Either someone blew his cover—how we don't know—or he stumbled onto information he should not have before he could relay it to us.

"Errol was investigating some of our suspicions about a Saudi nuclear weapon, or weapons, obtained via Pakistan with Chinese help. With their wealth, the Saudis can buy such devices off the shelf so long as a nuclear power makes them available; they have no need to first procure uranium and develop an elaborate program for enriching it to weapons grade.

"Our satellites at least have a chance of detecting those types of activity, but finding out about a purchased, ready-made weapon that can fit into a large traveling trunk is virtually impossible without human intelligence. Sure, we can get close and can even read a license plate number from the skies, but that doesn't tell us very much if, as it turns out, we lack access to Saudi data on vehicle registrations. I suspect they themselves don't even have much of that information: just look at how many twelve-year-old boys are driving around the cities."

At the mention of needing human intelligence, Nick thought he saw the direction this talk was going. His face had begun to blanch again, and he had momentarily bent forward, crossing his arms and taking his hands from the wheel, which slowly began to spin. Gewalt felt the boat turning and quickly reached over to the helm, steadying it. To help Nick concentrate, he took over the steering.

"I'm not going to ask you to take up where Errol left off. You're not made for that type of work, most of us aren't."

Nick's color came back in a flush of relief. "Sir, with the U.S. protecting them, why would the Saudis need nuclear weapons?"

"As Lord Palmerston once said, there are no permanent allies, just permanent interests. We cannot guarantee to act as the Saudis' strongman forever, and the Saudis know that. In the late 1980s, they bought Chinese missiles capable of delivering warheads several thousand miles. In 2002, shortly after the U.S. switched to a policy of preemptive deterrence against the so-called axis of evil, a high-level Saudi delegation visited Pakistan, which has been exporting nuclear know-how. As ostensible allies in our war against terror, those two nations were at least temporarily exempt from overt criticism, and Washington had no concrete evidence to object to what it suspected was going on. However, the timing of that trip raised concerns. Not long after 9-11 we were no longer handling Saudi Arabia with kid gloves: remember, we soon found out that it was primarily the Saudis—not Iraqis and not Afghans—who had attacked us on that day. Certainly, they must have felt that we might retaliate at some point and that we were waiting only to first pick off the easier targets of other countries."

"These days," Nick asked, "could their procuring a few nuclear bombs really serve as a deterrent against U.S. forces?"

"Look at North Korea. We've done nothing there, despite virtual proof for over a decade of their nuclear-weapons program. Why not? Because they have a huge military threatening the South. It's true the Saudi army is pitiful and poses no threat to any neighboring countries, but if you bring into the equation the Chinese as their allies, then the scenario becomes more complicated, and more ominous. For example, if any U.S. attack to take out nuclear facilities were inadvertently to kill Chinese workers in Saudi Arabia, or if the Saudis could draw the Chinese in by some other means—say, via a mutual defense treaty we don't know about—then you have the potential for a worldwide war.

"Personally," said Gewalt. "I don't think the Chinese would risk an open military confrontation with the U.S. They would see the rationale for our action in the context of preserving global security. What else could we do? To eradicate dangerous weapons that a few trucks can easily move from place to place, we would have to act quickly. There would not be time for a U.N. resolution, for economic sanctions, or for the cobbling together of multilateral forces.

"The same holds true if the U.S. had to act to protect oil fields from sabotage or from any other threat. Naturally, we would say we were taking the measures, not for ourselves, but for a government that might have come under siege, for the installation of a new, more reasonable regime, or if necessary, for international governance as a permanent U.N. protectorate with revenues distributed appropriately."

Nick noted he didn't define "appropriately" but hesitated to ask what he meant by that.

"I know I'm giving you an earful, Nick, and you'll need time to digest it. However, I'd like your own assessment of this key scenario: namely, how might the Chinese react if the U.S. moves militarily to occupy Saudi oil fields or to take out previously identified nuclear weapons."

"You may recall that we found Hart's vehicle and body not far from the remote Saudi Oil site of Udhailiyah, the same place your sources and our satellites have noticed increased activity during the past six to nine months. We think Errol may have stumbled onto something, and if so, the government quietly had him killed."

Nick thought that might be a bit of a stretch.

Gewalt paused to tend to the boat and was pulling the sail in, but Nick felt he should be easing the sheet.

"In addition to the transfer of nuclear technology, Errol was also looking into links between certain Saudi officials and al-Qaeda. If the Saudis do have the bomb, we want to avoid the nightmare scenario of someone passing one on to the likes of bin Laden. Several years back, we found ties between Pakistani intelligence, the Taliban, and al-Qaeda. Although the Saudi government and al-Qaeda seem to be at each other's throat, some of us think the Saudi intelligence service contains a fair number of sympathizers, supporters, or even outright operatives of al-Qaeda. If that were the case, we would have to act—most likely via back channels within the Saudi government to force them to take more systematic measures to root out al-Qaeda support in the regime. How they might do that is anybody's guess.

"However, as for Errol Hart, if someone killed him—and that's still an 'if'—the death has none of the hallmarks of an al-Qaeda execution, replete with videotaping and severing of the head. In fact, Hart's body had no marks on it. He died of dehydration, from exposure in the desert.

"With regard to the Chinese, one hypothesis is this: during the past several years they have been winning all these contracts—from oil to telecommunications—because they have helped the Saudis procure nuclear weapons and are now helping them in the care and maintenance of the facilities to store them."

Or maybe, thought Nick, the Chinese just sell their goods at lower prices than their competitors.

"A nuclear arsenal—even a small one of just a few bombs—requires a fair number of skilled technicians who know how to keep their mouths shut. We think the Chinese might be providing those people, under the guise of oil technicians in a remote location, namely at Udhailiyah."

"Wouldn't that be risky, sir? Terrorists have been choosing oil facilities as a prime target for attack. Why put nuclear weapons there that they could steal or possibly detonate on site?"

"We don't think the Saudis are actually keeping the weapons there, but just receiving training. If they needed a working device to show to trainees, the Saudis could ship one in temporarily from the hidden location, using, for instance, an oil truck as a cover. A few years ago, China won a contract to explore for oil in the Empty Quarter, but no oil has come from that. We think the deal might merely have served as a ruse to introduce Chinese personnel into the country and thereby help safeguard the facilities where the Saudis would store nuclear weapons. What's more, China Oil and Saudi Oil have recently started a joint venture to process Saudi oil imports in one of China's provinces directly opposite the island of Taiwan. I forget which one. Fujong or Fuzhou. . . ."

"That would be Fujian, sir. I've heard about that project. It's in the port city of Quanzhou."

"Yes, that's right. The countryside surrounding that port, due to its location, is said to be full of Chinese military installations targeting Taiwan. Any Saudis sent there to help run the refinery might also receive military training, and possibly even instruction in nuclear weaponry."

Nick felt on firmer ground when discussing China. "I wonder why the Chinese would want oil tankers moving into the Taiwan Strait. Less than a decade ago, it was a potential flashpoint with the U.S. navy."

"You tell me, my boy." Gewalt's left hand loosened its grip on the wheel. "Watch your head. We're coming around." His right arm pushed the tiller quickly to port as he simultaneously hauled in the mast's sheet line. The boat jibed while the two crouched beneath the swinging boom.

"There's another thing you need to know for our scenarios. The Chinese now have their first aircraft carrier, which means they can project military power far beyond Taiwan and their own coastal waters. In fact, a battle group led by that carrier is heading toward the Persian Gulf, ostensibly as part of a round-the-world 'good will' tour."

"Is that suspicious, sir?"

"Well, no, not necessarily. We do our own strutting on the world stage. But whenever you have two, potentially opposing military forces near one another, it makes for a riskier mix—if either side miscalculates."

Gewalt continued. "Over the years, the Saudis have bought off a number of U.S. government officials—both in country and in Washington, as well as CIA operatives. They used no outright bribes that we know of, but made—and delivered on—promises of lucrative consulting fees once these targeted individuals had left the foreign or civil service. Perhaps Errol had refused to be bought."

Gewalt frowned, as if recalling some overture the Saudis had made to him. Nick thought it would be hard to bribe a man like Gewalt who was already wealthy far beyond his needs, although blackmail might be an option.

Nick said, "Certainly, they couldn't buy *you* off, sir."

Gewalt looked at Nick, and hostility flashed briefly in the older man's eyes. "I started out as an errand boy on

Wall Street. Got a break and from then on, I moved up quickly, based on the results that I delivered—results from trades I made, relying on my gut as a trader—to make the firm and me a lot of money. I didn't advance one foreign-service grade, step by step, each year based on how well I kissed my boss's ass. You look at some of these career bureaucrats, and they're so goddamn cautious. Always waiting for just a bit more data to go on. Sometimes you just have to decide based on what you've got.

"Or take the CIA. They don't even recruit from outside the agency; there's no experienced new blood coming into that cabal, just guys wet behind the ears sent out to the field and expected to do the impossible. No wonder they burn out fast, return to cushy desk jobs at Langley, or leave the service entirely.

"You remember Morrison: the guy we talked with via video in March. Another case in point. He was with State's Bureau of Research and Intelligence a few years ago before the Iraq mess. Got his assessments right on WMD back then, no one listened of course, and we went in anyway. Now, however, since he got one call right, he thinks he has the judgment of Solomon. 'The Saudi ruling family is our baby,' Morrison says. 'We created them. So what if they're wallowing in filthy bathwater?'"

Nick wondered why Gewalt was venting. Frustrated by bureaucratic red tape, overworked perhaps? He looked tired and much older than when Nick had first met him.

The ambassador continued, calmer now. "Some of us believe that the members of the Saudi ruling family are now where the Shah of Iran was in the late 1970s—despised by their people and ripe for overthrow. When you do your assessment, Nick, focus on two scenarios. First, if internal unrest in Saudi Arabia got out of hand,

and if the king called upon his defense treaty with the U.S. to get us to come in militarily to help out, as we did before the first Gulf War, how might the Chinese react? Second, if radical fundamentalists seized control, and we acted after the fact to secure Saudi oil fields, what might the Chinese do? I suppose they wouldn't care who was in power so long as they were assured of a steady supply of oil, but I don't know. That's where I want your insights."

Nick silently mouthed the main points of the two scenarios to be sure he remembered: China reaction, if U.S. takes over oil fields, if takes out nukes.

"Remember this is all confidential. It may just be a game, but we don't want to unnecessarily alarm the Chinese or Saudis with someone's ill-advised question. That's why I'd like you to think over what I've told you this weekend and give me a verbal assessment Friday evening, that is, tomorrow at 8 p.m., so that we can proceed to put the cable together early next week when you're back in Riyadh. Come to my hotel suite for a drink—top floor of the Oasis Tower, room 543. I'd rather meet there than in the hotel lounge where someone could overhear us. The room should be secure: my guys routinely check wherever I'm staying for listening devices."

At last, Gewalt seemed to relax. "Time to take her home." He turned the rudder to bring the boat closer into the wind and began tacking back and forth. The deck slanted as Gewalt brought the boat hard against what had felt like a gale but was merely a steady breeze.

"You want to try, Nick? It should be smooth sailing: the wind isn't shifting at all right now. Just don't go too far off the mark." He pointed back to the clubhouse dock in the distance. "It's good to go fast, but I wouldn't want this baby to tip completely and have us get dunked."

Gewalt adjusted a grommet and watched Nick carefully keep the sail at close haul, bearing up to the eye of the wind and pulling the mainsail in and out of luff. He kept quiet for a few minutes, then as the boat sailed closer to shore said, "At the rate you're tacking, you may end up in irons, Nick. Your technique reminds me of my youngest boy, Hamilton, or 'Ham' as we call him. He's also smart and analytical, but oh, so cautious."

"I thought you had only two sons, sir."

"The middle one was born dead, but I still think of him as mine." He fell silent for a while. Nick wanted to kick himself for blurting out such a tactless comment.

Hoping his docking properly might make amends, Nick deftly steered the boat alongside the quay where a boatboy was waiting to catch him. With the boat safely moored, Gewalt grew expansive once again. "Anyway, Ham wanted to follow in his dad's footsteps. Against my advice, he joined Goldman Sachs, but soon began to hate it. He's the sensitive type, so I knew he wouldn't have the stomach for such a cutthroat atmosphere. He stuck it out for a while, and made a tidy packet as a research analyst. Last year he finally quit and is now a stay-at-home dad. Says he's never been happier."

Chapter 12

Tariq's eyes lit up when Rasheed told him the good news: they had found Tariq's father in al-Hair prison, and he was well. Rasheed hastened to add what he must have assumed were still more happy tidings. "Your father says to go ahead with marrying off Hajar. He has given his blessing for you to handle the negotiations with Sheikh Muamar."

Tariq's reaction was subdued, and the gleam in his eyes vanished. "Okay, thanks. Anything else?" Tariq studied the dirt covering the sidewalk.

"We told him of the move, and he understands the need for money—hence, he urges you to hurry with the marriage arrangements." Rasheed handed Tariq a slip of paper with Muamar's phone number.

After a brief glance, Tariq pocketed the note. "Do you have any idea when my father might get out? If soon, I will have to go back to Riyadh, albeit for just a short while. I know you need me here."

Rasheed shook his head. "No news on a date for his release. One other thing, however . . ." Rasheed laid his hand on Tariq's shoulder to soften the blow, ". . . my associate said your father's hair is now completely white. Those bastards must have tortured him."

Or withheld his hair dye, thought Tariq, who embraced Rasheed to signal he was going and said, "I had best get things rolling and contact Muamar." He would remain a dutiful son.

Within the week, Tariq had called the sheikh and verbally agreed on a bride price. To Tariq's amazement and disgust, Muamar had at first offered payment in camels. "We only accept Saudi riyals," said Tariq. "I'm not in the business of marketing animals." The blind sheikh did some quick mental arithmetic and suggested a price that Tariq thought more than fair, but Tariq haggled anyway to give the old man some satisfaction that he was not paying too much.

The next day, before he drove Hajar to work, Tariq told her. He had already mentioned several days before that Father wanted him to conclude the arrangements. He had seen that she was terrified, desperately trying not to break down and sob. Controlling her voice, she had argued that they didn't need the money, that she was earning more now and might even become an assistant manager. All to no avail, for Tariq had shrugged and said, "We must all accept our lot." Afterwards, Hajar seemed almost suicidal, as if searching for ways to kill herself but not knowing how best to go about it.

Tariq continued the conversation from the previous day. "All that remains is for Muamar to come here or for me to go to Riyadh, and together we will sign the papers before the required witnesses. He made no mention of whether he might come here, but as I have no plans to travel to Riyadh, I expect he soon will. You should prepare yourself. He even said he would send a down payment so that you might buy a pretty dress for the marriage."

Hajar did not reply, but made a motion to climb slowly into the back of the truck. Tariq helped her in, and she did not pull away when he supported her arm. He sensed the ineffable sadness that now enveloped her, where only a week before she had bubbled over with enthusiasm about life in al-Khobar.

Tariq tried one last time. "Sometimes," he said, "we must make sacrifices for what is bigger than ourselves. Your marriage is like that. You are sacrificing for the good of the family. I, too, am prepared to sacrifice. Know that I am not here merely doing the work of an errand boy. I tell you something big will happen, something that will turn Father's jailers into the jailed, and I am to be part of it. Mark my words. If I do not survive, so be it. I am not afraid, nor should you be."

The last words struck a chord with Hajar. She remained silent behind her veil, but straightened her back. Tariq thought he had plucked up her courage, but in fact he had planted the first seed of an idea—the steely determination to resist the inevitable.

The twins had noticed Hajar's despondency and stayed away from her at work, thereby displaying a rare consideration for her feelings. Nothing, however, would allay their curiosity, so they had asked Izzat, in whom Hajar had confided, what was the matter with her. Having learned of Hajar's impending fate, the twin who pretended to be her friend cooked up yet another scheme. On this day, the girl saw that Hajar no longer seemed so drawn and had more energy in her movements, so she made her move. As if to express the sympathies of both her and her sister, she said, "Oh, Hajar, you must not stand meekly by for this. Now is your last chance to find another man and run away with him."

Although Hajar politely declined to accompany her on any more Wednesday-night, closing-time walks, she noted with satisfaction that Hajar was finding more reason to use the stairs rather than the elevator and lingering longer there than she had in the past. It was common knowledge that the staircase presented an opportunity for serendipitously running into someone of the opposite sex. Yet the owners of the mall, it seemed, had not wanted, or merely not bothered, to incur the added expense of building another, separate staircase to completely exclude that possibility.

The twin had been correct in her assumption, for Hajar had resolved to find another man, any man, regardless of the cost. If only to have a fling—to experience pleasure once in her life—before having a blind husband lock her away forever, she was willing to take the risk.

Well aware of the dangers presented by the stairwell, the mall's *mutawwas,* who had argued in vain to have a second staircase built, took it upon themselves to patrol the stairs at regular intervals. They periodically rode the elevator from the first to the fourth floor and then walked back down the steps, often tapping their sticks as they walked. It was not easy to distinguish one completely covered woman from another. Although they saw Hajar on repeated occasions during their stairway patrol, she was perfectly attired from head to foot in black *abaya,* scarf, and veil. They looked past her, for that after all, was the intention of the dress: to render women invisible. One energetic *mutawwa,* however, began keeping track of the shoes worn by those he passed on his descent. Hajar owned only one pair—black with low heels, almost slippers—that made only the faintest sound as she climbed. He apparently realized one day that this was the same person, over and over again. Having no valid reason for confronting her, apart from the repetition, he nevertheless said, "Woman, why do you repeatedly walk these stairs? Are you looking for someone?"

Hajar had a ready reply, for she had expected this might occur. Reasoning that one can only prowl a stairwell for so long before attracting somebody's attention, she made a point of always riding down the elevator and walking back up the stairs—exactly opposite the path of the *mutawwas*. "It is for my exercise. I work all day and have no other opportunity," she said.

"For what reason does a woman need exercise?" the *mutawwa* demanded.

"I am to be married soon and must strengthen my body so that I may bear my husband many sons," she said.

That stumped the *mutawwa*, and he let her go. Thereafter, he seemed to begrudgingly tolerate her regular appearance on his rounds. He would frown when they met, but no longer stared at her shoes.

Despite the small victory and the strengthening of her thigh muscles, Hajar had no luck in attracting the eyes of men walking the stairway for a similar purpose as motivated her. On one occasion, a Western foreigner, coming down the stairwell, looked at her and said "hi" in the friendly way a Texan might greet someone on the ranch. Or maybe he was just trying to practice the one or two words of Arabic that he knew. At any rate, he didn't seem to realize the grave error he had made. If a *mutawwa* had been nearby, she would have been in a lot of trouble. The fool had been ignorant of the complicated mating rules, spawned by the strict segregation of Saudi society. Even so, she might have forgiven the mistake, but by the time she had thought of what to say in return, he had gone.

At another store in the mall, Hajar found a Bedouin veil, which covered the face but exposed the eyes. Allowed in the countryside, it represented a daring fashion statement for the city. Hajar was willing to try it. On several occasions, youngish Saudi or Arab men on the stairs walked by her and stared at her eyes, but they neither smiled nor made any other move in her direction, so she figured they were lost causes as well. After more than a week of these disappointments, she began to lose hope. Her step slowed and feelings of sadness and resignation returned. She believed in fate, but her hopes to tempt fate—to steer it in the right direction, had apparently failed. She stopped climbing the stairs at every opportunity, but did so only once at the middle of each day when she went to the ground-floor supermarket to buy a simple salad for lunch. Clutching her handbag, she no longer spoke to anyone on her break. The role of greeter, of forcing a smile and appearing pleasant, had become such a torture that Izzat relieved her of the duty and let her run the cash register; then as that too involved interacting with customers, she simply had her fold and hang clothes like the twins.

After a long morning of folding dresses, Hajar felt tired and almost decided not to bother with lunch. She went down anyway, and began the slow climb back up. On the second floor of the stairs, she heard someone running up behind her, bounding up the stairs, two at a time. No woman in an *abaya* could move that quickly: it must be a man. The guy in a hurry was on his way to a small computer store on the fourth floor to buy some parts. Hajar moved left to let him pass, but the fellow—forgetting the norms of the place where he was—also moved left and crashed into her. It was John Kaddish.

Hajar stumbled forward onto her hands, her scarf flew off, hair tumbled out, and the Bedouin veil dropped to her neck. The salad container had flown from one hand and her purse from the other, spewing its contents. Aghast at what he had done, John reached for the poor lady to see if she was hurt, and in whispered Arabic asked how she was and whether everything was okay. She nodded. Apologizing profusely, he scrambled to collect her things, all the while muttering in Arabic what a fool he was so that she might understand how badly he felt about colliding into her. Hajar picked up her scarf and was hurriedly arranging her hair while she watched the broad back of this strange man with the funny accent bending to pick up her things. He first handed her the salad, which thankfully had not spilled from the container. Looking full into her face, John flashed a broad smile in admiration. Her eyes locked on his, and for an instant, bright flashes went off, and she almost fainted. It must have been from the fall and quick rise, from the blood rushing from her head, or perhaps she had fallen instantly in love with what was the most beautiful face she had ever seen.

John picked up Hajar's cell phone, which had slipped out of the protective covering of the handkerchief that had softened its fall. He put the phone back into the purse along with the few coins scattered on the steps and handed the bag to Hajar, then noticed he had missed the handkerchief and went to pick it up. Just then, steps and a rhythmic tapping from above sounded on the fourth-floor landing. Steps that Hajar knew. It was a *mutawwa* on his patrol. John gave back the bound handkerchief, still containing its slip of handwritten paper, to Hajar who had by this time returned her veil to its proper place.

She held John's hand in hers and silently pressed the handkerchief and small note to his chest, turned quickly, and fled up the stairs and out onto the women's floor.

Bewildered, John looked at the handkerchief, seemed to recognize the perfume, but shrugged, as it must have been a popular one, and saw the note with Hajar's name and a phone number. He put both into his pocket just as the *mutawwa* reached him and passed by, not saying a word. Still in a hurry, John vaulted up the remaining two flights to buy the computer parts and get back to work. Later in the day, he thought about the chance encounter and pulled out the note to look at it before folding the paper carefully and placing it in his wallet. The handkerchief remained bound by the original string in his back pocket.

The next day on his lunch break, just before the start of the weekend, John dialed Hajar's phone number. He first entered a code to disable caller I.D. in case someone else happened to answer. The phone picked up after one ring with a brief request in Arabic to please leave a message, something John was not foolish enough to do. He hung up and wondered about the lilting woman's voice. It sounded strangely similar to that of Fatima. Thinking no more about it, John decided he might try again after the weekend to see if he could catch this Hajar during her break.

Hajar reached the landing of the clothing store breathless, her heart pounding. She felt hot and was about to tear off her *abaya*, veil, and headscarf, but thought better of it. Perhaps she should wait until she had composed herself.

She didn't want to attract attention from the ever-prying twins who had returned early from their lunch.

Hajar went straight to the ladies' restroom, combed her hair, splashed water on her face, and waited until her racing pulse calmed down. Back at the store, her entire demeanor had changed. The twins kept looking quizzically at her, and eventually she gave in, seeing no reason to hide her excitement. Within minutes the twin was at her side whispering, "What happened?" Hajar told the story as her listener nodded vigorously, exclaimed repeatedly, and clapped her hands in delight "No! . . . He didn't! . . . Really?"

After Hajar had finished, the girl assured her, "He will call. I am certain of it."

None of the three could concentrate for the rest of the day. They hung clothing on the wrong racks, gave customers erroneous information, and generally made a mess of what was normally a smoothly running shop. Izzat, who suspected something from the buzz among them, wondered aloud, almost in despair, "What has become of this staff of mine?" The twins giggled, but they often did that, so the manager decided not to push. At least, for a change, Hajar seemed happy.

The next day, Wednesday, Hajar repeatedly checked her handbag and kept it close to her side, but the phone never made the vibrating sound she had seen with Fatima. She cradled it during much of her four-hour break, cherishing the events of the previous day. Still the phone did not ring. Hajar skipped lunch and did not climb the stairs: she feared she might inadvertently jinx the magical experience from before. By day's end, no one had called, and she began to worry. The twin took some consolation by asking Hajar every thirty minutes, "Any call?" and evoking, at first, an annoyed, and then, an increasingly pained, expression on her face. Hajar was quiet when she went home that evening. Before leaving, the twin said, "You *must* tell us what happens this weekend."

Nothing happened for the two long days at home. On Saturday morning, back at work, Hajar was humming quietly to herself as if to boost her sagging spirits. The twin came up, saw the sadness welling again in Hajar's eyes and reached for her handbag. "Give me that. Let me see your phone."

The girl pulled it out and groaned, "Hajar! Your cell phone is off. Why don't you keep it on?"

"What do you mean, it's off? Won't it ring like that?"

The twin shrieked. Seeing Izzat look at her to see what was the matter, she waited, then hissed and made as if to pull her own hair. "Oh, girl! How naïve are you? Of course, it won't ring. Your handsome savior might have been trying to call you for days and gotten no response.

"Quick, I'll turn it on." The girl did and showed Hajar how to check for voice mail.

"There's a message!" She put the phone next to Hajar's ear and then, on tiptoes, leaned her own head against it to hear as well. Hajar moved away and listened. A message from Fatima the night before said she would be leaving tomorrow for several weeks to see relatives in London and asked if they could get together after she returned at the end of May, or in early June.

"The message is from my girlfriend." Hajar's face dropped, as did that of the twin, who thought for a moment, then said, "Of course! Your dreamy knight would not leave a message if he thought some man in your house might also use the phone. You absolutely must leave that thing on all the time."

The twin looked at the cell phone's screen and saw that the battery indicator had left less than half a charge. "Give me the charger. We need to keep this plugged in."

"Charger?"

"Don't you have a charger?"

"No, I don't think so." Hajar fumbled in her handbag. "I only have this phone."

The twin groaned again from the back of her throat. "Aacchh. So difficult! You must conserve the charge. When is he most likely to call?"

Hajar thought he would probably call during a lunch break, perhaps at the time when they had first collided. The girl and Hajar decided Hajar would turn the phone on each day for one hour before that time and one hour after. Otherwise, he might never reach her.

After a refueling stop at the port of Muscat, Oman, the Chinese naval battle group headed toward the Straits of Hormuz en route to a layover in Dubai. Inside the communications, command, and control center of *Ting Yuan,* the Chinese aircraft carrier, an ensign followed a green blip on a radar screen and beckoned for the captain's attention.

"The Americans are testing us again, sir. One plane is within fifty kilometers."

The captain nodded and spoke into an intercom to a group of pilots who were standing, suited up, near their planes on the flight deck. "Scramble two fighters to keep the American jet farther away. We'll relay its updated coordinates once you're in the air."

Two pilots from the group raced to their planes and climbed into the cockpits. A flight-deck controller flagged them into position for take-off, and within moments they were airborne. The two Chinese J-8F interceptor aircraft climbed in a steep arc toward the position of the American F-15 Eagle, which appeared to be slowly circling the battle group at a constant radius of just under fifty kilometers from the closest ship.

As the fighters approached from behind, the American jet dove and twirled, as if testing whether the less maneuverable Chinese planes could keep up. Within seconds, the F-15 had circled around to the rear of one of the J-8s, which had already separated to get a better sighting of their adversary. For a brief moment, the Chinese pilot, now being tagged, thought the American had locked onto his plane, but to his relief, the U.S. jet quickly spun away and headed toward the other fighter. From below, the pirouetting of the fighter planes must have looked like a mock dogfight. The Chinese pilots, however, were not amused. Less experienced than their battle-trained counterparts in the American air force, and finding themselves in an unfamiliar situation, they were bound to overreact. The second pilot, now ostensibly targeted, sent out a panicked radio message to his comrade.

"He's locked onto me. Help!"

The first Chinese pilot quickly maneuvered into position and fired two air-to-air missiles at the F-15. One missile spun harmlessly into the ocean, but the other held a deadlier aim. Too late, the American fighter tried to avoid the shot by banking sharply upward. The plane exploded in a huge ball of flame and smoke that briefly engulfed the second Chinese fighter, which continued on, unscathed.

Chapter 13

NICK ARRIVED EARLY at the five-star Oasis Tower Hotel and sat in the ground floor lobby to compose his thoughts before meeting Ambassador Gewalt. His mind drifted back to the images on television from 2004 when Saudi commandos had landed by helicopter on the hotel's roof, stormed into the building, and then inexplicably let the hostage-takers escape. The ambassador stayed at the Oasis whenever he came to the tri-city area, as he put it, "to show that terrorists will not intimidate Americans." Looking at the glass-enclosed atrium and the gated residential complex, Nick admitted it was still one of the most luxurious places in al-Khobar.

On the far wall near the elevators, a TV screen displayed the English-language news channel of an international cable network. A "breaking news" alert flashed on the screen, and Nick strained to catch the sound of the broadcaster's voice:

"A spokesman for the U.S. State Department disputes the claims of the Chinese pilots that they fired in self-defense. Search teams of the U.S. navy are now combing the area in the hope that a flight recorder might shed light on what happened."

Nick had heard about the story earlier in the day and tuned out. He went back over what he recalled from Gewalt's words the previous morning and thought of Ma Ling. Instead of a China Oil employee, could she actually be a Chinese agent facilitating the creation of a Saudi nuclear arsenal? It still sounded farfetched to him. He imagined what he might ask her to test that hypothesis. "So you won't talk, eh?" She stood helpless before him as he leaned forward, dressed in his finest Gestapo outfit and holding a tiny feather in his hand to tickle it out of her.

An image intruded on his fantasy. The elevator doors opened and out stepped John Kaddish.

"John! What are you doing here?"

John smiled and sat cattycorner on the leather sofa across from Nick. He ignored the question and looked over at the TV screen. "Our Chinese friends are getting frisky."

"But what brings you to the Oasis?"

John looked back at Nick and winked. "Ask me no questions; I'll tell you no lies."

Nick assumed he was visiting a female friend but wondered why this inveterate athlete smelled of tobacco. Must be from his companion. He did, after all, go for all types. "You're not the kind to kiss and tell."

"Nope, but I've got a good story for you. It involves a woman, but we haven't kissed yet, so my honor does not obligate me to remain silent on the matter." He made a flourish with his hand. Nick leaned forward to listen, and John told him about the collision in the stairwell of the al-Halal shopping mall.

"Some guys have all the luck," Nick said.

"For someone like me, Saudi women represent the final frontier."

"But you told me to stay away from them. Fatima, for instance."

John thought for a moment and did his poor imitation of an American accent. "You don't get your meat where you make your bread, *man.*" Nick looked puzzled, so he added more succinctly, "You don't shit where you eat." Nick still showed no sign of recognition.

"Look, I rely on Saudi Oil for much of my work, and most of that comes to me thanks to Ahmad. Why would I want to stink up that relationship? You think I want to tick Ahmad off by dating his sister? Besides, you're always mooning over her. I'd soon have no friends left."

Nick understood. "But this one, this 'Hajar,' she's anonymous, so it's okay?"

"And a real cutie, in a league with your dream gal."

"When you call, why not ask if Hajar has a friend?"

"You serious?"

"Why not? If you can live the life of adventure, so can others. I don't want to be a Caspar Milquetoast all my life. . . . That reminds me." Nick glanced at his watch. "I have to meet the U.S. ambassador in a few minutes and need some advice."

"Sure, go ahead."

"I can't go into details, but basically, he has asked me for an assessment and has given not-too-subtle hints as to what he wants me to say."

"So where's the problem?"

"It's just that I don't necessarily agree with the view that he's propounding."

"Nicholas. Give the man what he wants. That's the cardinal rule for any consultant—if you want to stay in business. If you disagree, even if you have the soundest arguments and turn out to be right, what good will it do you? You will have annoyed your boss, particularly if you show him up."

Nick didn't look pleased, but nodded, accepting the more worldly man's suggestion. John got up to leave. "I'd better let you think it through, Nick. I'll keep you posted on what happens with Hajar. If she takes my call, I'll ask whether there's the possibility of getting a foursome together."

Nick walked him to the hotel entrance and then paced the floor, thinking. Ma Ling had alluded to China's new assertiveness. Would the Chinese just stand by and meekly accept another U.S. grab for oil, particularly if Chinese died in the process? Nick remembered hearing how the U.S. had timed its bombings of Iraq's anti-aircraft batteries in 2001, before the war, specifically to avoid harming Chinese workers who were laying telephone cables there. Back then, the U.S. had been careful not to antagonize the Chinese, and it was in a much weaker position now. Our forces must have had good intelligence on Iraq—at least on a few targets—something they didn't seem to have in Saudi Arabia. Even the ambassador admitted his embassy's inside knowledge of the country was lousy.

In the elevator, Nick straightened his tie and brushed down unruly hair. He might as well look the part of a professional. On Gewalt's floor, the hallway was empty. Nick rang the bell, and the ambassador's bodyguard let him in, extending a beefy hand to grip his. The two-bedroom suite smelled of smoke, and Gewalt was stubbing out a cigar on an ashtray in the living room. Nick looked around the matching sand-colored décor, a desert motif that complemented the building's tan exterior. He saw that the place was twice as large as his own apartment. The guard must be staying in the extra room, he thought.

"Right on time, Nick. Sorry about the cigar smoke." Gewalt waved it about toward the air-conditioning vents near the ceiling and turned up the fan. "A man's allowed one vice in life: here in Saudi, these are mine, but I try to limit them to one a week. Smoking cigars is a bad habit I picked up working on the Street.

"You don't smoke, do you?"

"No, sir. Never even tried." Nick thought of the older smokers he had known, the ones with sunken, hollow cheeks and hacking coughs. He hoped Gewalt wouldn't end up like that.

"How about a drink?" Gewalt opened the mini-bar full of bottled juices, sodas, and tonic water. "Not much to choose from."

Nick didn't like to waste money, his own or that of others, or even of his employer, the U.S. government. If it had been John asking, he would have simply gone to the kitchenette and poured himself some filtered tap water but instead said, "A tonic water would be fine."

"Let's stand by the windows for a minute while the air clears." Gewalt looked back at the guard who went into his own bedroom, shut the door, and turned on the television. The sun had set and the city lights of Khobar and Dammam were twinkling on. In the distance, long boats were plying the waters to and from the King Abdul Aziz Port.

They admired the panorama. "Quite a view," Gewalt said. Through the glass, what sounded like a foghorn bellowed a distant acknowledgement. That's funny, Nick thought, this place doesn't have fog. Must be two ships passing in the night and signaling one another to avoid a mishap.

Nick took John's advice and told Gewalt what he wanted to hear. If no Chinese were injured, there would be little to worry about militarily in the near term. The Chinese might step up their feints toward Taiwan to mollify internal opinion. However, despite recent improvements, their navy was still no match for that of the U.S.

If the U.S. inadvertently killed Chinese workers in Saudi Arabia, their government would demand reparations and make noises of protest, probably more severe than what occurred after the Belgrade bombings, but would not confront the U.S. militarily. However, they might still use proxies and incite the North Koreans or others to misbehave. They would not take overt military action, Nick said. Since the late 1990s, the Chinese dictators had been stoking a sense of patriotic nationalism to deflect internal discontent, much like what occurred in the U.S. in the years after 9-11. The Chinese rulers might even secretly welcome yet another opportunity to orchestrate popular feeling against the U.S. Nevertheless, well before the Beijing Olympics in 2008, the government would have forgiven America. They wanted us there, to compete at the event, if only to knock out our stuffing on the playing field, something they couldn't do—for now—on the battleground.

Gewalt nodded, but seemed unconvinced. "And what about this recent fighter being shot down?"

"Reminds me of that incident over China in 2001. One of their fanatics brought down our spy plane over southern China, but we soon patched things up."

"Still, that kind of brazen attack bothers me." Gewalt thought for a moment. "Stay clear of your Chinese contact—that woman—until we determine what happened and settle the matter."

He continued to probe Nick. "What about the chokepoints?"

"I don't believe the Chinese would disrupt the global shipping lanes to get back at us because such a move would affect other countries, not just the U.S. Having said that, I think the Panama Canal represents the greatest risk—not for oil shipments, which are relatively minor, but because, of the five locations you pointed out, it has the highest share of U.S. shipping, which relies on that passage to move goods from the west to east coast and back again. Not much oil seems to move through there because it's too narrow for the largest tankers.

"At most, the Chinese might institute an economic boycott but would not undertake an outright blockade of U.S. ships like the one we used during the Cuban missile crisis. Even if the boycott were across the board, on all goods and services, by the time it began to pinch, we would presumably have won over world opinion to the necessity of America's use of force.

"In the final analysis, for the Chinese to conduct a sustained boycott or garner worldwide support for others to join against us would be a long shot. After all, the Chinese need our trade and investment as much as we need them."

"Well said, Nick. I like scenarios that keep our hands free. Just leave out the part about U.S. nationalism after 9-11. Otherwise, I agree. As for China, we probably still have just a paper tiger over there.

"Get a draft to me by Monday, and we'll have it out to Washington by Wednesday night. I'll see you on the plane back to Riyadh tomorrow morning."

Chapter 14

THE NEXT DAY JOHN CALLED Hajar's number. This time she answered before the first ring had finished. He started speaking in Arabic, and she answered him in faltering English, asking his name and thanking him for calling. She was not going to play hard to get.

Hajar explained that the only time she had free was during the midday break. John had expected as much.

"Would you like to go on a daytime date? How about a picnic at the beach tomorrow afternoon? I know a secluded area where no one will see us," John said.

Hajar would have agreed to go anywhere with him. She asked about his apartment, but he said that wasn't safe.

"By the way, I have a good pal from America who would like to meet a nice Saudi girl like you. He speaks no Arabic. Do you have a girlfriend who might be interested and could converse with him?"

Hajar thought for a moment, instantly ruling out the twin, even if her English were fluent rather than consisting largely of "thank you" and "hello." She thought of Fatima. "I do have a friend who speaks English much better than me, and she is much more beautiful. However, I do not think she would be interested in such a risky date. She has many opportunities to meet nice Western men when she goes overseas to school."

John accepted that. "It'll just be you and me then."

He said he would come by the mall and leave his vehicle in the garage's middle level at the northeast corner, out of sight of the lot's main pedestrian traffic going to and from the elevators. John described his SUV, gave her the license number, and told her he would put two large, green decals of the Saudi flag on both backseat windows. The Saudis did not allow black glass on any cars, even of diplomatic personnel, but only permitted light tinting, so that their *mutawwas* could look inside to see what might be going on. The decals would partially obscure the view. As soon as her break started at 1 p.m., Hajar was to climb into the backseat of the unlocked car as if waiting for the driver to take her home. John would wear his Pakistani outfit and would walk separately to the vehicle before getting into the driver's seat shortly after her. Once they cleared the automatic garage toll area, he would tell Hajar what to do.

"But you must bring me back to the mall by 5 p.m."

For the rest of the day and the following morning, Hajar concealed her excitement from the twins. She even managed to lie when asked if her beau had called. By 11 a.m. she was surreptitiously checking the clock every five minutes. She hoped the other girls would leave promptly for lunch since they never stayed at work a moment longer than necessary. At 1 p.m. the twins left, and two minutes later, not wanting to wait for the elevator, she rushed down the stairs, nearly tripping on the hem of her *abaya*. As usual at this time, the lot was busy, with drivers coming to take employees home for the break. Hajar merged with the stream of people walking to their cars, found the SUV exactly where John had said he would leave it, and got in. A minute later, John appeared, and glancing at her in the rearview mirror, said in Arabic, "Good afternoon, madam." Hajar noticed that a light blanket lay on the car floor and a similar one was folded beside her. John turned the air conditioning to high.

As soon as he had tossed the required change into the garage's tollgate, John said slowly in English so that she would understand, "Now pretend you are bending to pick something up, then lie down on the seat and cover yourself with the folded blanket." The SUV rode higher than most cars, so passing motorists could usually not see in. For those vans or trucks carrying *mutawwas,* if they looked into John's vehicle, they would not see the familiar black form of Hajar's *abaya,* but just an object under a light cover. If they examined closely and demanded he stop, John would claim his passenger was ill, and he was taking her to the hospital.

No one bothered to look in or challenge them. Like most others, the *mutawwas* took their breaks at midday and slackened in their vigilance during the peak of the heat. They were most active toward evening when they assumed the worst sins would occur.

Getting past the checkpoint outside town would be trickier, but John was a familiar sight to the roadside guards, as was his vehicle, which he typically crammed full of equipment on his trips to the field. Before they approached the checkpoint, John asked Hajar to lie on the car floor's blanket, to wrap herself completely with the other cover, and before doing so, to take some of the items piled high in the far back of the car and put them on the seat.

The precautions proved unnecessary. At the checkpoint, the guard stopped John, asked where he was going, when he'd be back, and made some light banter in Arabic before waving him through.

John headed south, past the Bahrain causeway, toward the western shore of the southern tip of the peninsula that extends past the town of al-Aziziyah. He went off the road and shifted the car into four-wheel drive, winding his way into the desert around the small hills that the area's few inhabitants called *jebels*. He parked beneath one of them, on a narrow strip of land surrounded on three sides by twenty-foot escarpments. Unless someone happened to look straight down from the cliffs above, only the western side of this land was visible—the side facing directly onto a sheltered bay and inlet off the Arabian Gulf. The regular patrols of the Saudi coast guard rarely went into the bay's shallow waters and only occasionally paused in front of its outlet to the Gulf. They had more strategic and more populated areas to watch. A few bathers sometimes came to swim in the warm, gentle waters, but generally only on weekends.

Hajar marveled at the view. She had never seen a beach up close. The afternoon sunlight was playing upon the water, shooting off fiery light from its undulating surface.

"Here at last. Wait in the vehicle for a minute. I'll keep the air conditioning on for you and get things ready outside." John removed his pants, shirt, socks, and shoes, leaving on just a pair of Speedo trunks for swimming. Hajar took off her black outer clothes and shoes but kept her dress on.

John pulled out two retractable poles from the back of the vehicle and, with the side of the car, made a kind of lean-to above one of the blankets that he laid on the sand. He took out a large icebox filled with fruits and two plastic gallon jugs of water. Pointing to the water, he said, "One of these is for drinking, and the other is for washing off the salt water.

"You can wear your dress if you like, but in this heat, I'm just going to wear my briefs. Besides we're going swimming first, so you'll either have to swim naked or use your underwear as your bathing suit."

Hajar didn't understand. She shook her head and said, "I'll watch. You swim. Then we can eat."

"No, no, young lady. I'm here to teach you. Your wet underclothes will dry by the time we leave. Come on." John put his arms around her and undid the back of the dress.

Hajar let him undress her. *If I am caught alone with this man, I am a dead woman, so what matter if they find me naked or clothed?*

John admired her body. "Don't be modest. You're gorgeous."

But not so beautiful as you, she thought. Hajar meekly stepped out of the clothing, and John led her by the hand to the water until they had waded up to her thighs. She nervously looked around as he dove in. Realizing she was more visible above water, she walked back a bit, then sat on the sandy bottom, exposed only from the neck up. John splashed around, demonstrating the various swimming strokes to her, then came and said, "Your turn."

"But I can't swim."

"Here. Lie back on my hands, and we'll practice floating." John lifted Hajar completely out of the water in his arms. She squealed and held his neck as he slowly walked in deeper and brought her body gently down to the water's level. "Now relax. Breathe normally. I've got you. . . . Yes, that's it. Put your head back." John's right hand cupped Hajar's bottom; his left supported her back. "Kick your legs up and down. Good."

Hajar laughed. "Is this swimming?"

"Almost. We'll turn you over now. Don't worry. I'm holding you. Remember the breaststroke I showed you? Try that. Bend your head up, and move your arms." Hajar's pelvis and stomach now rested on John's hands. She felt the side of his hand against her bra as he said, "Kick with your legs now. Spread and close."

Hajar tried hard to follow his instructions. "Don't drop me, please."

"Now I'm going to remove my hands."

"No. Let me hold something. I need to hold you. Otherwise, I'm afraid I'll sink like a rock." She stood, reached around to grip the back of his waist with her hands in a loose hug, and tried to float, kicking her feet. "That's not good, either. You carry me." She climbed on his back and ordered him to swim.

John tried to comply, doing the breaststroke back toward the shallow water, until he could rest his hands on the sandy bottom and hand-walk his way to the water's edge. He collapsed in mock exhaustion, turned over beneath her, and pulled her close. Their faces met. Apart from her father's hand, and his cheeks when she was a small child, Hajar had never kissed a man. Her lips were closed and eyes open as John kissed her, but soon she was copying his movements. She lay on top of his body as the water flowed up and back over them with the soft current of the incoming tide. Hajar forgot that anyone else could possibly come upon them until he said, "Let's go up to the blanket. It's more private."

They rushed back to the car. John unscrewed one of the gallon jugs, held it above Hajar, and slowly poured the water over her to wash off the salt. He caressed her body in the make-do shower, running his hands slowly over her curves, before lifting the jug above his own head.

They stripped off their wet clothes and hung them on a pole to dry. By this time, John was fully aroused, and Hajar looked at him, amazed. At the mall, she had heard married women trying to impress one another with talk of their husbands' organs, but she had never heard of one described like this. It was so big. No wonder her mother Layla had said that some women found intercourse painful. Hajar remembered the few times in the Riyadh apartment that she had listened to the noise of Suheir's bed creaking at night, the rhythmic noise mixed with the sound of stifled cries of pain. The following mornings Suheir would hobble about her side of the apartment with a dour expression on her face.

Before lying down with John, Hajar said, "I will do everything you want, but you must not penetrate me." She looked into John's eyes to see if he understood. "I am to be married against my will to a man, an old man I do not love, or even like. My family would have me killed if they found out my . . ." She didn't know what to call it, but pointed toward her feet, ". . . shield was broken."

"I know the rules, dear." They lay down together, and John began kissing Hajar about the face and neck, his hand massaging her breasts. He moved his lips down her body, as if sucking off from her skin any salt that remained. His fingers slowly rubbed her down below and his mouth then followed. Hajar didn't know what to do. She held his head in her hands. Embarrassed, she tried to pull him up, saying, "Please. Don't. You must stop." But he persisted, his expert tongue on her sensitive flesh, his hands on the insides of her thighs. Hajar had never felt this before. Words became moans and meaningless. Her repetitions, if he lifted his head, soon became, "Please, don't stop."

The skin on Hajar's chest and pelvis flushed as she moved her hips up and down, their insides moist. Gripping the back of John's head, she felt a wave of pleasure come over her, a wave so intense she nearly blacked out, crying aloud her love in Arabic, "*Habibee, Uhibak.*" Her arched back sank into the blanket, and she felt exhausted, a pure pleasure radiating through her limbs. She would do anything for this man.

John raised his head, bringing his mouth again to her lips, which she greeted hungrily. Then, reversing their positions, he explained to her what to do while he repeated his earlier caresses. Hajar climbed onto him, becoming still more excited and felt a second wave approaching. As her body swooned on top of his in a second orgasm, John ejaculated and her throat filled with his semen. "That's good," he cooed. She swallowed and coughed, exhausted but happy that she had given him pleasure in return. Their bodies, covered in sweat, stuck together. Climbing back into his arms, she rested her head on his chest, and stroked his hairs, drifting in and out of sleep, completely relaxed.

Half an hour passed. John got up, slid his arm carefully from under Hajar's neck, and prepared some watermelon, grapes, and dry dates. He was hungry. She woke and smiled, as if from a pleasant dream. Both sat up, eating the fruit he had brought.

"I'm afraid it's time to go." John helped Hajar dress. She clung to him, not wanting to leave. By 4 p.m. they were on the road again heading back to town. This time Hajar knew what to do. She asked John about his life and he of hers. Would he take her away with him? He'd have to think about that. She would love to be with him anywhere, anywhere but here. He spoke of New Zealand, of his parents raising sheep. Would you like to be a shepherd's wife? Anything, my love. They made it safely back to the mall, only a few minutes late. Hajar hated leaving him without a touch or a caress. John said he would call her but had to go away for a while on an assignment. Even if he never came back to her, Hajar knew she would cherish the brief hours she had had with him.

The days passed, and the memory of the beach faded. John left word for Nick that he would be out of the country for several weeks. Meanwhile, Tariq informed Hajar that Sheikh Muamar had had an accident and broken his leg, a mishap that would delay his arrival in Khobar by at least a month. Hajar tried to conceal her glee. The temporary respite raised her hopes about John, but when she heard no word from him, the disappointment became all the harder to bear. She began to wonder whether she had done the right thing. As her mood sank, remorse set in. Unlike in the past, when her appetite fell with her spirits, now she tried to comfort herself by eating and began gaining weight.

No one had ever taught Hajar about pregnancy and how exactly it happened. She wondered whether her swallowing that day might have somehow brought John's seed into her. Could she get pregnant? Was she already? How would she know? All she had as guidance were memories of the symptoms her mother had experienced when pregnant with her baby sister. Mother felt ill and sometimes got sick in the morning, her legs and back ached, she was always hungry, and her period stopped. Hajar began to imagine that she, too, was having these symptoms. Wasn't her period late? Wasn't she gaining weight, listless, and often feeling nauseous soon after waking? She couldn't confide in Suheir nor Aisha or Munira. If the family even suspected she might have been with a man, the taint on their names meant she would have to die. Honor killings of women by their brothers, fathers, or other relatives were common for much less than fornication. What to do? Fatima was back from her trip abroad. She must talk to her.

When alone during her break, Hajar dialed Fatima's home number, but she was at work. She re-dialed, and a nurse paged her friend, who came breathless to the phone. "Hajar! I should have called you, but you know how it is at work when you go on vacation. There's always so much to do when you return." Hajar didn't know and remained silent.

"Is anything wrong? What's the matter, dear?"

"Fatima, I am so sorry to bother you with my troubles, but I prefer to speak in person. Could we meet soon?"

"Of course. I will have Ahmad drive me there tomorrow and meet you in the mall for lunch. Or should I come today?" Hajar said tomorrow would be fine. Since Saudi Arabia had separate restaurants either for families or for men alone, Ahmad's joining them was not a possibility. He would have to eat on his own, while the food court of the women's mall was their only option.

The next day, Fatima arrived early and bought Hajar lunch. They took their trays to a spot in the far corner of the hall. Until the main crowd came, the table would afford a modicum of privacy. "I wish this were America and I could treat you to a nice restaurant—just two girlfriends out on the town together."

Hajar smiled, but looked sad, on the point of tears. Fatima put her hand on top of Hajar's. "Tell me now."

Hajar began speaking rapidly. "To get a good dowry, my father and Tariq have arranged for my marriage to Sheikh Muamar, and...."

"Who?"

"The one who taught us mathematics in grade school."

Fatima's eyes widened and she clapped her hand to her mouth. "No! We must stop that. Let me think."

"The marriage is to occur soon, probably this month, but...."

"I know! Here's what we do." She spoke as the thoughts came to her. "My family can pay the dowry for you ... on condition that you can then marry whom you want. We will buy your freedom. Then you can marry even a poor man, so long as you love him. How much do you need?"

"Oh, Fatima. You are so good. But it's not just that. I was foolish ... bad ... I...." Hajar stopped, unable to continue and looked down in her lap.

"Please go on, dear."

Hajar spoke rapidly again to get the horrid words out all at once. "I was desperate to be free, if only for a brief time. I went with a man. I ... I think I'm pregnant." She glanced quickly at Fatima, then looked down.

Fatima didn't, or couldn't, speak. She covered her face with her hands. "Oh, dear...." They both knew what this could mean. "Who is he? Does he know?"

"He doesn't know. I have not heard from him since and do not have a way to contact him."

Fatima turned pale, and Hajar continued. "He is a Westerner."

Fatima sat still, pressing her hand to her forehead as if to squeeze out some ideas. "Maybe we can find him. But still, as a non-Muslim, marriage is forbidden. He must convert! Tell me more."

"He's a very handsome man, talkative, and funny. I only know his first name, John."

"But that is too common."

"He's from New Zealand."

Fatima gasped and the blood drained completely from her face. "I know him."

Fatima told Hajar she would have her brother deal with Kaddish. They worked together. Ahmad and Fatima would demand that he convert and help take Hajar away—somehow—from the country, as soon as possible. If she was pregnant, there was no time. Her symptoms would soon become obvious. She hugged Hajar and told her it would be all right. She would talk to her brother immediately.

In the car, Ahmad could hardly believe what his sister was telling him, but he was less shocked than she. He knew how men were. "John should be back by now. He went away for a while. I won't confront him at work, but will invite him to the club, tonight if possible, and you shall come too."

Ahmad concealed his anger well, and John agreed to meet him at the club for drinks after work. "Sure, mate. But what's the rush?" Ahmad made up an excuse. When John arrived, Ahmad and Fatima were sitting at the table with drinks in front of them.

"This is a pleasant surprise. Always nice to see the lovely kid sister." John grinned, but neither smiled in return. Ahmad signaled the waiter over.

"John, what do you want?"

"Just a carcaday, mate." The waiter left. "Now tell me what's the matter."

Fatima spoke. "Do you remember Hajar in al-Khobar?"

"A shapely girl, about your age?" Fatima grimaced at John's characterization, but nodded. "Yes. Who wouldn't? She's your friend? What a coincidence. Like sticks with like," John said.

Fatima was angry now, apparently on the verge of slapping him. Ahmad seemed to sense an explosion, and placed his hand on her arm.

"What did you do to her?" Fatima's eyes glistened.

John spoke in an even tone. His smile gone, he watched them both. "Nothing. We just had some fun."

This time, Ahmad rose to his feet. "Why you. . . ." His sister stood and held onto him, fearing he would get the worst of any fight. She wanted to shame John into acting properly.

John remained seated. "So she's a kiss and tell. What a foolish girl."

"She's pregnant, John." Fatima hissed under her breath. She said this close to his ear and was standing behind him. John swiveled his neck, now clearly uncomfortable.

"What? That's impossible."

"She doesn't think so," said Fatima. She had moved in front of him again to see his reactions.

"Well, she's either mistaken, or it's some other guy."

"You bastard. How dare you!" Ahmad grabbed John by the collar and jerked the bigger man up out of his seat.

"Look, you're my friend. At least you were. Let's try and leave it that way." John pulled Ahmad's hands off and with a firm grip, held them down. People at the other tables were watching. The waiters began to approach.

"I'd better be going, as I see I'm no longer welcome." John turned and strode away. He got in his car, slammed the door, and drove off.

Fatima turned to Ahmad. "That didn't go well. Now what?"

Chapter 15

NICK WAS EXHAUSTED. He had worked nearly around the clock since arriving in Riyadh. Nick not only had full days of visa applicants to interview and assess, with written comments sent to his counterparts at Homeland Security in Washington, but also had to draft his share of the scenarios cable for the ambassador. His writing deteriorated when he got tired, and for this assignment, which he viewed as his most important yet, he needed to be in top form. On Sunday night, for the first time since freshman year of college, Nick pulled an all-nighter, stoking his brain with cup after cup of coffee to make the draft coherent. He typed entirely in capital letters, using the cabling convention, an anachronism that Nick found absurd in this age of e-mail. Imagine reading just that, all day long, with no relief provided by upper and lower case. Nick rubbed his eyes. He'd soon be as blind as Ahmad if he did nothing but read and write cables for his career. Nick had to finish this one by morning: he would have no time during the day to polish it before passing the text to Gewalt.

Late Monday, with a sigh of relief, he handed the cable draft to Martha Fischbein to give to the ambassador. She thanked him and brought it right to Gewalt's office. By week's end, Nick had caught up on his sleep and no longer felt the fatigue that his mind associated with jetlag even though he had crossed no time zones. Nick was looking forward to the weekend and a return to Dhahran. On

Wednesday afternoon, as most of the staff were leaving, Martha stopped by Nick's office—the one that was little better than a windowless cubicle—and gave him a curious look. Nick was surprised to see her distributing the packet of cables. Usually, a local Saudi staffer handled that, passing around the reading marked "classified," a copy to each division, for circulation before return and shredding. Must be something secret in this batch, Nick thought. But why would she be coming so late? He had a flight to catch and couldn't take the reading material with him. As a reminder, the folder was marked NICHOLAS HANSEN — NOT TO LEAVE EMBASSY. SHRED AFTER REVIEW. Then he remembered Gewalt had said he would send off the joint cable before the weekend. Sure enough, their cable, and nothing else, was in the manila folder that Martha left on top of his inbox. It was thicker than Nick had expected. Gewalt must have had a lot to say. The cover sheet was red and white, marked TOP SECRET—not the usual blue and white CONFIDENTIAL or even the green and white SECRET that Nick had once felt thrilled to get.

Like all foreign-service officers, he had a top-secret clearance, but he knew there must be many security grades above his. For most, the classification reflected the inflation that occurred whenever people tried to put one person above another. The arbitrary distinctions assuaged egos. At large multinational banks, weren't some of his school friends already vice presidents? Yes, it seemed an impressive title on a business card, but actually conveyed no more privilege than that due someone who had worked for five years in the same place. Such organizations had thousands of VPs, many of whom, he bet, had never met the corporate president.

Here he was, Nick marveled, not just reading something marked "Top Secret" but actually a partial author of it. He must have reached the inner circle of international affairs—a veritable "Agent 008" since the previous number already belonged to a certain member of the British secret service. Hadn't Gewalt said they had recently boosted his clearance? So this is what he meant: the privilege of reading—and writing!—material that the government allowed relatively few to see. But was missing his flight worth the distinction? He phoned the airline before their offices closed and asked for a seat on the last plane to Dhahran.

Nick always carefully read and re-read his draft cables, and then again checked the wording and punctuation once the copy of the actual transmission came back. He wrote well and was proud of his work. These lines were the physical manifestations of his efforts—what his remote colleagues in Washington, and often in other countries as well, would rely on to judge his ability.

Nick tried to write as succinctly as possible although he doubted the government had to pay by the word for its cable transmissions. Nick fancied himself old-fashioned, more suited to the 1950s than the world today. He would have fit in smoothly as the leading man in a Peter Lorre movie, sending off a telex, cutting out from the message all but the absolutely essential and discarding adjectives, adverbs, particles, nouns. Charged by the word, or most likely, by the keystroke, his urgent line might consist solely of AM ILL STOP SEND CASH STOP, or in his case, he hoped it might be: IN LOVE STOP TO WED STOP.

None of the others at the embassy seemed to care about the prolixity of their cables. Occasionally he spotted a kindred spirit writing succinctly from another mission somewhere in the world—probably someone naïve and misguided like him about how things really worked and what the bosses valued. Still, he reasoned, time had a value, and if he could save the readers' time, surely they would appreciate it. Multiply that by the dozens, or he hoped hundreds, who might read his cables, and one started having real savings.

Nick checked each cable transmission that came from his draft—not just the direct recipients, but those carbon copied as well—to see who was in the audience, like an actor peeking out from behind a theater's curtain before emerging for his command performance. If he didn't recognize an office acronym, he asked a colleague or looked it up and soon knew most of them. These three letters before the backslash meant this department, the following three signified that division, and so on.

Nick removed the paper clip that held in place the TOP SECRET coversheet over the cable, but as he did, a second coversheet, this one in black and white, marked ULTRA TOP SECRET — PRINCIPALS ONLY, slid out from behind the pages. That's strange, he thought. I didn't even know such a classification existed. Someone must have slipped it in by mistake. He put the two covers carefully aside and began reading the ambassador's text before moving on to check his own. In turning the first page, which largely consisted of the office acronyms of those sending and receiving the cable, he also noticed that Martha had badly stapled the sheets of paper together. Instead of the usual neat clip at the far top left corner, this one had three staples, two of which were bent and did not properly catch the papers at the back. Sloppy, but probably not entirely her fault. The embassy should replace some of the aging office supplies that management expected staff to use.

Nick started reading Gewalt's assessment. He certainly could use a good editor, Nick thought—for the umpteenth time—but Nick at least had the common sense not to dream of suggesting it. For that kind of insolence, he didn't doubt Gewalt would retaliate, perhaps assigning him to full-time proofreading of the mind-numbing text in standard embassy cable traffic.

Gewalt had let Nick touch on some of the economic implications of a U.S. intervention in Saudi Arabia, so the ambassador focused on what he knew best: the risk to financial markets. In Gewalt's worst-case scenario, the Saudis and Chinese, angered by the intervention—whether to destroy a nuclear arsenal or seize oil fields—would coordinate a combined selling of U.S. treasuries and dump their huge holdings, estimated to be over half of the world's foreign-held dollar reserves, onto the open financial markets to buy euros and yen. Other Arab countries would follow suit, almost overnight, ending the concept of petrodollars, whereby OPEC has stored its oil money in U.S. currency instruments. If unchecked by countervailing actions of the Federal Reserve and other central banks, the value of the dollar would tumble into a tailspin, causing financial markets—already spooked by the military intervention—to collapse, and interest rates to soar as the U.S. government desperately tried to prevent a flight from its currency. Hyperinflation—a phenomenon the U.S. had never experienced—would ensue. Prices could rise by orders of magnitude, at least by the degree seen in Latin American countries during the worst of the 1980s, possibly to the extent that occurred in Weimar Germany in the 1920s, when a populace, impoverished by the destruction of its savings, paid off small debts by carting around in wheelbarrows worthless deutschmarks. The U.S. economy would ultimately take on the characteristics of a large banana republic. A deep recession, likely spreading to the rest of the world, would follow, most probably culminating in a depression on the scale of that in the 1930s, when the nationwide unemployment rate had stood at 25 percent.

Needless to say, the American people would be upset. Demagogues would arise and call for drastic change in the political leadership, if not in the entire manner of government. Demands for peaceful change through democratic processes might slip into demands for a violent overthrow of an elected government, with those currently or subsequently in power removing civil liberties to maintain or restore order. America would in effect take on the very characteristics of its enemies. That was the worst-case scenario and assumed a paralyzed and hopelessly incompetent response by the U.S. government to the retaliatory acts resorted to by China and Saudi Arabia.

If, however, the Federal Reserve and the largest economies among U.S. allies—principally the G7 European countries and Japan—acted quickly to restore confidence in markets by buying up dollars, the concerted actions could slow, if not halt the slide in the dollar. At the same time, the president would have to issue an executive order to freeze Chinese and Saudi assets held in the United States, temporarily preventing their sale or withdrawal. Gewalt put the likelihood of a joint Chinese and Saudi action at less than 20 percent. The mere takeover of Saudi oil fields itself would, in all probability, cause the Saudi regime to fall, so their finance minister would have more pressing matters to worry about than meddling in world currency markets—like finding a country of exile to flee to.

Gewalt then delved into, and briefly explained, the details of measures that the U.S. Federal Reserve might take with regard to its regular auctions of treasury bills, notes, and bonds of varying maturities. He discussed discount and coupon securities, highest stop yields, sharp increases in the tails of spreads in bids' yields, over-the-counter secondary markets, the when-issued market of securities traded before issue, current-coupon issues, off-the-run issues, the bank-discount basis, and system or customer repurchase agreements with domestic and foreign individual, institutional, and government holders of securities.

Nick's eyes glazed over at the unfamiliar and arcane terms. He skimmed through quickly and reviewed his own section of writing, which now seemed almost childish in its lack of technical jargon. No matter, he thought, it's still better written. Then he turned what should have been the final page of the joint cable and, in shock, read what followed.

Labeled "Ultra Top Secret — For Principals Only" were four pages that someone had mistakenly tacked onto the rest of the cable. By convention, all official embassy communications from Saudi Arabia went out under Gewalt's name, with the actual author listed shortly thereafter. This one repeated Gewalt's name as the sole author and used the smallest, most select distribution list of recipients Nick had ever seen. Some of the acronyms at the bottom he didn't recognize. At the top were POTUS, the President of the United States, followed by SECSTATE and SECDEF, the Secretaries of State and Defense, respectively, and several persons Nick assumed were field commanders for the various branches of the military.

The text appeared to respond to several earlier cables and began, MISSION CONFIRMS MARCH SIGINT OF PLANNED HOSTAGE TAKING AND ATTEMPT TO SABOTAGE OIL FIELDS. Apparently, the U.S. embassy had evidence to support electronic intercepts picked up by the National Security Agency in March that pointed to a major attack planned by al-Qaeda. The headline paragraph continued, WE HAVE NOT REPEAT NOT SHARED INTEL WITH SAUDI GOVT AND ARE READY TO SUPPORT U.S. RESPONSE.

Nick read on. TIME AND PLACE OF INITIAL ATTACK UNCHANGED. BOARD MEETING, SAUDI OIL HQ, DHAHRAN 0900 2 JULY.

Saudi Oil, Saudi Oil . . . Ma Ling, Ahmad . . . Fatima . . . John, thought Nick, trying to compose his thoughts and grasp the meaning of what he was reading. Board meeting? But wasn't Fatima's father joining the board? He put his palms to his temples and bent close to the text. MISSION CONCURS. EVENT WILL BE IDEAL OPPORTUNITY. CHINA OIL CHAIRMAN TO BE PRESENT. HOSTAGE TAKING BUT NOT SABOTAGE REPEAT NOT SABOTAGE LIKELY TO SUCCEED. OIL FACILITIES WELL GUARDED.

Nick picked out the key sentences in the rest of the cable. USE PRETEXT TO URGE AMERICAN BOARD MEMBERS NOT REPEAT NOT TO ATTEND. IF NECESSARY, INTERCEPT THEIR TRIPS TO ARABIA.

PRE-POSITION U.S. SPECIAL UNITS NEAR OIL FACILITIES, MOVE LARGER FORCES FROM IRAQ OFFSHORE AND OVER LAND FROM NORTH TO SECURE FIELDS AFTER HPM DETONATED AND RESISTANCE DISABLED. What was HPM? Nick turned his computer back on and logged into the Internet rather than the secure network for State Department employees. Googling "HPM" and "detonate," he found the answer: high-power microwave, a form of electromagnetic pulse that could fry the inside of digital electronic systems, and thereby disable enemy military equipment. MISSION EXPECTS 12 TO 48 HOURS FOR COMPLETE CONTROL OF GOODS.

Nick knew that the Saudi national-guard base in Khobar and military airfield northeast of Dammam didn't stand a chance. Even if the HPM failed, U.S. forces had been training Saudi defense personnel for years and knew their capabilities inside and out. Moreover, the U.S. government had kept some advisors in the country, despite having quietly transferred the main contingent of its troops from Saudi Arabia to Qatar in 2002. Apart from a few pilots flying American planes, the Saudi forces had performed badly in the first Gulf War. Even if they fought bravely this time, their equipment was at least five years less advanced than what the U.S. provided to its own troops. Casualties, Nick thought. Why had the Ambassador been so concerned with that? Now he understood the rationale for an HPM. His Google search had said the U.S. had never deployed the weapon on a battlefield, although Nick suspected that the initial "Shock and Awe" campaign of the second war on Iraq might have used something similar.

Nick was now beginning to think of his own government as "they" rather than "we." They must want to minimize casualties, and not give the Chinese a reason to intervene. A successful HPM explosion would not kill soldiers or destroy the valuable oil infrastructure. However, when their communication systems failed, the defending troops would see the futility of resistance.

AMBASSADOR WILL STATE THAT U.S. EXPECTED SAUDI FORCES TO BUNGLE RESCUE—NO LONGER CONFIDENT IN ABILITIES TO PROTECT KEY RESOURCES.

This was no game after all. How could he have been so stupid! My God, the ambassador had lied to me, used me, he thought. Nick looked at his watch. He had better catch that flight. Carefully re-reading the part of the cable he was not supposed to have seen, he removed the staples in preparation for the shredding. Nick was tempted to take notes, but knew that doing so and trying to leave the compound with them would constitute espionage. The embassy guards usually just took a casual glance in the briefcases of departing employees, but Nick was in no mood to take chances. Instead he noted in Chinese the time and date of the meeting. That was harmless enough, he thought. Then he quickly crossed and re-crossed it out, nearly wearing a hole in the notepaper. Idiot, he thought. This isn't China. Writing even just a few characters in Chinese in a notebook would attract attention. Besides, the details weren't *that* hard to remember. The problem lay in what to do with the information.

On board the fifty-minute flight to Dhahran, Nick stared out the window at the dark sky. He hardly noticed who sat next to him and forgot to acknowledge the stewardess offering him a drink. "No, I said, 'No.'" He shook his head, and she moved on.

Nick was no fan of the Saudi regime, which he considered corrupt and abhorrent in its treatment of women. He had no opinion as to whether they secretly financed terrorism. However, he felt that the government's tolerance, if not outright advocacy, of hatred for non-Wahhabis, a hatred that its approved educators taught to school children, was at least partially to blame for the world's problems with Islamic fundamentalists.

At first, en route to the Riyadh airport, Nick had thought he'd just keep his head down and let events play out. He told himself he did not fear for his own safety—a bit of self deception, he admitted, as he ran a mental tally of whether he had accrued enough vacation time to spend a few weeks abroad at the end of June. Then, as he thought about the Wahhabis, about what they might do, and whether the Shi'ites in the province would welcome American troops as liberators, he realized with a shock that he did have a personal stake in the outcome.

Fatima's family were Shi'ites. Her father would attend the Saudi Oil board meeting. In previous hostage takings in Saudi Arabia and elsewhere, al-Qaeda had executed individuals considered apostates or infidels. No wonder the ambassador's cable warned against allowing the American board member from attending. But hadn't Ahmad said that the Wahhabis viewed Shi'ites little better than Westerners? If so, that would leave just Fatima's father—and presumably the China Oil chairman—directly in their line of fire, as the first to die. Even if the Saudi government did not purposefully or unintentionally bungle negotiations and a rescue, Sami al-Sayyid's chances of surviving were slim. Who knew al-Qaeda's motives for choosing this particular event to stage an attack? Maybe having a Shi'ite assume such an important position was motivating them. Nick could not simply wait to find out. How could he ever face the al-Sayyids—Fatima—having known that his own inaction had directly led to her father's death? The sweet girl had just lost her mother, now she would have no parents left. Yet, if Nick told anyone of what he knew, he would betray state secrets. He couldn't just blurt out to Fatima, to Ahmad, or even to Dr. al-Sayyid that he was in danger.

It was late when the taxi dropped Nick at his apartment, but he had no intention of staying indoors and looking at the drab furnishings of the cramped apartment. In his state, he would start talking aloud to himself, his concerns bouncing back off the walls at him as if mocking his plight. Nick dumped his bag on the bed, went out to his car, and drove to the coast. He parked near the causeway leading to Bahrain. Restless, Nick needed to think. Staring at the dual string of lights extending into the Gulf for fifteen miles beyond his view, he worked through the options. Appealing to the ambassador, to his boss Susan, or to any of his American colleagues for help was definitely out. So, too, was his somehow telling the Saudis of the impending attack. Even if they believed him, he might inform the wrong person, and word could get back to al-Qaeda. He'd be a dead man. Who else had a stake? Whom could he trust not to betray him?

Nick kicked the stones of the gravel on the road's edge. Traffic roared by, but he hardly heard it. Pacing, pacing, he kicked up dust, a gray cloud enveloping his knees as his mind turned to his father, to his studies, to what little philosophy he had learned. Confucius. What would he have done? To whom does one owe allegiance? First to parents—to one's own blood—then to spouse, but what about nation? Where did that fit in? The Chinese. That's it! They had a stake in this—a big one. Not only would a senior official of theirs be in danger, but a country they relied on for oil could fall into turmoil, or at best, lose its oil wealth to China's arch rival.

Ma Ling, he must somehow talk to her about this. She was shrewder than she made out, not just a flighty bird. She had influence, and she seemed to like me, Nick reasoned. Plus, she cared for the al-Sayyids, or at least appeared to. He would call her tomorrow and meet at the club.

The next morning as he arrived at his desk in Dhahran, Nick groaned. A week away in Riyadh and his inbox was already full again with requests from the province's American citizens asking for consular assistance. He just wanted to scream at them all and shout, "Get out now! Join your families back in the States!" He checked his calendar and remembered that John was back in town and would want to get together for their weekly tennis match. Nick's gear was stacked in the corner of his office. He looked at the racquet and saw that a string had snapped. Great, just what I need.

"Nick? Good to hear from you. Yeah, I had a good trip, mate. Your racquet string is broken? No problem. It's getting too hot to play now, anyway. Drop it off sometime, and I'll fix it for you. We'll pick up again when the weather cools off."

Nick hung up the phone, glad that John didn't mind his not showing up. He dialed Ma Ling.

"What a pleasant surprise. So you have finally succumbed and are asking me out on a date—just the two of us."

"Not exactly a date, Ma Ling. You know I'm too cautious for that, but I would like to meet at the club with you tonight after work."

"I'm not giving up hope. See you at six." Nick put down the receiver, imagining Ma Ling coming to the club dressed only in negligee and heels—an image that morphed into Fatima, standing amid a cloud of incense.

Chapter 16

After the confrontation with John at the club, Ahmad and Fatima went home to discuss what to do. They huddled together in the living room and spoke in hushed voices so that the servants, whom they had dismissed for the rest of the evening, would not hear any of their conversation. Their father was staying at his apartment in Riyadh.

"You're sure Hajar is pregnant? If not, this might just blow over with no one the wiser."

"She described her symptoms to me," Fatima said. "Of course, you can't know for sure without a pregnancy test. We cannot bring her to a doctor. Maybe we could use one of those self-diagnosing kits, but the problem is—"

"Could you get hold of one?"

"It would be difficult, even with my access at the clinic. People would ask questions. Plus, the timing is not right. She said her missed period should have occurred a week ago. It's too late now to test. Hajar would have to wait for four more weeks, and even if she did, these kits are not foolproof. There are often false negatives *and* false positives. She can't afford to take that chance and wait until the symptoms start becoming obvious to others."

Ahmad scratched his head. "So what do we do? It sounds as though we have to get her out of the country, and without her family's knowledge."

"Brother, you're the towering intellect in the family. What ideas do you have?"

Ahmad thought for a while, put off by his sister's tone, which he did not find conducive to brainstorming. "How about this? We convince the local imam, father's friend, to conduct a *mota'a*—a pleasure marriage between Hajar and me so that we can go to Bahrain, ostensibly to have a good time. Once there, I divorce her and she is free to stay."

"Oh, Ahmad, be logical. You're a Shi'ite; she's a Sunni. What Shi'ite cleric would ever conduct such a ceremony? Even if some might recognize the *mota'a,* the Saudis wouldn't. Besides, the cleric would have to tell Hajar's father or brother—to have their permission. And also. . . ."

"I get the picture. You think of something then."

Fatima said, "The main thing is to get her out of Saudi Arabia and far away. Bahrain is too close. Her brother could come across any day and find her. We need to get her to somewhere like England or the United States."

"But she has no passport," said Ahmad. "Even if she had, she could not leave the country without a father or brother's letter of permission. I doubt she even has an identity card. That family is so conservative—they would prefer she remain a non-person."

Fatima's eyes lit up and she hugged her brother. "That's it! Her identity—we change it. She leaves the country by pretending she is me traveling back to the U.S. to complete her studies."

Ahmad looked skeptical. Now was his turn to poke holes in the argument. "I don't remember Hajar well, but even as a girl, you and she did not look alike. How does she leave as you?"

"We substitute a photo of her for the one of me on my passport."

"You think it is child's play to doctor a passport?"

"Criminals do it all the time. That is what I hear. Why else would the authorities warn us against losing our passports or having them stolen?"

Ahmad objected. "We don't have any criminal friends."

"Never mind," Fatima said. "We'll find someone. For now, I must get back my passport, with the renewed student visa, as soon as possible. I will call Nicholas to urge him to expedite it. I think he already feels guilty for procrastinating on the matter."

Ahmad admitted that his sister's plan seemed more plausible than his. "I'll take you to see Hajar at work tomorrow. You can meet with her and explain what we need to do."

The next day, shortly after 1 p.m., Fatima arrived unannounced at the clothing store in the al-Halal mall. Hajar had stopped turning on her cell phone as the battery had died. The store was shut, and Hajar was sitting on the floor in the hallway, her knees against her chin, slowly rocking. Fatima sat down beside her and said nothing for several minutes. Hajar assumed she had bad news but did not ask. When Fatima put her hand on Hajar's back, a tear rolled down the younger girl's cheek: she sensed what was coming.

Fatima, however, did not mention John. Instead she said, "Ahmad and I have decided we must help you leave the country. It is no longer safe for you here or to go anywhere nearby."

Hajar continued looking straight ahead but had stopped rocking.

"You will go in my place back to the U.S. as soon as possible and stay with my brother Faisal. He will look after you and help you decide what to do about your pregnancy—whether to abort the fetus or keep the child. You will not want for money. I will see to that and will arrange your ticket."

Hajar turned toward Fatima, laid her arms on Fatima's crossed legs, and bent forward, her face hidden. She looked to the side only to plead. "Oh, my dear friend, I have ruined my own life. Do not let me ruin yours." Hajar's thoughts again turned dark. She would save her family the trouble of having to kill her—whether by stoning or some other method, she no longer cared. She would take her own life.

"Nonsense." Fatima pulled Hajar up, held her shoulders, face close to hers, and said, "Look at me. We shall have none of this talk. Show me the spirit that brightened my sad moments as a girl. You and I have had enough of this self-pity. What's done is done. You cannot change the past, but you can, and must, help me help you."

With surprising strength, she lifted Hajar to her feet. "Come with me to the restroom. You'll rinse your face, put on a smile, and we'll start from there."

In the bathroom, as Hajar leaned over the sink and splashed water on her face, Fatima checked that no one else was using the toilet, then put her hand on the girl's shoulder, and whispered, "Now we start. First I need some photos of you." She gave Hajar a handkerchief to dry herself and a comb for her hair. "Stand here and face this way." After stepping outside to see that no one was coming, Fatima quickly returned, pulled out a small digital camera from her handbag and began snapping photos a few feet from Hajar, with a plain cream-colored wall as the backdrop. "Turn this way. Now that. Put your hair behind your ear. Tilt your head and smile. Good."

Thirty seconds later she had finished and walked Hajar back into the hallway.

"I will print these and turn one into a passport photo, but we need someone to help replace my photo with yours. Do you know of anyone who might do that for us if we paid enough? You had said Ṭariq now hangs around a rough crowd, that they are the ones who brought you here."

"I don't know, Fatima. I'm afraid. You should not get mixed up with them."

"Ahmad will take care of it."

"The leader's name is Rasheed, and he has a small newspaper stand in al-Khobar, one block east of Dhahran Street, facing the clock tower, and near the new market and food center. According to Tariq, this Rasheed is there most of the time, so everyone knows him. He's a short, fat man with a long, unkempt beard, a few years older than Tariq."

"Has he ever seen your face?"

"No, I don't think so. I cannot imagine how he might have done so."

"Good, then we'll use him." She handed Hajar her battery charger and asked her to re-charge the phone. She would call when she had more details of their plan. In the meantime, Hajar was to dial Ahmad's cell phone number if she needed anything. They embraced, kissed each other on the cheek, and Fatima left.

Hajar had forgotten to mention that Tariq also spent much of his time at this same newspaper stand.

Nick stood to greet Ma Ling and her driver Huang, who were walking up to his table. Ma Ling came first and rose on her tiptoes to kiss Nick on both cheeks. "We are old friends now," she said. Nick was conscious of her perfume, the same she had worn at the Riyadh reception, but stronger now. Huang Lei cradled Nick's hand in what the younger man thought of as a large bear's paw without the claws. The driver said "hello," and moved away to sit alone in a seat several tables from theirs.

At about the same time, a large group arrived and occupied a number of nearby seats. Nick suggested that he and Ma Ling move to the far corner of the patio for some privacy. She smiled and arched her thin eyebrows as she agreed, and reacted with pleasant surprise when Nick sat next to her rather than opposite. They could have been a couple.

She touched his hand. "Now tell me what is so urgent. You must whisper it softly into my ear."

Nick didn't go that far, but began by saying, "Ma Ling, what I am about to say could get me in a lot of trouble if others found out, so I need to trust you not to reveal me as your source and to tell this to no one except those who absolutely must know." He hoped he didn't look as nervous as he felt. Nick's voice was shaking, and Ma Ling squeezed his hand to assure him she would not betray his confidence.

Nick told her that he had mistakenly seen highly secret U.S. intelligence indicating that Sami al-Sayyid and the China Oil chairman would be in grave danger at the upcoming Saudi Oil board meeting and that a hostage taking would occur. The U.S. military in the region would use the incident as a pretext for an invasion to seize control of Saudi Arabia's oil fields, in effect relegating the ruling family or whoever succeeded them to governing a worthless desert and the world's two holiest Islamic shrines of

Mecca and Medina. He did not mention suspicions of Chinese involvement in helping the Saudis acquire nuclear weapons.

Ma Ling immediately grasped the implications but frowned and said, "Why are you telling me this? You aren't trying to hurt me for some reason, are you?"

Nick assured her he was not part of some plot to trick the Chinese into a unilateral action. "You must trust me as I am now trusting you. I'm confident that the intelligence is legitimate. Why would the U.S. government purposefully try to mislead one of its own employees?"

Ma Ling did not seem entirely convinced by that argument and gently implied that perhaps her friend was an innocent dupe. Still she couldn't resist one last dig and said, "Have I done anything to you? Not that I wouldn't want to. . . ." and brushed his leg with hers under the table.

"Please, this is serious. I can't turn to my own colleagues or to the Saudi government, whom no one believes anymore."

"And, Nick, you are sure that the U.S. would not invade, even without a hostage taking?"

"I can't see how—the world would construe that as naked aggression. Even Germany needed a pretext before marching into the Sudetenland or annexing Austria." A dismaying thought shot across, ruffling Nick's forehead. What if Gewalt's allegations of a nuclear arsenal were just that—merely alleged weapons of mass destruction, as in Iraq?

"Nick, if this is true, and I repeat *if*, we don't have much time—just two weeks. However, if this is false, for whatever reason, and I wrongly convince my government to act, they would punish me severely. China treats suspected double agents in the harshest possible terms." Ma Ling's expression now looked as worried as Nick felt.

She said, "I need a few hours, perhaps a day, to think of a plan—one that would not harm my country's prestige and influence here if, in fact, a hostage taking does not occur. Then I will fly back to Riyadh and request an urgent meeting with my ambassador. Whatever action we decide to take, it would be best that you not know. For your sake, we should not meet or speak again ... unless I—or I should say—the Chinese ambassador decides not to risk trying to stop this crisis that you expect. Otherwise, you might fall under suspicion.

"Could you bear that, Nick? Being without me?"

Won't this woman ever stop? Nick smiled. "It would be a heavy sacrifice, but I would try."

"If you *do* hear from me—and I would merely convey some harmless message about playing tennis—you should understand that we will *not* proceed. Then you would have to go ahead with whatever your plan B is." Ma Ling paused. "I assume you have one."

Nick thought for a moment. "Could you and I have our own separate plan? Perhaps you might convince Sami not to attend the meeting, to go away with his family on vacation somewhere...."

Ma Ling frowned. "This is an important meeting for him. How could I ask Dr. Sami to skip his anointment as a board member without providing a valid reason? Even if I said his life would be in danger, he probably would not listen to me. The press has made this into an event. He cannot *not* go." She moved her chair away to look directly into Nick's pale-gray eyes. "One more question, Nick. Why are you doing this?"

Nick paused and swallowed before answering. "I don't want Fatima's father to die. Or any more innocent people, for that is what would happen even if everything went off, from our standpoint, without a hitch."

"I may have difficulty getting Ambassador Jia to believe me, based on the word of one man . . ." She rose to go and squeezed Nick's arm as if checking to see how much muscle was on the bone, ". . . but I will try."

Ma Ling left Nick to take care of the bill and hurried away with Huang Lei.

Chapter 17

THE TWO CHINESE WERE ON A PLANE to Riyadh the following afternoon and in the waiting room of the Chinese ambassador's office by early that evening. Ambassador Jia Guomin was clearing his desk and almost ready to see Ma Ling. Huang Lei would wait outside until called. A slight man in his late forties, Jia Guomin was rising rapidly in the Chinese foreign service, and many expected him to become a deputy foreign minister within a few years. Recognized early by examiners as having an aptitude for foreign languages, Jia had attended the Beijing Foreign Language University and graduated near the top of his class. He had been among the first to return to attend college after the ten-year Cultural Revolution when China had shut down all its universities and sent students to the countryside for re-education as factory and farm workers. In school, the state had assigned Jia to learn Arabic when few others were doing so. For several years after graduation, he served as a simultaneous interpreter in the foreign ministry and translated for Deng Xiaoping during the few state visits that Arab officials made to China. Simultaneous interpretation was a tiring job that only the relatively young could do well. Jia did not enjoy the work and was glad to go abroad for his first overseas posting. Never married and an admitted workaholic, he had spent much of the past two decades outside his country and had resisted lucrative offers to return and enter the private sector.

Jia was a cultured man, with a talent for calligraphy. He preferred reading ancient literary texts to making money and did not share the belief of so many of his countrymen that to get rich was glorious. His bookshelves were his riches, his ever-expanding knowledge a source of delight. Jia did not perch solely in an ivory tower, above it all. Rather, he ascribed to Western management practices and also read the books of the gurus like his favorite, the ur-management consultant Peter Drucker. Jia set high expectations for his subordinates, provided them with the resources to get the job done, and did not micromanage or second-guess their efforts. His approach seemed to work, and he had three years of stellar results in Saudi Arabia to prove it.

In the decades-long "special relationship" that had existed between the U.S. and the Saudis, the Saudi government had insisted that American ambassadors not be Arabists but instead that they have close personal ties to the U.S. presidents under whom they served. This arrangement helped the Saudis influence American foreign policy from afar while subjecting their own machinations to less scrutiny from ambassadors, who in theory were the president's eyes and ears, but in practice were generally clueless at reading the subtle signs on display at official or informal Saudi functions. To date, the Saudis had not bothered to enforce a similar policy with the Chinese. As China's influence in the country grew, however, that was bound to change.

Ma Ling stepped into Ambassador Jia's spacious office and sat quietly as he finished writing some notes to himself. She admired the scrolls of calligraphy that hung on the walls. Done in the ambassador's own hand, they represented the most obvious manifestation of his talents. Like most educated Chinese, Ma Ling recognized masterful work. Next to each piece was a similar sample of artwork, in Arabic calligraphy, that the ambassador had collected or that various dignitaries had given to him over the years. In a corner, on a low glass-covered table that Jia used for tea was also a bright red paper cutting, another of China's traditional arts.

Jia looked up from his notepad and addressed Ma Ling by her title in Chinese, "This sounds important, Director Ma. Shall we go into the secure room?"

"Yes, sir. I believe that would be best."

The Chinese had built their embassy in Riyadh not long after establishing diplomatic relations with Saudi Arabia in the late 1990s. To do so, they had used their own workers brought in from China. After an embarrassing incident when the Chinese discovered that the U.S. had bugged their president's official plane, the government made sure that key embassies each built a secure, windowless room, sealed in lead and impervious to electronic eavesdropping. Guards routinely swept the rooms for listening devices, as one could never be too careful about security.

On their way out of the ambassador's office to the nearby room, Jia paused to greet Huang Lei. He did so respectfully, almost as a pupil might to a master, bowing and inquiring about his health. He asked Huang to please wait and he would call for him, if needed, once Ma Ling had provided him with sufficient background to the problem.

Ma Ling closed, but did not lock, the heavy metal door behind them. She briefed the ambassador on what Nick had told her and concluded her remarks with, "I promised to protect the source's identity."

"Excellent work, Director Ma. You continue to justify the confidence I have placed in you." Ma Ling modestly demurred to accept the praise.

With a teasing smile, Jia added, "As for your source, it is not hard to guess who he is. Do you think this fellow would like to work for us on a more permanent basis?"

Ma Ling could not conceal a flash of anger in her eyes, a silent response that Jia did not fail to notice.

"I'm sorry, Ma Ling. I had to ask. It seems that Hansen already has stuck out his neck and may be in hot water soon. I assume you would not be here if you did not trust him and the accuracy of his information."

Ma Ling nodded. "We can ask no more from him. He is little more than a boy when it comes to this kind of work."

"I'm sure you've thought through the consequences if you are wrong. Not only will a fine career be over, but much worse might occur." Jia Guomin paused, and Ma Ling felt he was not just speaking about her.

After a prolonged silence, Jia's expression brightened. "However, I would be remiss to treat you as Xuande did with your illustrious ancestor Sanbao." Jia was referring to the Ming dynasty emperor and Ma Sanbao, a Muslim eunuch renamed Zhong He, who went on to become one of the world's greatest explorers, China's equivalent of Christopher Columbus. In the early 15th century, Zhong He commanded a huge armada that traveled to the Middle East, explored the coast of Africa and, some said, circumnavigated the globe a century before Magellan. Emperor Xuande ended Zhong's explorations and China turned inward for several centuries thereafter, a policy that caused the country to slip far behind the West in its technological prowess.

"You realize," he continued, "there is no time to seek guidance from Beijing. We will have to handle this matter entirely within this country and limit knowledge only to those directly involved in the operation that you propose." Jia was referring to the impossibility of communicating via secure phones or encrypted cables with his superiors in the Chinese government. If the Americans could crack al-Qaeda's messages, they presumably could do the same with those of the Chinese. Jia Guomin did not know this for sure, but it was not worth taking the chance of tipping their hand.

"Very well," Jia said. "Let's proceed. Ask Huang Lei to join us."

Ma Ling stepped outside and returned with the driver, his broad bulk squeezed into the tan uniform.

"Master Huang, I asked of your health for a reason, and not just out of politeness. Director Ma has informed me of an operation we must undertake in twelve days' time. It is a dangerous mission that will require all of your skills and those of the other Shaolin masters. We have little time to train but will do what we can."

Like a number of the Chinese drivers, who doubled as bodyguards, Huang Lei was actually a Shaolin monk from Henan Province. Famed masters of Chinese martial arts, these men trained from early childhood in the physical and mental powers needed to excel in *kungfu*. The elite monastery in Shaolin, for centuries, had produced the world's most skilled practitioners in hand-to-hand combat. The monks emphasized defensive practice and used deadly force only as a last resort. Once skilled in hand fighting and traditional weaponry, the best were taken by the government and trained by the PLA in modern warfighting and soldiery. Of these, approximately ten now worked under cover as drivers and bodyguards for key Chinese officials in Saudi Arabia. Huang Lei was one of them, and by virtue of his age and skills, their *de facto* leader.

"Ma Ling, please brief us on how you feel we should approach this."

"Thank you, Ambassador Jia. As I think you agree, we need to allow the hostage taking to occur but must disrupt it as soon as the assailants announce their intentions. We will use the element of surprise to disarm them before they have time to entrench and secure their positions. We don't know how many al-Qaeda men will take part but have to assume, based on previous attacks like the one at the Oasis in 2004, that there will be only a handful, not dozens, not one or two. That means we will require a similar number of martial-arts masters to ensure we control the situation, and if possible, prevent the loss of life.

"Having worked at Saudi Oil's headquarters for the last twelve months, I know that their security detail will not allow weapons of any kind into the main building. Our official security officers must surrender control for protecting the chairman to Saudi Oil's guards once he has entered the compound. In this case, we agree with the American suspicions that al-Qaeda has compromised Saudi Oil security, just as they appear to have done with Saudi intelligence. How else could they hope to get into a highly secured facility?

"So our ostensible security detail will escort the convoy containing Mr. Yang Pangzi, the China Oil chairman, into the Saudi Oil compound, but will not be able to follow him into the building. They will have to wait outside and should position themselves far enough from the main compound entrance to prevent any direct entanglement with al-Qaeda, in the unlikely event that the terrorists try to shoot their way in from the street.

"Chairman Yang will be bringing four aides, all men, to Saudi Arabia with him. They are supposed to attend the presentation—one to operate the computer and electronic presentation, one to serve as interpreter, one to carry briefing materials and supplementary information, should it be required, and one, a technical expert based at the joint-venture facility in Fujian. At the last possible moment, we need to replace these four with our Shaolin masters. We must even deceive Chairman Yang as to the reason: he cannot know what is to happen; otherwise, he may get nervous, raise suspicions, and give away the operation. We will make up some excuse—for instance, that there was a last-minute problem with the visas of his entourage, and we needed to replace them.

"Ordinarily, as the China Oil liaison, I would serve as the chief aide to the chairman at the presentation. However, with the governor, the king's son, present at the board meeting, we must defer to custom and keep all women out of his presence. That presents us with an opportunity.

"I will ride in a separate car from the chairman and along with me, disguised as female aides, who we shall say are part of the supporting technical group, will be three additional Shaolin masters, hidden under black veils, scarves, and abayas. We four will drive around back and enter the much more lightly guarded women's entrance. Typically, only one or two *mutawwas,* armed with sticks, guard that back door and the doorway separating the men's and women's part of the building. We should be able to easily overpower them, and al-Qaeda would least expect any rescue attempt coming from that direction.

"Once inside the back of the building, we will wait near, but outside, the board room and monitor what's going on via closed circuit camera and head gear linked via radio communications to the laptops of our colleagues within the rooms. Those same laptops will have unobtrusive Web cameras attached to them and each agent will position his to cover a different angle of the room. When one of the Shaolin agents speaks a code word, it will signal for our men outside to attack and storm the door. Simultaneously, the four inside will spring into action.

"Unlike the attackers, who will likely be heavily armed, none of our Shaolin masters will be able to carry conventional weapons, although it may be worth trying to have the ones disguised as women carry them under their cloaks. Instead, the four in the boardroom will use Ninja throwing stars or flying knives, carried within their laptops' DVD disk drives. We will have the PowerPoint presentations printed onto them in case someone inspects the computers. The only difference between these flying circular knives and regular DVDs will be their jagged edges, which become deadly in the expert toss of a Shaolin master. If we have time to rig them properly, we might also enable the laser pointing devices used in presentations to act as mini stun grenades, emitting tear gas or smoke when tossed hard against an object."

The two men listened closely. The ambassador was visibly impressed by Ma Ling's thorough plan, hatched in under a day. He said, "Splendid. That sounds viable, but I have one concern: the interpreter. I don't think any of our Shaolin masters can handle that. Do you have anyone, Master Huang?"

"You're right, sir. Overall, I also believe it is possible to do as Director Ma describes, and I can think immediately of six others to accompany me on this mission. However, none of us is able to act as a simultaneous interpreter. One speaks good Arabic, but not at your level, sir."

The three fell silent, and the ambassador mulled over an idea. "Let's still go ahead and replace the interpreter coming from China with your fellow, Huang. I have decided I will accompany the delegation. That way, if necessary, I can step in and relieve your man if it becomes too difficult."

Ma Ling looked aghast at Jia. "But sir, this is not an ordinary meeting. You might die!"

"It's a chance I'll take. My presence there is plausible. Besides, if this mission fails, I'm as good as dead anyway. I will ensure that I get the chairman under the table as soon as our attack begins. We'll let the others take care of the rest."

"Thank you, Ambassador Jia, for your honesty and courage. It will be an honor to have you with us," said Master Huang. "I do still have two additional concerns: first, my men know little about computer presentations and the oil industry or details of China Oil's operations and joint venture with Saudi Oil. They will need a thorough briefing on that, particularly if any are expected to answer questions. Second, what happens if the Saudi guards ask the men disguised as women to unveil their faces?"

"Good points, Master Huang," said Ma Ling. "We definitely need to train you and your men in the areas you mentioned, but I wouldn't concern yourself too much about any questions on China Oil or the oil industry. We will have your men defer to the chairman, which would be natural for aides to do. He's a career oilman and knows the business inside and out.

"With regard to the disguises, the three you select for the *abayas* should be the ones most capable of passing as women. They will have to wear make-up, lipstick, wigs, perfume, nylon stockings, and women's shoes, albeit flat ones so that they can run and kick in them. In other words, they will need to play the part."

The ambassador laughed. "Are your Shaolin brothers up to that?"

"They have endured worse, I assure you," said Huang.

Ma Ling continued. "We will also have to provide the supposed females with I.D. cards. I suggest we collect some the day before the meeting from women in the embassy. The Saudi guards won't look too closely for a match. Normally, they never ask a woman to unveil, as local customs make that shameful—both for the man asking and the woman asked. In the off chance that the Saudis do want to check, however, we Chinese all look pretty much alike to them, so I wouldn't worry about an I.D. not resembling its carrier's face too closely."

Huang asked, "Director Ma, can we get hold of a blueprint for the Saudi Oil building?"

"I doubt it, Huang, but I can sketch for you the layout of the women's floors of the building. We should expect that the top floor with the boardroom has roughly the same structure." Ma Ling quickly drew the rectangular cross section of the ten-story building, giving approximate dimensions. "The four stairwells are here and here, facing each other at either end; you'll find the two banks of elevators in the middle, also on opposite sides. This side of each floor has several adjacent meeting rooms. I expect that they have combined the spaces into a single boardroom at the top. If so, that would make a room of approximately ten by forty meters, large enough to seat up to about 100 persons arranged around a large central table, with seats along the walls." Huang had driven Ma Ling many times past the building on the way to the Saudi Oil club. For the ambassador's benefit, she continued. "The headquarters' main entrance, facing north, opens to a courtyard, set back about 100 meters from Spruce Street, site of the main gate that one drives through. The women's entrance is directly opposite on the other side of the building. Our convoy will drive from here, the security detail should park at this corner, and the vehicle carrying me and the disguised men should park at the back as close to the women's entrance as possible."

Huang said, "We will have four masters in the room. Each should have responsibility for taking care of a particular quadrant and any attackers in it. We will assign those in advance and have each man sit, if possible, in chairs off the main table with views of their respective corners."

"That's good, Huang. We will have only a small delegation compared to the Saudis so it won't be necessary that all sit on one side of the table behind the China Oil chairman. You can spread out."

"At most, we will have only a few minutes between the time that attackers enter the room and when we must act," Huang added. "We cannot afford to let them start tying people up." He paused. "I hope they don't come in with guns blazing."

"Do we have a schedule for the meeting?" Jia asked.

"The meeting begins at 9:00 a.m. on July 2nd. After some introductions, Chairman Yang is to give his presentation of about 45 minutes, beginning at 9:15 a.m. The

Saudi Oil board has set aside 30 minutes for questions and answers about the joint venture, which takes us to 10:30 a.m. Then we are to leave, and the board will discuss its own business, such as formally inducting Sami al-Sayyid as a board member and voting on key new projects for the next fiscal year, including the level of expenditure to commit to our venture. I am not sure whether the governor will stay for the entire session. He is not part of the board, but keenly interested in hearing what we have to say."

Jia looked worried. "Let's just hope that if an attack occurs, our men are still in the meeting room to take care of it. We cannot plausibly hang around the building once they have dismissed us, nor would we have a rationale for intervening."

Each of the three had a lot to do in the days ahead, so they broke up the meeting soon after and agreed to coordinate on a daily basis beginning at the same time each day until the arrival of Chairman Yang, shortly before his scheduled presentation to the Saudi Oil board. The three had not had time to discuss what to do if the presumed hostage taking did not transpire as anticipated or if it even failed to occur at all.

As a precaution, later that evening, Ambassador Jia wrote a handwritten memorandum of all they had discussed and arranged to have the sealed memo sent via immediate diplomatic pouch, hand carried by a personal courier to his superiors at the foreign ministry in Beijing. Jia stressed in his letter that the ministry contact him only via a similar "old-fashioned" means, that he would take full responsibility for any failure in the mission, and that Beijing should prepare for possible unilateral military action by the U.S. in Saudi Arabia. He did not suggest what the Chinese government should do, but only asked that any preparatory measures not alert the Americans to the Chinese embassy's attempt to foil the expected attack on Saudi Oil.

That night, Jia tossed and turned in bed. To relax, he got up, took out some scissors, red paper, and pencil. He began an elaborate paper cutting, a skill he had first learned as a child. Although Jia would never admit to holding folk superstitions, he secretly hoped the cutting's bright red, a symbol for good luck, might keep future evil spirits at bay.

Chapter 18

Fatima rummaged through her purse and found Nick's business card. *Nicholas D. Hansen, Consular Officer.* She looked at the "D." What was that? David, Daniel? She turned the card over to read the Arabic version. Maybe he should change his name to N. David Hansen or N. Daniel Hansen or to whatever that D was. Anything would be better than Nick. After she got her passport and visa back, she might try to tactfully suggest it. After all, some American men of her father's generation, professors at school, had used their middle names after a first initial, and it seemed somehow sophisticated, or at least she thought so. Maybe they were just rebelling against their parents or correcting a badly chosen name. But when she had asked one of them what the unused initial stood for, it had seemed no worse than the middle name given prominence in its place. She hadn't said so, and the older man she asked had seemed flattered by her attention, too flattered in fact. Perhaps she should have implied he had made a mistake, that she liked the other one better, and not gotten his crazy imagination working. A simple question and he had wanted to take her for coffee, go for a walk after class. Men. How they get so worked up. Just like here.

Fatima sighed and dialed Nick's office number. He said he usually went to work early, so maybe she'd catch him before he got busy and distracted with other matters.

"Fatima! It's so good to hear from you!"

Oh, no. Was she giving the wrong impression again? But she had to be nice, so she made chitchat. "Nicholas, we haven't seen you for a while. How are you? Yes, it is getting hot out. I guess we won't play tennis for a while. Maybe we can have you over—sometime soon, for sure. I'll ask Ahmad.

"What? Oh, my father is fine. He's spending most of his time in Riyadh, but will be coming here the week after next. That's right, for his first board meeting. A bit exciting really—we may have a little party to celebrate. So you have met him? Yes. That would be good for you to have a chance to talk to him some more."

Gently steer it now. "Nicholas, you must be awfully busy, and I hope I'm not being a pest. What? Oh, you're too kind. Thank you. As I was saying, I was thinking I may need to go back early to the U.S. Of course, I'd come back here over the holidays, for the semester break, to— Why not? Oh, the tougher guidelines. Yes, of course. Anyway, I'm sure I'd see you when you go to Washington—you do go sometimes, right? For meetings, yes. Good. As I was saying, I don't want to bother you but was wondering about the visa and how soon you can have it ready.

"Really? That's great." The singsong lilt of Fatima's voice rose and softened as a broad smile spread across her face. "So when— Clearance from? Oh, yes—that homeland group. Pestering him? Yes, like me." She laughed.

"You'll call me as soon as it's ready," she repeated. "Nicholas, that's wonderful. Thanks so much. Personally? Where? Saudi Oil. I'm afraid they won't let you in my building. Great. Ahmad and I will meet you at the club. Just tell us when."

Fatima said goodbye and hung up. From her purse, she pulled out the sets of photos Ahmad had touched up, printed, and cropped for her. They looked almost professional. She thought the one straight on was most becoming, but maybe Hajar had to show a bit of ear on hers. She would check her own passport photo and choose which pair of photos to give to Ahmad, just in case they needed two. You never knew with those criminal types—they also had their little bureaucracies . . . or just screwed up sometimes and needed a backup.

Fatima thought of what Nick had said. This might turn out okay after all. Later she would call Hajar, tell her to get ready. That might cheer her up. As soon as they had the passport, Ahmad would get the photo done, and then he and Hajar would leave right away.

How would Hajar feel going from her home, perhaps never to return? Frightened. The poor girl was already frightened. Terrified. Going into the unknown and alone. At least until Faisal. . . . Oh, she must contact Faisal! Would he be okay with having a beautiful, young woman staying at his apartment? No, not his sister. She smiled, and then shrugged, remembering she now might not get back to school for another year, or at least not until the start of the spring semester. She would have Ahmad speak to Faisal. Send an e-mail, then call him tomorrow to explain.

Fatima wondered whether Faisal still wore the thin, manicured beard, the one he stroked while preening in front of the mirror. He was too vain about his looks, she thought, and he valued that in others. Like his older brother, Faisal could be a prude sometimes, although he was more relaxed in the States. Always chaperoning. Asking her about boys. "No, nothing serious," Fatima would tell him. As if he wasn't constantly chasing after girls—younger women actually, trying to impress them with his job at that big defense contractor. As if they cared how big his projectiles were or whatever he called them. She'd tell him to stay off Hajar. She'd been through enough. But they *had* gotten along. She remembered the three of them had occasionally played together until Faisal and Tariq started fighting. Faisal and Hajar? Maybe. . . .

A week later Nick met Fatima and Ahmad at the club but didn't stay with them for dinner even though it was already late and night had fallen. Fatima was surprised that Nick wouldn't accept their invitation. Normally, she thought, he would have done the polite thing and agreed, after an initial reluctance and perhaps even a refusal. She saw that Nick's face was drawn, the pudgy blush of his cheeks less noticeable, and he seemed worried. Getting the passport back was harder than he had expected, he said. Such matters usually were. Nick seemed relieved to have the passport back to them, but apologized profusely for having taken so long. Now he seems anxious to get rid of me, thought Fatima. Why the change of heart? Nick asked whether the al-Sayyids might be going on vacation. "No, I was recently in London," Fatima said, "although Ahmad and my father could use a break." She saw Nick momentarily brighten, but the cloud hanging over him returned. What is going on? Then Fatima thought of the incident between John and Hajar. He must know. That was it. Fatima certainly wouldn't bring up the subject and hoped she never saw John again. Ahmad seemed to have forgiven him. Maybe he had to. They saw each other nearly every day at work. Maybe he felt bad about challenging John, or relieved that John had let it go at that. Men. Always fighting about one thing or another. Then changing their minds. Like Nick. What was wrong with him? He almost seemed more attractive now that he wasn't fawning over her. Hajar, Nick. A sadness was spreading like the flu. Would it infect her, too?

They were standing. Nick wouldn't sit any longer. He hugged Ahmad in the Saudi fashion as if he were going somewhere. He almost did that with me! Fatima thought. But Nick seemed to think better of it, stepped back, and awkwardly looked at her, not even extending his hand in that silly American manner. Were tears in his eyes? Oh, the poor guy. I'd better look away. "Goodbye, Nicholas. We'll see you again soon."

Nick was walking away. Fatima called back to him, "Nicholas, what does D stand for?"

"D?"

"Your middle initial."

"Dudley." He gave a half salute, half wave of the hand and turned away.

Fatima couldn't suppress a small smile. Dudley . . . dud. No wonder Nicholas sticks with Nick, she thought. But anything would be better than that. Dudley Do Right. Dudley Hansen? Deadly handsome. John. Yes, *he* was deadly. What had Mother said. . . .

"Why were you smirking?" Ahmad asked.

"Nothing. Was I? Just playing games in my mind with the name of Mr. Nicholas Dudley Hansen."

"You should be nicer to him. He seemed upset."

"Yes, I wonder why. He certainly went out of his way to help us," she said.

Fatima changed the subject. "Now you can take care of the passport. You're not nervous, are you?"

Ahmad shrugged and they spoke no more about it.

The next day after work, Ahmad carefully taped a thin piece of paper over Fatima's name on her passport. His sister gave him the pair of Hajar's photos that she thought most appropriate. They all looked alike to him, so he was befuddled as to why she had to make such a careful selection. Fatima told Ahmad to be sure not to reach the newsstand too early. "Get there around 9 p.m. when Tariq has gone to pick up Hajar," she said.

Before leaving, he said, only half in jest, "If I'm not back by midnight, send out a search party. You may have to dredge the Gulf."

Ahmad drove his father's white Mercedes to al-Khobar and parked not far from where he thought the newsstand of the forger might be. The name Rasheed was all he had to go by. Starting from the food center east of the clock tower and heading north, Ahmad walked the length of three blocks and then part of the way back. He walked briskly, wondering just how bad the neighborhood was, and carried the passport and photos in a brown paper bag inside a small satchel, the kind he might use if he were going to pick up a few groceries. Ahmad had put in his wallet 400 Saudi riyals, the equivalent of about US$100, and stashed a similar amount in his back pocket as insurance. That should more than cover a deposit, he thought. After all, the amount of work involved was minimal: removing and replacing a single photo. It just had to be done right. He hoped this Rasheed could do the procedure while he waited.

The street had several newsstands on one side. As he walked past the first, he paused, pretending to scan the headlines of the print on display and debating whether to get a paper. By now, he realized, the day's news was decidedly stale. He thumbed through a few magazines, glancing up to see whether he saw anyone that matched the description of Rasheed. After a few minutes, he realized that two Indians were running the stand, so he moved on to the second.

A man about Ahmad's age, with a long scruffy beard, was sitting next to another and munching a sandwich by the open entrance to a small shop with papers on display. Flecks of crumbs covered his beard and tunic.

"Are you Rasheed?"

The man wasn't pleased to have someone interrupt his supper and even less happy to be addressed by name. "Who wants to know? And how do you know my name?"

"I'm Ahmad, an acquaintance of Tariq. I need your help."

"I'm not in the business of helping people. Tariq should know better than to send strangers looking for me." Rasheed spat on the sidewalk in front of him, narrowly missing Ahmad's shoe.

"It's a simple matter—just a few minutes of work—but I'll pay you well for your efforts." Ahmad took off his glasses to wipe the sweat from them. He couldn't see Rasheed's expression, but sensed he was more interested now that Ahmad had mentioned money. "Could we speak alone in the back of your shop, off the street?" Ahmad said. He didn't like going anywhere on his own with this guy, but was nervous that the police, driving about the area in their periodic patrols, might see him.

Rasheed put down the half-eaten sandwich, picked his teeth with a toothpick, and sized up Ahmad. "What's the rush? How do I know you're not working for somebody—people I don't like?"

"You mean the cops? If I were, I wouldn't be on my own, and we wouldn't be having this conversation right here. You'd be in the back of a police van on your way to a cell. We both know what you do."

"A little tough guy, huh?" Rasheed laughed. "No, you don't fit the profile of an undercover officer. Tell me then, what *do* I do?"

Ahmad looked at Rasheed's acquaintance as if the force of Ahmad's stare might push him off the stool and out of earshot. The fellow got the message; he moved several paces away and started whistling. Ahmad stepped closer into the garlic halo surrounding Rasheed's personal space and, in a conspiratorial tone, said, "forge passports."

"Hah! *I* don't do anything, but I might know someone who does." Rasheed looked at Ahmad, who was already backing off, dismayed by the smell. "You said, 'a few minutes of work.' Are you crazy?"

"I just need a photo replaced, not an entirely new passport."

"Okay. How much is it worth to you?"

"Two hundred riyals."

Rasheed waved him away. "Don't insult me. A thousand is the price."

"Never mind. I'll go somewhere else." Ahmad began walking down the street in the direction of his car. When he had gone halfway down the block, Rasheed's voice flew past: "Five hundred!"

Ahmad turned and walked slowly back to within range for him not to shout. "Four hundred, but do it while I wait."

"That's impossible. You can come tomorrow. Let me see what you have."

They walked to the back, and Ahmad pulled out the passport. Rasheed thumbed through it, apparently making mental notes of all the stamps. "Well traveled.

Student visa in America. This could be quite valuable." He flicked open the front page, and whistled through his teeth. "Wow! You didn't tell me it was a woman. Sorry, but I had to look." He noticed the paper covering her name. "What's this for?"

"She's from a prominent family and cannot be mixed up in this matter."

"I see now that I gave in too easily on the price. Maybe you'll make it up to me. Is she, by any chance, unmarried?"

"None of your business."

"From your arrogance, I assume you must be from the same family." He walked behind Ahmad so that Rasheed's fat body blocked Ahmad's way to the exit. "It would be my business if I decide to keep you here for a nice ransom, now wouldn't it?"

"Look. Others know where I am and will come looking for me if I'm not back soon. Don't be a fool. Just do what you agreed to."

"Easy, friend. I wasn't serious, but tell me one thing. Why are you doing this? Someone respectable like you—and the lady—coming to a place like this."

Ahmad had expected the question. Like many novice liars, he gave too many details. "I am marrying the other woman six months from now, but taking her to Bahrain for a 'get acquainted' weekend. She has no passport, and her father would never allow her to leave with me before the marriage. Get it?"

Rasheed seemed to accept the story. "All perfectly above board as far as I'm concerned. Give me the photo. I'm sorry I'll have to look at this one, too."

Ahmad handed him both. "Here are two—one as back-up—but I expect you'll return the one you don't use."

Another whistle. "You're a lucky guy. I wish I had women like that in my harem." Ahmad flushed with anger and was about to tell Rasheed to keep his comments to himself, but heeded his own advice and kept his mouth shut. Instead, he slammed 200 riyals onto the table and before walking out, said, "Here's your fifty-percent deposit. I'll come back at the same time tomorrow."

After Ahmad had gone, Rasheed studied Hajar's photos before putting them and the passport back into the brown paper covering. He called his colleague over and said, "Take these to Farouq and have him replace the passport photo with one of the others. Get them back to me tomorrow."

The man left and Rasheed sat stroking his beard. Soon after, Tariq stopped by after having dropped off Hajar at home.

Rasheed's face was contorted with anger. "Why the hell have you been telling people about me?"

"I haven't said anything. What do you mean?" Tariq stumbled a step backwards, as if to avoid the range of Rasheed's arms.

"A guy came by—a real snot—saying he was your friend and wanted me to change a passport photo for him."

"Who?"

"Ahmad something. Thick glasses, wimpy, slouching physique. He didn't give a last name, but implied that he was some hot shot, maybe a royal."

"How on earth would I be friends with someone like that?"

"Who knows? But you'd better not be talking about me. I did him this favor because of you. Now I wish I hadn't. I don't like it. We've got the operation in a few days, and strangers are coming up to me, saying they know what I do."

"Can I see the passport?"

"I've sent it on. Come by tomorrow night. Let this guy meet you in person since you're apparently such good friends that you don't even know him."

The next day Tariq called Hajar at work to tell her he'd be late picking her up that night. He had a "friend" to meet. She should wait for him in the first-floor supermarket, which stayed open until 10 p.m.

For most of the day, Ahmad had been busy at Saudi Oil, had skipped lunch, and realized he might be late if he didn't leave soon. It was 8:30 p.m. and Fatima had already had their driver fetch her to go home. Ahmad hopped in his car, the one he borrowed from his father, and drove back to al-Khobar. He was famished and stopped at a small food court in the market center to get some fast food before going to Rasheed's newsstand one block up the street. Among the other men eating in the food court that evening was Tariq. Neither man took any notice of the other. Ahmad was trying to decide between pizza, burgers, or a local dish. Shortly before 9 p.m., Tariq got up and hobbled to the exit before walking slowly toward Rasheed's shop. Ahmad thought he recognized the gait and took a close look at the man's face as he passed by the glass window. While Ahmad watched his back swaying from side to side, Tariq stopped at a white pickup parked halfway up the block, opened the cab door, and tossed a bag inside. Yes, it must be him. In a moment of panic, Ahmad thought of rushing back to his car and driving off. Then, steadying himself, he reasoned,

Rasheed's shop is open much of the night. The guy is probably just late going to the mall for his sister. So he waited inside.

Thinking he might need his wits about him, Ahmad had no more doubts about the choice for tonight's dinner. He'd have a brain sandwich, a Gulf specialty made of fried goat's brain with garlic sauce. Ahmad remembered freshman year at M.I.T. at the cafeteria with his pals. He bemoaned the perpetual lack of brain sandwiches on the menu, and they just thought he was kidding. Then he got exasperated and asked the food manager about it, almost by way of complaint. "Don't be an ass" was his reply.

Well, he'd try not to be a jackass tonight. Play it smart. He munched slowly on the sandwich and waited. At 9:30 p.m. he peeked outside and saw the pickup was still there. He ordered some French fries, but only nibbled on them and hoped his hanging around so long in a fast-food joint wouldn't attract attention. At 9:45 p.m., another peek. The car had gone, so Tariq must have left. Ahmad hurried to the shop.

"Sorry, I'm late. I got held up with some errands. Is my package ready?" he asked Rasheed.

"I don't know. We'll find out."

"What do you mean?"

Rasheed didn't answer, but whistled for a boy. "Go to Farouq and see if it's done."

Turning to Ahmad, he said, "You just missed your friend Tariq who, by the way, has no recollection of you. Funny, that."

"Did I say 'Tariq'? Actually, it was just a guy I ran into a few weeks ago—medium height, taller than you, long beard. I think he had heard it from a Tariq."

Rasheed obviously didn't believe him, but said nothing. He just sat watching Ahmad. A few minutes later, the boy returned with the package.

Ahmad inspected the passport, and it seemed fine. The paper still covered Fatima's name. There was no evidence of tampering, at least none that he could see. Ahmad handed Rasheed the remaining 200 riyals.

"Stick around. Tariq will be back in a few minutes. He'd like to meet you."

"You know, I'd like that, but I've got to work tomorrow." Ahmad looked inside the brown covering of the paper bag that contained the passport. "By the way, where's the second photo?"

Rasheed asked the kid, who shrugged, and ran back outside. "I guess my colleague Farouq must have needed both."

"That's a nuisance. I'd like it back, so please check whether he has it. I'll call you in the morning. If you've got the other photo, I'll come back tomorrow around this time. Maybe then I can meet Tariq." Ahmad had no intention of returning and hoped he and Hajar would be long gone. He had asked Fatima to call Hajar earlier in the day and tell her to be prepared to leave the following morning.

"Suit yourself," said Rasheed as Ahmad hurried down the block waving with his arm but not looking back.

Chapter 19

Hajar's stomach churned with butterflies all day after the call. Fatima had said Ahmad would pick her up the following morning in the mall's parking lot as soon as Tariq had dropped her off. She was not to bring anything except what she normally wore to work.

In her last evening at the store, Hajar was especially solicitous toward Izzat whom she would miss. Before leaving, Hajar told the older woman how she was a role model, that her giving Hajar a chance had changed her life. Izzat smiled and said she did not want to pry into Hajar's private affairs but hoped they would settle down: the girl's mood swings concerned her.

During the afternoon break, Hajar wrote a note to Aisha. She would leave it that night in the bottom of the container where her half-sister kept the sewing materials she used for her piecework.

Dear Aisha,
You've always been kind to me. I'm sorry I couldn't say goodbye, but I have had to leave and go far away. You told me to find happiness, which is what I'm trying to do. Please tell my mother and baby sister in Riyadh that I'll come for them some day but can't say where I've gone. I'll think of them constantly, as I have since we parted.
Your sister,
Hajar

That evening on the ride home, Hajar noticed that Tariq was edgy. He had called to say he would be late, which was not unusual. According to Aisha, he had been spending a lot of time away, staying out the entire day and returning only when he brought back Hajar from the mall. Tariq was angry with Hajar about something, but would not say what. As always, she had smiled and said "hello" when he drove up to the curb in front of the mall's elevators, but Tariq said nothing in reply. Once she had climbed in, he just slammed the back door of the pickup, told her to shut up—even though she hadn't said anything else—and drove off recklessly, almost careening into a pole as he left the mall's garage.

At home, he yelled, "Get out!" and Hajar, rushing to climb down from the truck, nearly tore her *abaya*. "What's the matter, Tariq?" She feared that he somehow knew of her plan. Again he was silent, but pushed her toward the door. To her relief, no further abuse awaited her that night. Later Hajar only pretended to sleep, but listened until her stepmother's snoring and the softer rumbles of Aisha and Munira began. She tiptoed past and left her note. The following morning, Tariq took Hajar to the mall for the last time. She let herself out, but asked him to wait a bit before driving off and walked over to his car door. He had rolled down the window. "What do you want?"

"Are you all right, Brother?" she said. "I hope you will be okay." Tariq snorted and raced the car engine with his foot.

Hajar continued. "I think I understand why you get angry with me. I haven't been a very good sister."

"What? What are you talking about?" Tariq looked at her through the thin veil. "Well, you'll have to do better as a wife. Muamar may not be so indulgent as I have been."

"Take care of yourself, Brother. Goodbye."

Tariq left in a huff, muttering to himself, "How could she know? Was she talking about the Saudi Oil assault?"

Not far off, watching them from the white Mercedes, sat Ahmad. He flashed his lights as the pre-arranged signal, and Hajar rushed over to get into the back seat. Ahmad started driving immediately, without a word. If anyone in the parking lot asked what they were doing, the previous driver had been just that, a driver. He, Ahmad, was the brother of this woman, now known as Fatima. She had a passport to prove it, and they were traveling from al-Khobar to visit relatives in Bahrain. On the way, Ahmad stopped at the bank and withdrew 20,000 riyals in cash, more than enough to buy Hajar's plane ticket and provide her with initial spending money in the U.S. In the car's trunk was a suitcase filled with some of Fatima's jewelry, a bit of her clothing that might fit Hajar, and other pieces of apparel that she had hurriedly bought for her friend. Ahmad and Hajar drove on, heading the few miles south to the Bahrain causeway and, Hajar thought, freedom.

After dropping off his annoying sister, Tariq pulled up next to Rasheed's shop, got out, and found Rasheed sitting next door in a café smoking from a water pipe.

"Tariq, last night that guy came by just after you left. He had changed his story, saying something about 'maybe it wasn't you' who had told him about me. Said he'd stop by this morning."

"I'll be waiting for him this time. Do you have the passport?"

"I gave it to him."

"What?"

"Farouq's kid brought it when the guy came by with the money. I couldn't very well say 'come back tomorrow.' I had the thing in my hand. Besides, he implied his tip about me had come from a different Tariq, although I don't know many others by that name, do you?"

"Rasheed, what were you thinking?" Tariq slammed the palms of his hands on the table. "Now what reason does he have to come back?"

"For the copy of the photo that we pasted into the passport. Farouq hadn't thought it necessary to return it. I had the kid bring the girl's picture early this morning."

"Let me have a look."

The two went to the shop and Rasheed pulled down the passport photo. He had tacked it to the wall, at eye level, by a small table where he liked to take his tea. Hajar's face smiled at him like a pin-up girl, the Saudi version of what auto mechanics in less repressive countries sometimes enjoy looking at for an extra boost during the day. Rasheed passed the photo to Tariq, whose face changed into progressively deeper hues of pink, red, and purple. He screamed at Rasheed. "Where did you get this?"

"Easy, man. I told you. The guy brought it."

"This is my sister!"

"You're kidding." Rasheed thought for a while. "That must be how he knew about me. Naturally, I didn't recognize her."

"You said he was going to marry her? And go where?"

"Bahrain."

"That bastard. Have your guys wait here for him—if he shows up. I've got to find Hajar."

Tariq dashed to his car and sped back to the mall. He skidded his vehicle to a stop in the parking lot.

"Come on. Come on!" Tariq said, waiting for the garage elevator. Finally it arrived. He got in and then cursed as the lift took him past the third floor. He stepped out on the fourth and shuffled quickly down the flight of stairs. Tariq frantically looked around, then right in front of him, he spotted Hajar's clothing store. He strode in, demanding of the terrified twins to know where Hajar was. They screamed and, covering their faces with their elbows, fumbled to put on their *abayas,* headscarves, and veils. Izzat had no such compunction. She stepped up to Tariq, her squat body like that of a bulldog, and asked what he was doing on the women's floor. She said, she had been wondering where Hajar was herself. By this time, two *mutawwas,* hearing the commotion, had run to the shop and grabbed Tariq as he was about to head back down the stairs. He struggled with them and might have gotten the better of the old men. Their sticks had fallen to the ground, and he had yanked himself free. When they said they would have him arrested, he decided it might be wise to provide a brief explanation. Regaining his composure, he disdainfully told them the ten-second version of Hajar's elopement.

They let him go. As Tariq scampered down the stairs, they yelled at him not to come back—him or his sister.

Tariq drove home, barely stopping for red lights, honking pedestrians, animals, and other cars out of the way. He hit the apartment like a whirlwind, pushed Aisha aside, and rummaged through Hajar's things. "Do you know where she has gone?" No one did. Tariq sat down to think. He'd have to go to Bahrain to look for her. Although just a few miles away, Tariq had never gone to Bahrain nor had he ever left Saudi Arabia. He had no reason to. Tariq thought his Saudi I.D. card should be enough to get him through the border control, but to be sure, he grabbed a fake passport that his al-Qaeda handlers had made for him—just in case he ever had to leave the country in a hurry.

Um Tariq and her two daughters gasped when her son told the startled women that Hajar had probably fled to Bahrain—with a man. He would find them, bring her back, and deal with her suitor. Tariq took some money from Aisha, grabbed a switchblade knife from his drawer, and said, "Don't expect me back tonight." Suheir had just enough presence of mind to urge him to be careful. Her words were hardly out before the front door slammed shut behind him.

Tariq stopped briefly again at the shop. The guy had not shown up. He wasn't that dumb. As Tariq was driving off, Rasheed came running out. He was waving both arms.

"What is it?"

Breathless as he reached the pickup, Rasheed said, "You don't have the gun in here, do you?" Embarrassed, Tariq didn't reply, but Rasheed saw the familiar case under the driver's seat. "You fool. Don't compromise our mission for a lousy sister. If they found that on you at the border, you'd be in prison by nightfall and tortured by morning." He took the case. "I'll keep it for you when you come back. Don't be any later than tomorrow afternoon. We have some final preparations to do."

Ahmad didn't speak much on the short drive to the causeway and the border crossing. He was nervous. Hajar sat veiled in the back waiting for instructions. Ahmad merely repeated to her their cover story. She was returning to the U.S. to study; she would live with her other brother Faisal; they would only spend a few hours in Bahrain to say hello to their uncle Omar, who did in fact exist and lived in Manama. They hadn't yet bought a ticket because they weren't sure whether Omar would insist that they stay for a few days before leaving.

The preparation turned out not to be necessary. Ahmad pulled the car up to the booth of the Saudi customs official and handed him both passports. The man looked at the names and checked that there were only two persons in the car. He spoke only to Ahmad who said, "We're brother and sister." He waved them through.

Ahmad drove straight to an office of Gulf Air, parked, and put the envelope with the cash into a small satchel. He helped Hajar out of the car and said, "You should take off your veil, Fatima." After a brief wait, the airline agent was ready to help.

"Roundtrip to Washington Dulles, please." Ahmad thought it would look less suspicious to buy a roundtrip ticket. The additional cost was negligible.

"I'm sorry we don't fly there. The closest we go is Newark, New Jersey. You could clear customs there and then switch to a domestic U.S. carrier."

"That's no good."

"We could fly you to Riyadh for a connection."

Ahmad shook his head. Can you suggest another airline?"

"Try British Airways next door."

At the neighboring office, the agent said, "We have one flight a day, sir, departing at night, 1:20 a.m. You fly to

London Heathrow and complete the trip from there on United. There's a bit of a layover. Total flight and transit time is 18 hours."

"Okay, I'll take it. Is tonight available?"

"I'm sorry the flight is very full. There's only one economy seat left. You'll have to go standby."

"Only one of us is flying." Ahmad waved Hajar to the counter. "My sister, Fatima."

"Shall I issue it then? Yes? With tax, that will be 3,455 dinars."

"Damn, I forgot to convert my riyals."

"You're paying cash?" The agent looked at Ahmad more closely and then said, "No problem. We'll take riyals." He calculated the exchange. "That's 4,278 riyals."

Ahmad counted out the bills, collected the ticket, and walked out with Hajar. "That's a relief. We're all set now. Just twelve more hours to kill, and then I'll take you to the airport." He smiled at Hajar. "Hungry?"

She was, so they drove to Seef, one of Manama's mega-malls. At lunch, Ahmad went over with Hajar all that he could think about her upcoming trip that she might need to know. He would escort her to the departure area for check in, but after that, until she got through customs in Washington, she was on her own. He described the process. "After you get the boarding pass at the check-in desk, you'll pass through security. Put your handbag on the conveyor belt, make sure you aren't wearing or carrying any metal, and then walk through what looks like a doorframe. Pick up your handbag, line up where it says "Other," not "Bahraini citizens," and show your passport. The boarding pass will have your gate number and your seat. Go to that gate.

On the plane, they will serve you meals. You need to buckle your seatbelt when the plane takes off and lands, but otherwise you can usually walk around, unless a stewardess or the pilot says not to. Once you arrive at Heathrow, ask for directions to the connecting flight, but be sure to stay within the international terminal. Follow the signs for transfers. You'll have plenty of time. Try to sleep on the flight to London or from London to Washington. It's a long way. At Dulles airport, Faisal will be waiting for you. I will call him in a few hours to tell him the flight number and time of arrival."

Hajar nodded, sure that she would forget something important. Ahmad was relaxed now and asked about her life. He thought he had only met Hajar once or twice when she was a small child before he went to college. Of course she looked different then, although he was surprised at how Tariq looked much the same, apart from the facial hair. He mentioned he had seen him outside the shop and had been lucky to get away unnoticed.

Ahmad paid the bill, and said, "Time for a treat. This mall has a cineplex with 16 movies to choose from. You can watch a movie on the plane, but it's better here on the big screen." Movies were banned in Saudi Arabia, so Hajar had never been to one. She had never even watched TV, although she had seen flickering television screens from a distance while driving past shop windows at night.

"Most of the newer ones aren't very good," Ahmad said. "Let's go to that one." It was *Lawrence of Arabia*. Hajar sat speechless throughout, enthralled.

The Saudi border guard flipped through Tariq's passport, saw no stamps, and checked the date of issue. It was new. "Why are you going to Bahrain?"

"To find my sister."

"Haven't heard that one before. Pull over and step outside, please." He looked through the cab of the pickup and ran a mirror underneath the vehicle. By this time, Tariq was holding the photo of Hajar in front of him and asking, "Have you seen this woman come by, maybe an hour ago, with a Saudi man, about thirty, wearing thick glasses?"

The guard was about to pat Tariq down, but seemed to change his mind. He took the photo. "Sorry. Most women go by here in veils. You might try filing a missing persons report at the central police station. You can go now."

Tariq sped off. Once in Manama, he asked a pedestrian how to get to the police station, and then at the station asked for 'missing persons.' He no longer felt too proud to ask for help.

The clerk handed him a form to fill out. "I'd rather speak to someone in person," Tariq said.

"Very well, speak then."

He handed the man Hajar's photo and said he needed to find her. She had come across the border today with a man, without her family's permission.

"Was she abducted?"

"No. I don't think so."

"Name?"

"Hajar bint Saleh al-Qaatil, but she used someone else's passport."

"Name traveling under, or name of companion?"

"I don't know."

The clerk put down his pencil. "How do you expect us to find her? We don't put photos on milk cartons." The clerk ignored Tariq's look of perplexity. "Even if we did, what good would that do if she's wearing a veil?"

"I think she came here to get married, or else to have one of those 'pleasure weekends,' or maybe to go away somewhere."

"You might try checking at the major hotels, or the airport." The clerk took Hajar's photo, made a photocopy, and returned the original to Tariq. Above the xeroxed picture he wrote in large letters "Wanted—Missing as of June 28." Underneath he wrote Hajar's name, followed by "traveling under assumed name with male companion, possibly with stolen passport. Accompanied by 30-year-old Saudi male, approximately 1.7 m, 65 kg, light skinned, wavy black hair, thick glasses, Western dress." He made some copies for Tariq.

"We'll fax this to airport security, and they'll circulate it to the passport-control officers for you. If they find anyone matching your sister's description, they'll contact us. You might also take the copies and leave them with the reception desks at the major hotels." Tariq had no phone, so the clerk handed him a card with the number for the missing persons office.

Tariq thanked the clerk and spent the rest of the day going to hotels. The desk clerks were, by and large, sympathetic, but had no information on the alleged fugitive. In the evening, Tariq went to the airport to make sure that security personnel had the photo and were working on it. The head of security found the fax but had not yet made copies to circulate. "Frankly," he said, "we've got bigger problems to look out for, but we'll do what we can."

Tariq sat on one of the benches to watch passersby, but it was late, and Tariq was tired. He had done all he could.

As Tariq was about to get up from the bench to leave the departure terminal, ten yards away, Ahmad and Hajar walked in the entrance. Hajar saw him first from the side. She let out a tiny yelp, dropped to her knees, as if doubled over in pain. Pushing the cart with her bag, Ahmad stopped and turned. He bent down and put his hand on her shoulder, "Fatima, are you all right?" Under her breath, she whispered, "It's him! My brother. Give me my veil." She fumbled with it, trying not to attract attention. Once Hajar had the veil in place, she got up and continued walking. Ahmad followed. As he approached Tariq, Ahmad rubbed his forehead to obscure his face. Tariq looked their way, but walked by.

Ahmad whispered to Hajar. "I can't go with you any farther. Keep your veil on unless someone insists you remove it. If they're looking for you, they'll probably be watching for two persons traveling together and won't know the name you're traveling under, just your face. I'll wait here in the hallway until your plane has safely taken off."

After security inspected her bag, Hajar went to the British Airways check-in counter and presented her passport and ticket. The agent asked her to lift her veil, compared her face to the passport, and then gave her a boarding pass. As Hajar walked away, an agent called after her, "Madam!" Hajar's heart dropped. She turned. A uniformed man was rapidly approaching, his hand extended. "You forgot your baggage tag."

At passport control, she saw an officer going from booth to booth and handing out to his colleagues a paper with writing on it and what appeared to be a photo. Some looked at the paper immediately. Others put it aside. When her turn came, she saw the paper more clearly and read upside down her name written in large letters above a copy of her passport photo. Hajar's stomach tightened in fear. She felt like running back to Ahmad, but others blocked the way. Gripping her purse, Hajar hoped no one would notice her hands shaking. The officer asked her to lift her veil, looked at her, and stamped the passport. She was free to go.

Chapter 20

Faisal waited in the arrival hall of Dulles Airport. His patent-leather white shoes tapped impatiently. The plane had landed an hour ago, but no one arrived who matched the description that Ahmad had given him over the phone. Faisal had checked the baggage-claim area, then ran back to the arrival gate, waited some more, tried to peer inside, returned to baggage claim, and then came back again. They wouldn't let him into the secure zone: it was one way only—out. Faisal had thought of bringing a sign to hold up with "Fatima" written in Arabic, but how would he have explained not recognizing his supposed sister? The same United Airlines agent whom he had been pestering for information during the past half hour finally checked the passenger manifest: a Fatima bint Sami al-Sayyid had been on board, but a yellow light now flashed next to her name. The woman said, "ICE—Immigration and Customs Enforcement—are detaining her. Come with me. I'll take you there."

Nick was arranging his files before shutting off the light and leaving. Just over twelve hours until D-Day he thought. Nick was relieved he had not had to return to Riyadh in the past few weeks: he had not seen or spoken with Gewalt and wondered how he could ever face the man again. Does one betrayal cancel another?

Another e-mail arrived. Don't they ever stop? This one came from Washington, and its subject line read, "Detention of Suspect." As if Nick didn't have enough to worry about, now they were dragging him into criminal cases. Unless it was obvious spam, Nick never liked to leave an e-mail unopened in his inbox. Maybe that's why he was always struggling to catch up.

In the text of this message, an agent from ICE was alerting Nick, as the consular officer who had issued the suspect's visa, that ICE had stopped an alleged Fatima al-Sayyid at the border in Dulles airport. The woman had been trying to enter the country illegally. They suspected a possible connection to terrorism. Terrorism? There must be some mistake. Nick hadn't even known Fatima would be leaving Saudi Arabia so quickly: he had only handed her the passport three or four days earlier. The ICE officer provided a contact phone number in Virginia for Nick to call if he needed more details. He sure did, but when he dialed the number, an answering machine started. Not wanting to leave a message, Nick hung up and dialed Ahmad's cell phone.

"Ahmad! It's Nick. Fatima has been arrested at Dulles airport!"

Ahmad's voice, to Nick, seemed oddly calm. He should have been frantic to hear the news.

"Yes, Nicholas. I know. We have a bit of explaining to do, and could use your help. I'm actually on another line now to my brother in Washington. He's there handling the situation. Can I call you back? Or better yet—this may take a while—could you come by the house tonight, around 7 p.m.? We're having a small party for my father. There will be others there, but we could talk then in private."

A party? Hardly seemed like an appropriate time to celebrate. Nick said, "See you at seven," and hung up. So he wouldn't be seeing Fatima again ... and she was a criminal to boot. Great.

A male servant of the al-Sayyids opened the door and ushered Nick into the parlor. Nick heard guests talking in the living room and some Arabic music playing in the background. The servant asked him to wait and went upstairs. A minute later, Ahmad peeked his head over the banister, saw Nick, and said, "We'll be right down." We? Who was "we"? Nick wondered.

Ahmad continued. "In the meantime, make yourself at home with the drinks and *hors d'oeuvres,* or mingle if you'd like. Ma Ling is in the living room; you know her at least."

She's the last person I should be talking to right now, Nick thought. He went into the living room and saw nine or ten persons standing and talking, some with drinks, others with canapés in their hands. As he was taking in the scene, a man came up to him, gently touched the sleeve of his jacket, and in Chinese, said, "Mr. Hansen. What a nice surprise. I am Ambassador Jia Guomin. It is so good to meet you at last." Nick knew who he was—someone had pointed him out to Nick at the Riyadh reception, which now seemed years ago, another lifetime. Nick was surprised that the ambassador recognized him or even knew his name. Then he saw Ma Ling standing at a slight distance looking uncomfortable, and he remembered the connection.

Nick flushed and said, "I'm flattered, sir, that you would know of me." Nick gave Ma Ling a dirty look.

"Let me introduce Chairman Yang of China Oil. He is in town to give a presentation tomorrow." A short, balding man in a broad, ill-fitting suit looked at Nick. He held his glass with stubby fingers, the square nails stained yellow from decades of tobacco. Nick saw that he had the rough face of a country peasant, the ones who reach positions of provincial power through their Party membership. An apparatchik, Nick thought, and a chain smoker like virtually all the men of his generation. At their meetings, they handed out cigarette packs like sweets. Nick guessed he was in his late 60s and instantly disliked him. If it had been just this guy attending the board meeting, I wouldn't have lifted a finger. It probably showed, too. The chairman, in a gruff, gravelly voice, was saying something unintelligible and repeating it. *"Dobriy vyecher! Dobriy vyecher! Ha, ha, ha!"*

"Excuse me?" Nick said in Chinese. "I don't understand."

"You're not Russian? You look Russian. I thought they said you were a Russian. That blond hair, rosy cheeks. I was saying the few words I remember. Ha ha!" said Chairman Yang.

"I'm American."

Nick assumed the chairman must have studied in the Soviet Union.

"When I was your age—nineteen?—they sent me to Moscow, our fraternal comrades at the time. The next year they pulled me out. Our friends one moment were our enemies the next: a bit like you Americans and the Saudis. Ha ha!"

Nick turned to the ambassador. "And what brings you to Dhahran? Are you escorting Chairman Yang?"

"Yes, and I'll be attending the presentation with him."

"Really?" Nick gave a worried look to Ma Ling, who made a small nod.

Ahmad had come into the room and was pulling Nick's arm. Ahmad said to the ambassador in English, "Excuse me for dragging my friend away, but I need to speak with him in private." They went into the parlor where Nick was dumbstruck to see Fatima sitting on a couch. The two men sat beside her, Nick in the middle.

Fatima began, "Nicholas, I'm so sorry to cause all these problems for you...."

"But you're supposed to be in the States." In a whisper, Nick said, "I thought you were under arrest!"

Ahmad said, "That's just it, you see...."

"Let me explain," Fatima said. Nick's head was turning from one to the other and back again. He leaned onto the couch cushions to put both into his field of vision. His hand rubbed his neck.

Fatima adjusted her body on the sofa to face Nick. "You see, Nicholas. I wasn't entirely honest with you. I was at first, but my girlfriend got into trouble: she needed to escape Saudi Arabia, in a hurry so I gave her my passport. We replaced her photo with mine."

"Why would you break the law like that?"

"It's not so simple," Fatima said. "This girl was engaged to be married, but pregnant by another man. Her family would have killed her if they found out. How can you hide a pregnancy? An abortion was not an option."

"The scoundrel who made her pregnant—what happened to him?"

"He's still here. It's John Kaddish."

"John! Oh my God...." Nick paled.

"But it turns out," said Fatima, "she wasn't pregnant after all. The customs officers have her in detention. My brother Faisal said they took a blood sample to check her story, and the sample came up negative. But I know Hajar—that's my friend—I know she wouldn't lie like that. She must have really believed she was pregnant. She said she had all the symptoms."

Fatima's face darkened and her throat tightened. "But she did sleep with John. That much we know. He seduced her and admitted as much in front of me and Ahmad."

"Now I remember. John had mentioned he had met a Saudi girl. We . . . I mean, I had no idea she was a friend of yours. A few hours ago, before I called Ahmad, I received a brief e-mail about her—I thought it was you—but haven't been able to get through by phone to find out more. The e-mail mentioned 'suspected terrorist'!"

"That couldn't be. I've known Hajar since we were small girls. Besides, what Saudi terrorist organization would allow women to participate? They found she was lying—she was, in fact, but only to impersonate me—and because of that, since she's from Saudi Arabia, they think she's a terrorist. . . ." Fatima was too upset to continue. She put her face in her hands.

Ahmad said, "They even thought my brother was a terrorist. That could have been very serious. By this time, several FBI agents had appeared and wanted to pull Faisal aside for questioning. But he's feisty and kept his wits about him. He showed them his I.D. card for his employer, Lockheed Martin. They made a call, confirmed that he had a high-level security clearance, and released him. I hope he won't get into trouble at work for that."

Nick wasn't happy to be reminded about the FBI and his other potential problems. He changed the subject back to Hajar. "How did they catch her? If she got out of Saudi Arabia, she must have been quite smart."

Fatima motioned to her brother. "We can thank him for that."

Ahmad said, "According to Faisal, who spoke with one of the customs officials, Hajar wasn't hard to spot: a woman traveling alone wearing her veil at immigration. She had never been on an airplane before. I had told her what to do, but she must have forgotten. It's a lot for a girl to handle on her own. So, despite my instructions, she didn't know how to act when she arrived. The INS guy started asking her a few questions and must have wondered how a student supposedly returning to the U.S. could be so clueless. Then they brought a bomb-sniffing dog, which freaked her out. Before long, she and her bags were in detention.

"I hope they don't take her to one of those 'undisclosed locations,'" said Fatima, on the verge of tears. "Oh, it's horrible!"

"They promised Faisal they wouldn't, dear." Ahmad tried to comfort his sister across Nick's knees. He looked over at Nick. "But they won't let Faisal see Hajar or bring a lawyer. Fatima and I—our father knows nothing of this—were hoping you could contact the INS officials. As a diplomat, your word carries weight. You could vouch for us, and ask that they at least treat her as an asylum seeker. Faisal said the immigration lawyer he spoke to suggested she claim political asylum."

Nick knew the rules. "That won't be easy," he said. "Political asylum applies to identifiable groups suffering political persecution." He recited from memory what he had learned, first at Human Rights Watch, then at State: "But international and U.S. laws on asylum are anachronistic when it comes to women, who are not formally recognized as having special gender-related problems. Immigration officers have published guidance on the subject but the guidance does not have the force of law."

After a pause to let it sink in, Nick said, "However, there have been some legal precedents, so I think we could make a strong argument, particularly if repatriation would put Hajar at risk of an honor killing.

"Usually, they would set a hearing before a judge, but that may not occur for several months. At least a good lawyer should be able to get her treated as a refugee, not a terrorist. Maybe if I argue for you on her behalf—over the phone—that might do the trick. Regardless, they will probably require the posting of a bond to ensure she appears at the hearing and doesn't try to disappear into the country as an illegal immigrant. A bail bond could be quite expensive—perhaps five thousand dollars."

"That won't be a problem. Faisal should have the money," said Ahmad.

Nick nodded. "I'll have to speak with the officials detaining her and will try calling again this evening." It would be a long night, he thought.

"One other thing," Nick said. "I will tell the U.S. not to report any of this to the Saudis. Ordinarily, with an asylum case pending, they would not do that, or even afterwards, if we assume a favorable outcome, they would say nothing about the matter. I'll just emphasize again that any mention of the incident could put Hajar, and even you, at risk of reprisals from the Saudi authorities or her family."

Fatima blanched.

Nick said, "Don't worry. I hold myself partially responsible. I knew in advance of John's plans and did nothing to stop him.

"With regard to the passport, Fatima, there's no point in asking Immigration and Customs Enforcement to return it to me. Its stamps would show your already having left the country, but with no re-entry, and hence would set off alarms if you ever tried to use it again. Ahmad should just report the passport as lost. That way, he can apply on your behalf for a new one. With any luck, you might get it in time to attend school this fall. I would do my best to expedite the visa once I had the passport."

"But wouldn't U.S. immigration object this time? After all, we tried to trick them into letting Hajar in," Ahmad said.

"They might, but I would argue you were acting for a noble purpose—saving a friend's life. Sometimes we must break the law to serve a higher good."

The brother and sister nodded in vigorous agreement.

"Thank you so much! You're too kind to us." Fatima said, and Ahmad apologized for the trouble they had caused. Nick understood, but was tired.

He would have enjoyed sitting next to Fatima for longer. Her perfume was intoxicating, but he knew he'd better be leaving. He rose to go.

"Won't you stay to meet our father? He's a bit late in arriving tonight." Fatima said.

"Thank you. I've met him before. Please convey my regards and congratulations. I'll be thinking of him tomorrow."

Nick had no intention of facing the Chinese again, so he said goodbye and left.

Chapter 21

DURING THE NIGHT, small teams of U.S. Special Forces parachuted into remote spots of Saudi Arabia's Eastern Province. Trained in desert survival, they would spend the next several days scouting the perimeters of Saudi Oil's facilities and major oil fields. Meanwhile an AWACS plane was circling just outside Saudi airspace and relaying military communication traffic to NSA headquarters for decoding and interpretation. During the past week, U.S. troop carriers had stepped up their evacuation of soldiers and heavy armor from southern Iraq, leaving via the Iraqi port of Basra and slowly—too slowly in the minds of external observers—making their way south along the Arabian Gulf. The ships transporting the men and materiel were not far from the major oil port of Dammam. Other U.S. troops, elite light-armored units, were massing in makeshift camps along the southern Iraqi border with Saudi Arabia to the west of Kuwait. When given the signal, they would make a dash to the southeast to hold and occupy Saudi Arabia's key oil fields. At the same time, overwhelming U.S. air power would deter any Saudi air force that dared to take off and approach the area.

The U.S. military planned to demobilize the King Fahd Airbase, a nerve center for command, communications, and control, with a targeted high-powered microwave blast detonated several hundred meters off the ground. Low-altitude detonations would enable the destruction of electronics systems among those whom the U.S. would soon term the enemy, without affecting nearby U.S. forces. Given the concentrated location of Saudi Arabia's oil fields away from major centers of population, the American Joint Chiefs of Staff estimated they could secure them on a permanent basis with as few as five thousand troops on the ground.

Although monitoring the movements of the U.S. military and aware of their intent, Chinese forces did not take any public or covert actions. They could have prepared to respond in the region itself or elsewhere in the world at places like the straits of Taiwan or along the major shipping chokepoints to inflict countervailing pressure. However, the rulers in Beijing honored Ambassador Jia's request not to communicate any aspect of his message electronically or take measures that might inadvertently inform the Americans that the Chinese knew of their plans.

The Saudi military still relied on the U.S. for much of its intelligence, which various branches of the U.S. foreign service, military, and covert agencies had in recent months turned into disinformation to trick the Saudis—and anyone else who might be listening—about U.S. motives and likely responses in the event of a crisis in the country.

Much of the country was slumbering through the late June heat. It was the peak of the summer, and a large contingent of Saudi Arabia's rulers—the king and his key advisors—were vacationing with their families abroad in Europe or at palaces in the cool mountain highlands of Taif, a Saudi resort town overlooking the Red Sea.

The night of July 1st, Tariq slept with Rasheed and two others in a bare, rundown apartment that the al-Qaeda cell used for its clandestine meetings. The other four, two of them still just teenagers, would meet them at first light after morning prayers, and they would drive together in a rented minibus. Inside the bus were duffel bags filled with rope, knives, ammunition, machine guns, a video camera, executioners' swords, explosives, and national-guard uniforms that they would use to make their entry into the Saudi Oil compound. That morning, the two guards on duty at the main Saudi Oil gate, whom Rasheed had assiduously courted with cash and other favors over the preceding months, would let them pass unhindered, thereby allowing them to drive right up to the entrance to the Saudi Oil headquarters building.

They had obtained a schedule for the board meeting and a list of attendees. Rasheed told the men he was pleasantly surprised to see the added bonus of the Chinese ambassador among the prospective hostages. He wondered aloud whether the ambassador or the chairman of a major Chinese oil firm held more currency as a bargaining chip with the Chinese government. Probably roughly the same, he figured. At any rate, their big prize for extracting concessions from the Saudi royal family would be capturing alive the king's eldest son, reputed to be in line for succession after the elderly crown prince, the last remaining full-blood brother of the current king.

The van of eight drove out into the desert a few miles past the Saudi Oil compound. There they would change into their uniforms, check their weapons, and make sure they were clear on the plan and possible fallback options if problems occurred. There were always problems, but each man was ready for the glorious end reserved for martyrs. "Be ready, but don't be too anxious for such a death," Rasheed told them. "We should want, above all, to succeed in our objectives." Rasheed had kept the details of the operation secret—a technique he had learned from other missions that he had participated in but never led. On this day in the desert, Rasheed finally briefed his team as to the mission's goals, the logistics, and the tactics. The men already knew the long-term strategy: to bring down the ruling family and replace it with clerics amenable to a truly fundamental state like that once enjoyed by their Afghani brethren, the Taliban.

Some influential clerics already had tremendous sway over daily life in Saudi Arabia, but absolute power still eluded them. The royal family, weak and bloated, corrupted from decades of misspent oil revenues, was teetering on the edge. Rasheed hoped the prospect of a videotaped beheading of the king's heir would give the final push and force an abdication to save the man's life. To demonstrate their seriousness, the al-Qaeda group would methodically execute the infidels on a daily basis, or on a publicized schedule to maximize the impact. He counted those first for the knife as the two Chinese and the Shi'ite apostate. To build the drama and show their resolve, they would start with a methodical slaughtering of the underlings of these three, with the executions shown live on an Internet site, procured specifically for the purpose. Rasheed calculated that the boardroom of the world's largest oil company must have a connection to the World Wide Web. The pressure internally and from abroad to stop the killings would be intense. Rasheed, therefore, instructed his men only to fire on the hostages as a last resort. Their deaths were too valuable to waste indiscriminately.

To deter any rescue of the hostages, two of the al-Qaeda operatives would booby-trap the doorways leading to the top floor of the building. Two others, also versed in explosives, would wear suits wired for detonation as a way of dissuading attacks from outside. They would position themselves at opposite ends of the captives' space. Once activated, the suits each contained enough plastic explosives to destroy a large ballroom.

Rasheed also imparted his philosophy to the men. He wanted them to act like trained soldiers on holy jihad, not an unruly pack of killers, baying for blood. He showed them the two executioners' swords, the blades of which he had personally sharpened like razors. "Why two?" he asked rhetorically and then answered his own question. "We want executions to be quick, clean, and painless." Rasheed had studied the methods used at chop-chop square and often found them wanting. He told his fighters that the quickest cut required two men: one to prod a sword's point into the victim's lower back from behind and the other to deliver the killing blow. The prodding would force an arching of the back, an arch that would make the neck hang backward for the single decapitating cut. "We must not make an execution into torture by inflicting unnecessary pain," Rasheed said. He offered an analogy for dealing with infidels. "A man stomps out an insect. He does not pull it apart slowly, limb by limb. To do so demeans one before the eyes of God, and only a sick person, one destined for hell, would purposefully commit, or take pleasure in, such torture."

After the main briefing, Rasheed pulled Tariq aside. "Tariq, of these guys, you're the one I most worry about. Are you okay?" Tariq had appeared distracted and unable to concentrate after returning empty-handed from Bahrain.

He was sure he had just narrowly missed his sister, who now would never return. "I know she'll come back," Rasheed had said, but Tariq didn't believe it. What would he tell his father? He supposed after this mission, nothing would matter any more, but he couldn't take his mind off her.

"I'm going to have you carry the bags with the video camera, swords, and other equipment. You'll have your gun, of course, but you'll be the back-up guy, not the one likely to take any first hits when we go in there," Rasheed said.

Tariq nodded he understood and fingered the string of prayer beads in his pocket.

At 8:45 a.m. a convoy of three cars led by a police escort reached the main gate of the Saudi Oil compound. In the front car sat the Chinese ambassador and the China Oil chairman, driven by one of the martial-arts masters. The middle car contained their security detail of heavily armed embassy guards—in uniform and in plain clothes. Behind was a vehicle for the women, driven by a regular embassy driver. Ma Ling sat in the front passenger seat, unveiled, so that the Saudi Oil guard would recognize her. In the back were three masters with thin veils and covered in headscarves and *abayas*. At the compound's main gate, the driver of the police escort spoke with the Saudi Oil guards, who stepped back to let the convoy in. Once inside, the Chinese security detail pulled off to the right and parked, the front Chinese car drove up to the main entrance of the Saudi Oil headquarters, and the other went to the back of the building to let out the female staff assistants.

Because the provincial governor was attending this board meeting, employees who normally worked in the same headquarters building were told to take the morning off and come to work only in the afternoon, with the unspoken expectation that they would work into the night past their normal hours.

Ma Ling had been correct in her estimate of the boardroom's dimensions. A handcrafted table of inlaid mahogany occupied the room's center and extended for two-thirds of its length. On the north face, floor-to-ceiling windows covered the entire wall opposite the room's main entrance, which the builders had fitted with double doors wide and high enough to drive a truck through. Each of the approximately thirty high-backed, brown leather chairs surrounding the table had a retractable microphone in front while jacks along the table's edge enabled those seated to plug in individual laptop computers. The room had wireless Internet access, but persons not properly equipped could also use jacks along the table for broadband connections. A projector hung from the ceiling, and a screen covered one of the end walls.

On the morning of July 2nd, Minister Abdul-Zayyat, the chairman of the Saudi Oil board, and the governor sat in the middle of the table's north side facing the entrance. To the governor's immediate left in a position of honor sat Sami al-Sayyid, who today was joining the board of directors. Directly opposite them were Chairman Yang and Ambassador Jia, able to enjoy the commanding view of the Gulf, desert, and scattered settlements in the distance. Eight other board members, all Saudis, sat around both sides near the table's center. The three American board members were inexplicably absent. Initially, the aides to the Chinese and the assistants to the Saudis occupied the chairs surrounding the perimeter of the room, but the governor waved them to the table and said, "There's plenty of space. Take seats at the two ends."

The Saudis wore a mix of Western and traditional clothing. The Chinese sported light-colored suits. The clothing on the four martial-arts masters, disguised as aides, was well tailored but loose in cut. In each of the two inside pockets of their jacket breast, every master carried a throwing star, inside a cover labeled with the day's PowerPoint presentation: one version in Chinese, one in Arabic.

The meeting started badly, perhaps because of Minister Abdul-Zayyat's annoyance at the absence of the Americans, two of whom had assured him that they would come specifically to Saudi Arabia to attend the meeting. He tried to cover his embarrassment at their failure to appear, first by whispering to the governor that their planes must have been delayed and then by opening the meeting with a dig at them: "It seems our American board members have not shown up this morning. I hope that in no way reflects their attitudes toward our Chinese friends."

Chairman Yang was also not in a good mood, angry at Ambassador Jia, and poorly prepared for the presentation. Jia had told him only the night before at Dr. Sayyid's party that his aides had a problem with their visas, so Jia was substituting his own personnel. Yang had had no opportunity to meet these people because, as Jia explained, they were busily huddled with his normal contingent and learning what to do. Yang assumed that Huang Lei, as the oldest of the four, was replacing his right-hand man who ordinarily would either answer the difficult questions for him or discretely pass him scribbled notes with the appropriate responses. To make matters worse, Yang was hard of hearing, and one of his two earpieces was malfunctioning. He would have to jerk the left side of his head toward the interpreter if he was to have any chance of hearing questions properly.

At the boardroom table, Yang waved the ambassador away from sitting next to him and snarled, with a fixed grin on his face, "I need my interpreter on my left, my right-hand man on my right. Is this fellow . . ." he pointed to Huang, ". . . going to serve as my aide-de-camp?"

"Yes, he'll also operate the projector and electronic pointers for you if you wish."

The martial-arts master who was acting as interpreter could speak reasonably well in conversational Arabic but had no grasp for technical terms. The Saudis first began to suspect there might be a problem when the fellow translated the governor's welcoming remarks. Accustomed to translators, the governor knew to pause at judicious points but sometimes got carried away with his own eloquence and went on for longer riffs before remembering to allow the interpreter to catch up. This was one of those occasions. He wanted to impress the Chinese visitor with the importance of moving rapidly ahead with the joint venture in Fujian. The governor spoke for twenty seconds, the interpreter spoke for five; the governor then spoke for ten seconds, paused for the interpreter, who said nothing, but looked back at him, waiting for the governor to continue. He spoke for another ten or fifteen seconds; again the interpreter spoke for five. The stand-in interpreter was condensing whole paragraphs of thought into brief sentences, and as Ambassador Jia realized, guessing at the governor's meaning and making some things up as he went along. Jia sat quietly, not wanting to cause the master to lose face. He, Jia, would not say anything, but would step in only if the Saudis became exasperated. They soon were. Board members exchanged glances, then whispered to one another, then started making snide remarks, first in Arabic, and finally even in English to help the Chinese understand their point. Minister Abdul-Zayyat at last intervened after having completely missed Chairman Yang's introductory remarks and having guessed from his paper handout in Arabic at the meaning of the first few projected slides, which were in Chinese.

"Ambassador Jia," the minister said. "Your facility with Arabic is renowned in this country. Unfortunately, your interpreter is having some difficulties conveying what must be very deep thoughts coming from your Chairman Yang. Might you suggest a solution?"

Jia apologized profusely and explained in Arabic that the original interpreter had fallen ill, and this man was kindly standing in for him. He turned to the struggling master and asked in Chinese, "Would you be offended if I interpreted for the remainder of the presentation? I understand how tiring it can be, so you must need a rest."

A look of relief passed over the master's face. He smiled and went to sit in an empty chair at the end of the table, opposite one of his colleagues. Earlier in the week, Jia had had Chairman Yang's office e-mail his presentation to him so that the embassy could send it out for translation into Arabic. Afterwards, Jia had gone through both versions and was now thoroughly familiar with the contents. He had even looked up the meaning of arcane technical terms that only oil specialists might know.

Jia's ability impressed Yang and took the edge off the older man's morning gruffness. At one point, during a pause, Yang muttered under his breath, "My word, you're good. I don't even know what some of these terms are that I'm reading off the slides." Unfortunately, while Jia knew how to translate, he didn't know the intricacies of the business, of how the parts of the venture fit together; namely he lacked the details that some board members were keen to know. It turned out that Yang, the old oilman, normally relied too heavily on his right-hand assistant, and today's nominal replacement had only a cursory understanding of the venture's highlights. During the question-and-answer period, Yang's most frequent refrain became "We'll have to get back to you with an answer on that one," an unsatisfactory reply to his listeners because the board that very morning would be discussing, and then voting on, funding levels for the Saudi side of the venture. The earlier tension and discomfort of the start of the meeting again settled on the faces of the listeners during the time allowed for Q&A, a 30-minute session likely to end more quickly than that. Next to Chairman Yang, Huang Lei fiddled with two electronic pointers, rolling them between his fingers and occasionally glancing at his watch. He looked across at the ambassador, who had no trouble reading his thoughts: "Would they have to leave the room soon? Was the attack coming? If so, when?"

Chapter 22

Shortly after 10:00 a.m., the minibus carrying Rasheed and his men, outfitted as Saudi national guards, stopped at the main gate of the Saudi Oil compound. One of the Saudi Oil guards ran a mirror underneath the vehicle while another boarded the bus and idly looked at the men and their bags. He got off and waved them on. The driver of the minibus had called out, loud enough for the other nearby Saudi Oil guards to hear, that they would be escorting the Chinese from the meeting to the airport.

Near the entrance to the compound, a local TV crew was setting up their television camera. Two Westerners, apparently from Reuters, were also waiting by the gate; one held a regular camera with a long telephoto lens and the other a microphone and a recording device. They were hoping for interviews with the governor, the OPEC minister, or the Chinese ambassador after the board meeting. For the Saudi television network, it was a slow news day, particularly in the province, so an otherwise ho-hum story might even make it to the top of their nightly broadcast.

In the back of the bus, Tariq looked at the familiar Saudi Oil gates and spotted the media personnel. Good, he thought. We'll have lots of coverage right from the start. Rasheed had given him a pill to take, said it would relax his nerves, and it did just that. He felt almost euphoric and wondered why he had never had such wonderful medicine before.

The minibus parked near the entrance to the headquarters. Rasheed and his men hopped out, slung their bags over their shoulders, and jogged the few steps into the building. Once inside, they pointed their automatic weapons at the attendants and told them to lie face down while they tied their hands and put tape over their mouths. The team closed and locked the front doorway. Two operatives went on ahead to begin laying booby traps on the top-floor doorways. The six others soon followed in the elevators and a few minutes later burst into the boardroom.

Yelling "God is great!" they pointed their automatic weapons at the horrified faces of the Saudis and the startled Chinese. Tariq noted that one odd old man, with his back to them, hardly even turned to look. His hands stopped playing with two small objects and he crossed his arms. "Hands over your heads! Heads down! Now!" Rasheed shouted in Arabic. His men circled the table, standing behind those seated. The two with suits wired to explode took up positions on opposite ends of the room, and like their cohorts trained the weapons on those who now sat captive.

Downstairs on the fifth floor, reserved for women, the shrouded masters had been listening to events on their ear pieces linked to microphones wired into the masters' suit jackets upstairs. At the same time, they watched the boardroom on a central monitor via the closed-circuit link established with the two laptops that the Chinese had placed on the table, their webcams discreetly facing opposite ends of the room. Ma Ling described to the others what was going on at the meeting. She, too, had become increasingly anxious as the Chinese neared the end of their presentation. One of the four in the ladies' section had been watching the elevator bank. As soon as they saw the first elevator go to the tenth floor, they knew something was on. The men, still shrouded, crept up the stairwells and waited just outside the doors leading onto the tenth floor. They heard the Saudis burst into the room, but stood motionless, silently waiting for the signal from Huang.

Hearing Rasheed's commands, the Saudis at the table immediately placed their hands over their heads and leaned forward, faces down. The governor had tried to object, demanding to know what these troops were doing, but quickly stopped when an al-Qaeda operative behind him grabbed his head and unceremoniously shoved it to the table. The young terrorist then stood behind Sami al-Sayyid, tapped on the back of the man's silver head, and said, "This apostate is going to die early."

Chairman Yang was the first of the Chinese to comply with the shouted orders. His frightened face had turned from one commando to the next. Lifting their hands and bending forward, they were already miming to him what the instructions were. Ambassador Jia was slowly raising his hands but said aloud in Arabic, "Stop this at once. If you lay down your weapons now and go back where you came from, we won't hurt you."

Like Rasheed, Tariq was momentarily taken aback and looked around the room, wondering which ventriloquist was talking through this Asian's mouth. His Arabic was flawless. Then Rasheed sneered and said, "You're the ones who are going to get hurt, my preening infidel friend. Shut up! Such fine words in our language won't help you now." Rasheed motioned for one of his men to begin tying the hands of those seated, but first he wanted everyone in the same position. To his annoyance, the other four Chinese appeared particularly stupid and sat with arms tightly crossed at their chests, hands hidden in their jacket pockets. Three of them seemed to be watching a fourth, the older man, a broad slab of a fellow, seated near the monkey who could prattle in Arabic. Tariq knew that Rasheed would show him a lesson that the others would not soon forget.

Rasheed walked up behind Huang and used the palm of his hand to smack him on the side of his head. "Are you deaf, old man? Or just an imbecile?" He shouted into the impassive Huang's ear, mocking the placid man's posture to his comrades who laughed, expecting a good show. With one hand now on each of Huang's jacket sleeves, he prepared to yank the man's arms over his head and teach him a lesson. But Huang beat him to it. With a deafening Chinese cry of "Jack Rabbit," Huang flung open his arms, hurling with each hand a light pointer at opposite ends of the room. The pointers hit the walls with a bang, sending blinding flashes and smoke billowing out. Huang's outstretched arms then reached up and behind him, collaring Rasheed's shirt. With a tremendous judo swing, Huang flipped the man up and over his head like a rag doll crashing him onto the table in front. The blow knocked Rasheed unconscious. At the same instant, the three other masters uncrossed their arms. Deadly throwing stars flew in all directions, hitting their marks. The two commandos, armed with body suits ready to explode, clutched their necks.

Tariq felt his bladder empty as he wondered what to do. Shoot, run, or nothing? The final option seemed most likely, for his muscles had frozen and seemed not to be obeying any of his mind's commands. As smoke began to fill both ends of the room, Tariq recovered his poise. He started to shoot, but the gun aimed high, shattering the windows opposite him. He felt a burning pain in his trigger hand. Looking down, he had just enough time to see half his index finger dangling, a knife point still stuck in it. A heavy blow crashed on the back of his neck. As his knees buckled, and just before Tariq's vision slipped into darkness, an image flashed through his mind: his father Saleh al-Qaatil was holding down Hajar's face in a sink full of water.

It was all over in a matter of seconds. Ambassador Jia had barely reached for Chairman Yang to pull him under the table, when Huang called out that it was safe to get up. Shortly before the shots rang out in the boardroom, the veiled masters stormed onto the floor and quickly dispatched the other two al-Qaeda men outside the room. The two hapless operatives, huddled over the mines they had been laying, had only enough time to stand upright before flying kicks from women, appearing from nowhere like hideous witches, knocked them senseless. Many of the rescued Saudis, unsure of what was going on, got up and fled down the stairs. Some lingered behind to watch those they had thought were incompetent aides quickly tie the hands of the would-be hostage takers. Jia gathered up a confused Yang and shooed him along with the other Saudis out of the room and down the staircases. "Let the men finish their work. It still may be unsafe if there are others around," Jia said. The governor, minister, and remaining board members needed no further encouragement to leave.

Soon after, the Chinese martial-arts masters walked the now conscious commandos down the stairs.

Miraculously, apart from Tariq, no one else had gotten any shots off. Some had minor cuts from shattered glass, but apart from two al-Qaeda operatives lying motionless on the floor, everyone else emerged intact. Two of the masters, still dressed as women, remained behind to clean up. They gathered the guns into one of the commando's duffel bags, and bent over the bodies, defusing the bombs. One of those on the floor appeared to be still alive, so the older of the two masters hastened to save his life by stopping the blood gushing from his neck. Pausing from his work of collecting the guns, the younger master spotted the video camera that Tariq had brought. He turned it on and did a slow scan of the room, the lifeless body, and his colleague trying to save the second figure on the floor.

"Xiao Lin, What are you doing?" asked the kneeling man, his hands covered in blood.

"Recording this for posterity. These killers would have thought nothing of filming and showing the execution of their hostages. Let's see how they like having their defeated images broadcast to the world." Lin thought for a minute. "Besides, we should have a record of this assault in case they ever try to deny that anything had occurred. By tomorrow, I'll have a copy of the tape transmitted to CCTV in Beijing." Lin needn't have worried. The television crew outside had their cameras rolling, and the Reuters correspondent was clicking away as soon as the first Saudis fled from the building. The Chinese ambassador walked up to them and gave an impromptu interview in Arabic, explaining what had happened.

"Our intelligence had intercepted communications among al-Qaeda operatives indicating a planned assault on the Saudi Oil board meeting. We felt we were in the best position to intercede and hope that the Saudi government does not object to our taking the necessary actions to protect our important visitor from China as well as the Saudi dignitaries attending his presentation."

Still inside the building, the older master lifted the gravely injured commando's shoulders and said, "Help me carry him out through the elevator." He motioned with his head toward the dead body. "Leave that one behind. The Saudi security forces can handle him: he's no longer dangerous." As they exited and emerged into the sunlight, the two lay the limp but still breathing body on the grass and waved an ambulance over to take him away.

Uncomfortable in the hot sun, Lin pulled off his *abaya*. Seeing a woman disrobe in public, two *mutawwas* who had entered the compound from the street to gawk at the spectacle pushed their way past the crowd. They ran toward Lin, who faced in the opposite direction. The *mutawwas* each seized Lin's upper arms with one hand and lifted their sticks with the other. They intended to beat this woman's uncovered but shapely legs, now indecently exposed. In a flash, as a crowd of onlookers gasped, Lin had flipped them both to the ground. One lay motionless; the other slumped against a low brick wall and made as if to climb again slowly to his feet. With a terrific scream, captured by Saudi news cameras, Lin brought the edge of his hand down hard against the bricks with a karate chop next to the stunned *mutawwa's* head. The bricks crumbled and the *mutawwa* fainted in fright.

Lin's more sober companion rebuked him. "What are you doing? It is against our code to show off!"

"Just teaching him a lesson. Maybe they'll think twice now before assaulting a woman."

Chapter 23

News of the stunning attack and rescue quickly spread. The Saudis so heavily edited their film coverage of the aftermath that their initial broadcasts referred to the defused crisis as a minor event. However, when the still shots of the Reuters cameraman and the Chinese video of the destroyed boardroom got out of the country, the story broke wide open. The cameraman, familiar with press censorship, quickly shot his pictures of the grinning Chinese, some dressed like men in drag, leading the shackled Saudi terrorists, in uniform with heads bowed and badly bruised, across the compound's front lawn. His companion intended to get his microphone close to Ambassador Jia and whispered to the photographer: "Just snap a photo of the ambassador and leave quickly. Send out the copies through e-mail before the censors come looking for the photos." That he did.

Saudi and American officials hastened to congratulate the Chinese on the daring rescue. A day later, news media in the U.S. led with a headline that none of the three American board members had attended the ill-fated meeting. That absence raised questions, and soon members of the international press were hounding the one board member they could most easily locate. They wanted to know why this retired CEO of a major oil company had not gone to Saudi Arabia as planned. A forthright Texan, he told them what had happened. Federal agents had stopped him from boarding a plane in Houston. They detained him for hours and caused him to miss not only his flight but also any chance of taking another and of making a connection to get to the meeting on time. At first, they said there was a problem with his tax returns. Then they changed that to a temporary ban on all Americans flying into Saudi Arabia. When he demanded to have his lawyer present, they initially refused, then relented. By the time his attorney had arrived and secured his release, he was ready to file charges, but later decided against it when the news broke on the attack.

The press became suspicious. Had the U.S. government known in advance of the impending attack and done nothing? Finally, the president came out and admitted that, yes, they had intercepted both al-Qaeda and Chinese communications. The president had decided to let the Chinese take care of the problem, which they had appeared determined to do. Besides, the U.S. had no authority from the Saudis to intervene militarily. The American forces were merely positioning themselves nearby in the event the Saudis asked for help. The president did not mention the teams of U.S. Special Forces that had parachuted onto Saudi territory. A squadron of stealth helicopters picked them up in the night following the Saudi Oil crisis. If the Saudi military detected anything that night, they kept silent.

The Chinese government did not contradict the Americans, but issued a statement saying that from now on the Middle East, its resources and stability, were a vital national interest. They would be increasing their military presence in and around the key facilities of the Arabian Gulf to prevent any aggressor, whether internal or external, from ever trying to seize them by force. The Americans countered by re-iterating their intention of keeping the oil region a nuclear-free zone but made no specific charges against the Saudis or the Chinese.

Ambassador Gewalt was privately upset at how events had transpired. He told himself he had never wanted innocent hostages hurt, but he had been thinking strategically—of the long term, of the greater good as he saw it. Not only were the corrupt Saudis still in control of their oil wealth, but also the Chinese were now more firmly entrenched then ever and had gained new standing in the eyes of the world. China had made the U.S. look ineffectual or worse, and Washington was sure to question his competence in cheerleading the Americans' aborted intervention.

Gewalt couldn't prove anything, but he suspected Nick had learned the truth and talked to the Chinese. He doubted that their listening capabilities could crack U.S. codes. The day after his and Nick's joint cable had gone out, Gewalt's secretary Martha had sheepishly returned an ultra-top-secret coversheet to his desk but not said why she had not brought it back earlier. The old woman was getting careless. Could she have inadvertently distributed a copy to Nick?

At a minimum, Gewalt wanted a scapegoat. Someone—not just him—would pay for this. The evening after the rescue, he had Martha call Nick at home and ask him to come to Riyadh the following day. He didn't say why because he didn't have to. Nick would know. Officials in Washington had already asked that they both come back for "consultations." Gewalt would send Nick first and then recommend that he not return due to classified or unspecified reasons. He'd think of something: "not a team player, friction with colleagues, incompetence." He was sure he could get Nick's boss, Susan, to write something negative. She was already taking every opportunity to bad-mouth the kid behind his back. Must have been jealous that I had taken her out of the loop, Gewalt thought.

He stared out his office window. So what if his actions ruined the boy's career? Nick wasn't cut out for diplomacy. Nor was I, the ambassador mused. Maybe it's time to take up sailing full time. No! He wouldn't leave under a cloud but would stick out his promised three years. Maybe he could eventually salvage something to redeem himself from this fiasco.

On the night before the attack, Nick had stayed up past midnight trying to get through by phone to the FBI case officer who was in charge of Hajar. Nick urged the officer to turn the girl over to immigration, that she had no connection to terrorists and was seeking asylum. After a few hours of questioning, the agent had already concluded the same and was in the process of reclassifying Hajar. As Nick expected, she would have to post bail for release and appear in September at a hearing to determine her ultimate status. The case officer assured Nick that, as far as he knew, the customs and law enforcement agencies had followed proper procedures: no one had alerted, or would alert, the Saudi authorities.

The following day, to keep his mind off the attack that he knew was coming, Nick wrote a draft cable with instructions to re-issue Fatima's student visa once she received a new passport. Nick had a premonition that he might not last much longer in the country, so he wanted any successor to know what to do. He was not surprised when the call came from the ambassador's office. He had no illusions that Gewalt was calling to have him attend the ambassador's annual fourth-of-July party. Nick wanted to contact Ma Ling to congratulate her but didn't dare. On the morning of the third, he flew to Riyadh and soon after, met Gewalt in the ambassador's office.

Gewalt didn't mince words. "Nick, I have a hunch you knew this attack was coming and may even have facilitated the rescue." He looked closely at Nick who was trying to maintain a poker face. "We have no evidence of that, and even if we did, we would still find it awkward to publicly punish, or even to discipline, you for interference. Some might call you a traitor; others a patriot. I have my own thoughts about loyalty and where one's allegiance lies.

"Martha has booked you on a flight leaving tomorrow morning from Dhahran back to Washington." Nick's expression said, So soon? "You need to go back to debrief your superiors in Washington on your assessment of what occurred with the Chinese. Personally, I don't want you around on July 4th—here or anywhere else in this country. I'm going to recommend that you not return."

The ambassador turned his back on Nick and spoke while looking out the window. "Do you have anything to say for yourself?" Nick didn't. "Very well, then. I'll give you some parting advice. Unless you're planning to join China's secret service, you'd better be careful in how you manage your career at the State Department. Frankly, I don't think you have much, if any, career left, but I'll let others decide."

He paused, waiting for any comment from Nick. None came, so Gewalt sighed and said. "That's it. Game over. Now get out of here."

Nick knew he'd have to rush to catch the next flight back to Dhahran and then do what he could to get his affairs in order. There was little time even to pack. He'd have to ask someone to help out after he'd gone. Nick wasn't sure whether he felt bitter toward the ambassador or merely pitied him—that someone in his position could end up so petty. But nothing surprised Nick any more. He felt years older than when he had arrived, barely eight months before, as a freshly minted foreign-service officer, filled with enthusiasm at a challenging new assignment.

As soon as Nick landed in Dhahran late that afternoon, he called John to tell him he was flying out the next morning, probably for good, and would he mind helping him clear up a few matters after he had gone.

"What's this, mate? Packing it up after all the excitement we've had? You didn't have a hand in it, did you? I don't believe that for a minute. Sure I'll help out. I'll come over right away. No? Okay, tomorrow morning then. Let me call Ma Ling and the al-Sayyids. On such short notice, we can't do much of a send-off, but at least we can take you to the airport."

The irrepressible John had forgotten that Fatima was no longer on speaking terms with him. He arrived early the next day to help Nick pack and get instructions on selling Nick's car, closing the bank account, and all the other minutiae of repatriation.

Nick confided to John, without going into specifics—that he was leaving under a cloud. To John, his explanation sounded as if the ambassador was unhappy that Nick had somehow not alerted him to the amazing capabilities of the Chinese in Saudi Arabia. For some reason—no good reason, in John's mind—Nick assumed that none of his colleagues at the consulate, who would have been in a better position to help, would do so once word had gotten out that Nick had left at the ambassador's displeasure.

John tried to buck up Nick's spirits and reminded him that Ahmad and Fatima's father was safe, although surely shaken, by the ordeal. Nick said he was most happy about that.

John continued. "Leaving on the fourth of July? How fitting for an all-American kid like you, Nick. I'm going to miss you. I'm sure we all will."

Nick thanked John, and then told him what had happened to Hajar. John's jaw dropped. "That kid, she was sweet and all that, but so naïve—or maybe she had us all fooled?"

"I'm sorry for egging you on with her."

"No worries. As far as I'm concerned, it was much ado about nothing." The news from Nick reminded John of Fatima's lingering hostility. "Listen, mate. Your dreamboat has got it in for me now. I'll bring you to the airport, but had better keep my distance from her."

The previous evening, John had called Ma Ling and told her of Nick's imminent departure and what flight he was taking out of Dhahran International. Could she meet them at the airport for a little send-off and ask Ahmad and Fatima to come, too?

"Ma Ling was just as shocked as I was that you're leaving. I think you broke her heart, Nick. She'll definitely be there and will make sure that Ahmad and Fatima go, as well."

When it was time to leave, Nick approached John's car. John had cleaned out the entire back area so that all of

Nick's luggage could fit. "Hey, you didn't forget." He saw his tennis racquet leaning against the dash, pulled it from its cover, and strummed the strings.

Before Nick sat down, John brushed aside some sand that the desert winds had blown in. As if recalling another, unpleasant incident, John muttered, "These damn sandstorms are always leaving a mess behind." Nick didn't comment, and John added, in a brighter tone, "Anyway, I replaced the snapped one, so it's now as good as new. You can play mixed doubles as soon as you get back to D.C."

"If I can find anyone to partner with...."

At the airport, as Nick was checking in, Ahmad drove up to the curb of the departure terminal and let out his sister and Ma Ling before parking. John said, "I'll take care of this for you, mate. You go say 'goodbye.'"

Fatima rushed up to Nick, "Oh, Nicholas, so much good news, and now this. How can you leave us so suddenly?"

Nick apologized, but said he had to go back for consultations, possibly for quite some time. He might even still be there for Hajar's hearing, in which case he'd be sure to testify on her behalf. Nick said he had left written instructions for his replacement to take care of Fatima's visa as soon as she had the new passport.

"I hope we'll see each other in the freer environment of the States," he said.

"But why are you going, Nick?"

"I think the ambassador is not very happy with me. He thinks the Chinese outsmarted us. They were part of my bailiwick, so he holds me responsible." Nick smiled. "Maybe, I'll end up selling real estate like my dad in some backwater in California."

Ma Ling interrupted. "Nonsense. You have a promising life ahead of you, Nick. To me, you'll always be a hero." She put her arms around Nick, and pulling his head down toward her, kissed him full on the lips. Looking around the departure hall, she said, "I don't care what anyone thinks."

By this time, Ahmad had arrived and embraced Nick. "Sorry, no kiss on the lips from me." In a more serious tone, he looked at Nick and, in a quiet voice added, "Ma Ling told us our father owes his life to you. I don't know what you did, but Fatima and I—and Faisal—are eternally grateful."

Last came Fatima. She and Nick walked to the side to have a few moments alone. Nick took from his pocket the silver necklace he had kept in his wallet for months since the Bedouin woman had given it to him.

"This doesn't look like much, but it has special meaning for me," he explained to Fatima. "A kind woman gave it to me soon after arriving and said it would bring me good luck. I have held onto it for that reason, but knew that there would come along a special person to give it to." He saw his own reflection in Fatima's dark eyes. "In meeting you, I found that the woman had spoken the truth. May I?" Nick unclasped the chain.

"Yes."

"I don't care about silly rules any more, not touching a woman and all that. So what that I might burn in hell? If such a punishment comes from touching you, then that would be heaven to me."

Nick reached around Fatima's neck and sealed the locket in place. Fatima hugged and then kissed Nick. "Nicholas Handsome, come find me when I am back at school. I'll welcome you with open arms." She whispered in his ear, "Who knows? One day I might even start calling you by your nickname."

That was good enough for him, Nick said, and waved goodbye. With John still standing apart, but tipping the brim of his hat at the other three, the two friends walked to the departure hall. Shaking Nick's hand and then giving him a rib-crushing bear hug, John said, "I'll miss you, man. Now I have reason to visit Washington, a place I've always been interested in seeing. Perhaps I'll also stop in to see how Hajar is, if she'll speak to me."

Nick walked off, and John waited at the airport until his plane had safely departed. As the Boeing rose gracefully into the air, John's unexpressed, but parting thoughts came to him, in Hebrew. *Shalom, hakhaver sheli. Tikkun olam.* Goodbye, my friend. Heal the world.

About the author

During a varied twenty-year career, Paul Ulrich has worked as an economic, telecom, and policy consultant in nearly sixty countries, including China, the Middle East, and the Arabian Peninsula. He has an undergraduate degree from Yale and graduate degrees from Harvard and Stanford. In addition to economics and public policy, Paul has studied Chinese and Arabic, among other languages. Before devoting himself full time to writing, Paul's jobs have ranged from foreign-aid worker to government bureaucrat to multinational consultant and software entrepreneur. He is a patented inventor, with two high-tech U.S. patents to his name. *Saudi Match Point* is Paul's first novel.